To farmgirls everywhere: drive
make waves in a man's world. You got this, girl.

Sydney,

Happy reading!

Jessica

Amber
Waves
of
Grace

Jessica Berg

Amber Waves of Grace

Red Adept Publishing, LLC

104 Bugenfield Court

Garner, NC 27529

http://RedAdeptPublishing.com/

Chapter One

Perched high in her Peterbilt semitruck, Corrie Lancaster winced as the leather seat sucked at her tanned arms. She swiped at the sweat dripping down her nose. Didn't matter. She loved harvest time. Consistent and efficient. Just what she liked.

Enclosed in the cab cocoon, she waited out the cloud of dust and chaff spewed out by the back end of the combine as it inched across the wheat field. She counted down the seconds until the last of the dust storm passed, then she opened the door and hopped down from the sweltering cab. Even a hot day felt like a fresh breeze after being trapped like that. Filling her nostrils with the smell of wheat and dirt, she shuffled through the stubble and knelt. With deft fingers, she moved aside the chaff and scoured the ground for wheat kernels.

Seeing only two, she exhaled. The old girl kept chugging along. If the 9600 John Deere combine could keep doing that for the next two thousand acres, they'd be set. With the years of drought and bad grain prices, the piggy bank had squealed its last a long time ago. A good harvest was the only hope for reviving it.

Corrie straightened, brushed her hands on her jeans, and readjusted her dark aviators as her gaze darted over the field she'd planted and cared for. Ambling to the semi to wait for the next load, she groaned when a familiar rusty-orange Ford F-350 tore into the field, wheels spitting up chaff in their wake. George, her hired man, slammed the door, the pickup shuddering with the force.

"Here we go again," she mumbled, posting herself next to her semi, careful not to touch the black paint molten in the sun's heat. She waited for the large oaf to close the distance. "George, what's the rush?"

His tongue darted out and licked his chapped and peeling lips. His licentious gaze raked her while still communicating disdain. Quite a trick for someone with mush for brains. She hugged her arms around her chest.

"The rush?" George spat. "Rush is, I quit."

Her arms fell to her sides. "What?"

"You heard me."

Corrie balled her hands into fists and kept herself from planting them in George's overfed face. "You can't quit."

"I ain't about to work for no woman for minimum wage. Especially a woman like you."

Bright? Diligent? Caring and responsible? Words he probably didn't know.

She narrowed her eyes. "Fine. Quit."

"Or you could do what any *reasonable* woman would do. Sell the farm. To me."

Corrie snapped her mouth shut on a nasty swear word. "When pigs fly." She clambered up the semi steps and slammed the door.

Hot, humid air and her heavy breathing filled the cab as George sped from the field, truck tires making a permanent rut. Corrie pawed at the window knob until the coolest breeze a ninety-five-degree day could muster blew through. Laying her head back against the headrest, she closed her eyes and, for the first time, longed to be back in Sioux Falls with a juicy story to unfold to the readers of the *Argus Leader*. Impossible, of course. Her family needed her.

"Corrie?"

She jumped in the seat and banged her knees on the steering wheel. She couldn't remember praying for patience, but she made a mental note to remind God she didn't need any more for a while.

"Nathan! You scared the living daylights out of me." She quirked an eyebrow. His fifteen-year-old face resembled a Cheshire cat's. "Did you scare me on purpose?"

"No." Tinges of crimson crawled up his neck. "I swear on my ability to drive, I didn't mean to." His blue eyes radiated innocence, but he'd made her look like a fool before.

"If I even get a hint, a breath of a hint, that you did it on purpose, I'll take Old Bertie away for two days."

"How am I supposed to practice driving if you take the truck away?"

"You shouldn't have sworn by it then, should you?" She reached out and ruffled Nathan's hair. Ignoring his scowl, she asked, "Why are you here, anyway? I thought you had a grain bin to clean."

"The auger's broken, and I couldn't get ahold of George to fix it. I thought he'd be here with you."

"George quit." And all she wanted to do was find ways to exact revenge upon him. *Ex-lax in his morning coffee? Too messy. A new mouse infestation in his pickup? Too mousy. "Losing" his last paycheck—*

"Corrie? Are you there?" Nathan waved a hand in front of her face.

"What?"

"What do you want me to do?"

Go find the loser and run him over. No. That wouldn't help. He would be only slightly less useful dead. "I'll figure something out. Did you finish the rest of your chores?"

"Yeah. I was just about to finish cleaning out the grain bin when the stupid auger broke. Can I still go to the lake with my friends?"

His large boots thumped on the running board. Just this morning, he'd complained they were getting tight on him.

"Yeah, you can go." Before he could hop down, she grabbed his arm. "Double-check with Mom and make sure you're home by five to relieve Nikki. She's been in that combine since eight."

He beamed at her and walked away with a lanky stride caused by a six-foot frame and an arm span to match.

She hollered, "Why didn't you just call over the radio?"

"Broken," he yelled over his shoulder before he slammed the door to the old red manual pickup he'd learned to drive.

Rage exploded from deep inside of Corrie. With a scream, she scrunched up an empty Pepsi can, and pretending it was George's head, she chucked it out of the truck cab. For all his horrible qualities, George had worked hard. And he didn't earn minimum wage. He earned a dollar an hour more.

An approaching tractor's purr drew her attention. Her cousin Joey bounced up and down as the John Deere inched closer. He lined the grain cart up with the semi and began dumping golden wheat kernels into the trailer. After several minutes, he pulled away and headed down the rough field to await another combine hopper.

She started the truck and drummed her fingers while it aired up. When the red light signified the truck was ready, she shifted into first, exited the field, and began the twenty-mile drive into Sandy. Metallica screamed through the truck's speakers, and she bobbed her head to the vicious beat.

They would have to hire another person. A person crazy enough to work for a dollar an hour more than minimum wage.

A full moon illuminated the well-kept Lancaster farmyard as Corrie pulled into the driveway. She hauled herself out of the pickup, every muscle in her body threatening mutiny.

"Well, Old Bertie, you did well today. I hope Nathan's treating you right." Giving a tap to the pickup's hood, she chuckled. "I'll have to remind him you're three hundred thousand miles old."

Trusting that Nathan had fed the dog, she rattled the doorknob on the barn to check the lock and trudged to the large two-story colonial-style farmhouse. Its brick façade with white windows and a red front door welcomed her home. She scratched the panicked idea of going back to Sioux Falls. As much as she enjoyed the city, she needed the country and its peaceful quiet and meandering back roads.

She inhaled the cool summer air bursting with the scent of her mother's pansies planted snugly in terra-cotta pots. She sank into a white wicker rocking chair. A plane's red lights blinked in the starlit night, and a shooting star soared into the black abyss.

Nearer, farm equipment not being used in the field hunkered down in the tree belt, far past the reach of the single farm light on the barn roof. Most of it would have to wait until spring to be brought out and put to use. Corrie shook her head. Although perhaps idiotic and slightly neurotic, she couldn't help feeling as if the planting equipment stewed in jealousy and dejection for most of the year. Maybe her parents had read her too many *Corey Combine* books. Apparently, they had thought she would be a boy and had chosen the name before she drew her first breath. Surprised but not beaten, her parents had ditched the spelling and kept the name.

With a grunt, she heaved herself out of the rocking chair and tiptoed into the dark house. Nikki, Nathan, and her mother would have gone to bed hours ago.

One person, however, would still be up. After kicking off her shoes, Corrie walked into the living room. The fresh scent of furniture polish spoke of her mother's Friday cleaning. The television glow illuminated vacuum tracks in the plush white carpeting. A solitary figure sat in a brown leather recliner.

"Hey, Dad." She stooped and kissed the top of his head, noticing for the first time the lines and wrinkles edging his eyes, signs of aging he'd always hidden.

Jake responded with a slurred variation of her name and a wobbling smile. She muted the game show. He'd never liked game shows, and now the Game Show Network was the only thing on when he was in the house. The no-nonsense man she'd known all her life had died when a semitrailer slammed into his truck one icy December evening.

As she did every night, she sat by his slippered feet and told him about her day. The damage hadn't touched the part of his brain that loved and lived off farming. Every day convinced her even more that his love of the land was nurtured not in his head but in his heart. Nothing could kill that.

"George quit today." Corrie saved the worst news for last.

Her father's eyes met hers and reflected the anger he couldn't formulate with words. Then a sliver of worry crept around the anger in his eyes.

Wanting to reel the words back in and swallow them, she sighed. "Don't worry, Dad. I'll take care of it. I'll find someone to replace George."

The worry and anger didn't leave his eyes. With a sigh, she got off the floor and laid her hands on his once-broad shoulders. "Don't stay up too late. Morning comes early on the Lancaster farm." She pressed a kiss to his forehead and left him watching *Deal or No Deal.* He would be up for hours.

CORRIE groaned into her pillow and hid from the protruding fingers of sunlight soaking through her window shades. If only she could cover her head with her comforter and fall back into her wonderful dream about Middle Earth and hobbits. But she couldn't afford the luxury. Not with a truck full of grain to take to the elevator. Not if she wanted to beat the line so she could get back and service the combine. Nikki could take care of the other morning chores, but the combine was Corrie's baby. Nobody greased it except her.

Bacon and eggs sizzled as she entered the bright kitchen. The west wall, full of floor-to-ceiling windows, faced her mother's garden. As a child, Corrie had loathed weeding and watering the garden. Now, a day in the garden would be a nice reprieve.

"Good morning, dear." Corrie's mother, Cynthia, greeted her with a smile.

"Good morning." Corrie took the proffered tongs and flipped the bacon, careful to avoid the splattering grease. "How's Dad this morning?"

"Fine." Cynthia no longer cried when she talked about her husband. A steely reserve now crept into her eyes and flared whenever Jake was mentioned.

Corrie took the hint to shut up. After transferring the bacon to a paper towel–lined plate, she set the table. She watched closely as Cynthia stirred the scrambled eggs with a little more force than necessary. Corrie stopped herself from chewing on her bottom lip, a bad habit carried over from toddlerhood. She wanted to ask her mom about her dad, needed advice about the future of the farm—of them—but all was cut short when a herd of stampeding feet echoed down the stairs.

"You two make enough noise to scare the dead," Corrie scolded as Nikki and Nathan scooted around the corner.

"We're just hungry. That's all." Nathan nipped a piece of bacon. "Where's Dad?"

Before Corrie could intercept the question, Cynthia spun around with a spatula covered in scrambled eggs and whipped the air with it. "Eat. Now."

Nathan ducked his head. "Sorry. I just wanted..."

Corrie's hand squeezed his shoulder, stopping his comment.

Cynthia threw the spatula into the pan of eggs, tossed a potholder on the table, and slapped the pan down, egg shrapnel exploding over the table. She left the kitchen, and when the master bedroom door slammed shut, Nikki and Nathan jumped in their seats.

Several minutes of awkward silence thicker than bacon grease permeated the kitchen. The cheery yellow of the walls and crystal-clear glass of the cupboard doors did nothing to stop the shadows of doubt lurking in every corner. No one mentioned the unspeakable but not improbable event they most feared.

Nikki exhaled. "Do you think they will... you know... get a divorce?"

Corrie shushed her and grabbed the salt and pepper. She no longer had an appetite, but it would be a while before a meal came her way. Forcing herself to swallow, she glanced at Nathan as he scraped at his full plate. "You need to eat, Nathan."

"I'm not hungry." He scooted back his chair and stalked out of the house. Nathan ran across the farmyard and into the barn, where he would most likely find solace in the soft fur of his miniature Australian shepherd, Bacon.

After the barn door slammed, Nikki turned back to her food. "So, do you think Mom will want a divorce?"

Corrie winced at the pain radiating from her seventeen-year-old sister's eyes, the same glacier blue of their father's. Nikki twirled her curly blond hair around her index finger, warming Corrie's heart for a moment with memories of holding her baby sister, mesmerized by the tiny index finger creating equally tiny curls. Her chest swelled as she surveyed her sister, a combination of dirt and the most delicate of wildflowers struggling to soak in the last raindrops.

"I don't know. I really don't." Corrie finished her orange juice. "I can't imagine what Mom is going through right now. I don't think I want to." She started cleaning up. "We need to keep praying."

"It's not working." Nikki swirled the rest of her scrambled eggs around on her plate.

Corrie abandoned her task of clearing off the table and sank beside her sister. "I know things are hard right now. Trust me, I feel the weight of all this. Sometimes, we can't see where God wants us to go. And sometimes, instead of smoothing the mountain for us, he gives us the tools to climb that mountain, and only from there can we see the beauty and majesty of his plan."

Nikki laid her head on Corrie's shoulder. "I'll keep trying. I'm just really tired."

"Me too." Corrie pressed a kiss to Nikki's hair. "Tomorrow is Sunday. We can rest then. Until then, we've got work to do. I'll take the truck into the elevator and meet you at the field later." She headed for the door. "Don't forget to pack a lunch. I don't want to have to go to the café again."

Nikki rolled her eyes. "One time and I'm branded for life."

"Forget again, and I'll brand 'lunch' on your forehead," Corrie teased. She laughed at Nikki's pouty face and rushed across the yard.

Nathan was busy gassing up Old Bertie and making sure the fuel tank on the back of it was full of diesel. Corrie slipped into the passenger side and waited until he finished turning off the tank.

He ambled over to the passenger door, opened it, and blinked in surprise. "You're going to let me drive?"

She chuckled. "Don't expect this every day."

He sprinted around the front of the pickup, hopped in, and started the old girl up. Stomping on the clutch, he slammed the stick into low gear then let off the clutch while easing the gas pedal down. Old Bertie responded with a grunt and spasm but obeyed with jerking movements.

"Okay. Now let the clutch fully out. Good. Give her a little gas. You're choking her. Okay. Now ease in the clutch again and shift to first."

He complied, and soon the pickup was soaring down the road toward the field. She glanced at his profile and wondered when he'd grown up on her. Gone was the scrawny boy who cried every time he came across a dead bird or a hurt farm cat.

"Nathan?"

"Yeah."

"Are you okay? You know, with what's been going on and stuff?" *Good grief. As a reporter, I should be able to ask a better question.* But this wasn't some stranger or some big news-breaking story. This was her brother, and his soft heart was breaking.

His pronounced Adam's apple bobbed up and down. "I guess."

"It's just this morning you seemed... I don't know..." The countryside whizzed by in a blur of color.

"I just miss Dad. I want him to be him again. You know?"

She nodded and bit the inside of her cheek to keep her tears in check. "Yeah. I do. But Dad will always be your dad. You have to know that. He still loves you, loves us, but he can't show it like he used to. You have to have faith and believe he will get better. You never know. He might play football with you again or take you fishing."

Nathan shrugged. "Sure. Maybe."

In other words, conversation over. From the time he'd learned to walk, Nathan had been Dad's sidekick. Now Jake hardly noticed his son.

Nathan brought the pickup to a jerking halt in the field, and she stepped out. "I've got to take this truckload in." She poked her head through the open passenger window. "We'll be okay." Before he could reply, she jumped in the semi, started it, and after it aired up, drove into town.

After twenty miles of rolling cropland and pasture, she crested the hill into Sandy, South Dakota, a small town nestled against the Sandy River. At this time of year, it was more of a creek, but a river it would always be to the residents who'd grown up around its banks. She downshifted in the truck's descent. Judging from the myriad trucks and cars, Corrie guessed Mabel must have cheese buttons as the café special. Corrie's stomach rumbled. She could almost taste the cheese-and-onion mixture tucked deliciously in dough and cooked in cream.

The knife of memory slid and cut its way into her mind as she passed the VFW dance hall where she'd won her first dancing competition. Her father had been her dance partner for the waltz.

She blinked her stinging eyes. Amazing how one phone call could change a life forever. Like a tornado, it sucked her up, spun her around, and spit her out. If only he'd stayed home that snowy night nine months ago. He would be the one harvesting. He would be the one shouldering the farm's responsibility.

Coming to the end of town, she turned right at the only stop sign on Main, pulled up behind a mile-long line of trucks, and inched up off the highway and onto the elevator's graveled property.

"Good morning, Corrie."

She beamed at the old man who hopped on the truck's running board and stuck his head in her truck cab. "Good morning, Baxter."

A proud working octogenarian, Baxter tipped his stained and dusty DeKalb seed cap. Upon close inspection, his crinkly face mirrored his life—full of happiness with a dash of adventure and a few sprinkles of sadness and loss. She loved to hear his stories even though she knew most of them by heart.

"You're looking good." He patted her arm with a veiny, rough hand.

Without a doubt, her wrinkle-free skin had grown new fissures over the past nine months, and baggy, dark circles sat like bloated toads under her eyes. No matter how many promises different shampoo brands boasted, her hair had lost its luster and hung limp in a ponytail every day. "You're much too kind. But thank you. It's nice to hear."

"How are things holding up on the Lancaster farm, dearie?"

"Not so well." She could never pretend with the old man. He was far too wise and knew far too much. "George quit yesterday."

Baxter took off his cap and slapped it against his thigh. Dust flew. "That good for nothing..." He slammed his hat on his bald head. "That rat! Sorry to hear it, Corrie. If you need anything, please let me know." He peered at her with wizened eyes. "I mean it, young lady. All you have to do is ask." Someone inside the main building called for Baxter. With an apologetic pat on her head, he hopped off and ran to the weigh house.

"Spry old man," she muttered as she shifted the truck from neutral into first gear for her turn on the scales. The red light turned green, and she eased onto the scales. She waited until the mechanical arm swung over from the weigh house and sucked grain into its proboscis and into the building. The red light flickered green, and she drove through the obstacle course of trucks and grain bins to the correct dumping site. She watched in her side mirror as elevator employees swarmed the truck's hoppers like worker bees. Eventually, they signaled her to leave, and she waited in line again. Several smaller farm trucks waited ahead of her to go back on the scale. Ten minutes later, she stopped the truck on the scale until Baxter came out with her ticket telling her the bushels and moisture of the load she'd just dumped.

"Here you go, little miss. See you again soon for the same song and dance."

Corrie laughed. "Save me a spot." She glanced at her ticket before veering onto the highway. After doing some quick math, she gave a whoop. Eighty bushels an acre. "Praise the Lord!" That number was exactly what she needed to hear.

All day, she trucked back and forth between the quarter of land they were combining and the elevator. With all that time to think, she couldn't figure out where she would get the extra help she needed. At eighty bushels an acre of wheat, it was really necessary.

Chapter Two

Corrie jabbed her elbow at Nathan's rib cage. He glared at her and rubbed his side. She raised a warning eyebrow then refocused on Pastor Luke and his sermon about trusting the will of God. An apt sermon for the times. The full meaning of what trusting actually meant drilled into her brain. Maybe because of her lack of control, she felt an overwhelming need for it.

The congregation stood to sing the last hymn, interrupting her reverie. "On Eagle's Wings" was usually her favorite hymn. Today, it only reminded her that no eagle had landed on her property in a long time. She snuck a glance at her mother and wondered what was going on behind the plastered-on smile. Her mother, once a beautiful woman, was slowly crumbling under the pressure. Whether it was the pressure to fix her husband or the pressure to stay with her husband, Corrie didn't know.

The song ended, and Corrie and the rest of her family filed out into the foyer. Men who used to crowd around her father, laughing and joking, now stood awkwardly with him for a short time before walking away, shaking their heads. Jake seemed to shrink with every back turned, every prolonged stare, every pitying look. Maybe it was harder on him than it was on the men he'd considered his friends. Maybe it was easier to stop pretending everything was going to be okay. She fought the tears stinging the backs of her eyes.

"And how are the Lancasters doing today?" Pastor Luke laid a hand on Jake's shoulder.

"Doing okay." Jake slurred his speech.

Luke's caring green eyes said he believed none of it. "I've been thinking of coming out and doing some hard work. I've been lazy lately and need some farm work to get me back on the straight and narrow." He looked at Corrie. "Could you help a poor man out and give his hands something to do?"

Her stomach did little flip-flops. And she hated that. Although the question was innocently posed, when it was asked by a man with green eyes the color of the shallows around a tropical island, a straight nose, and cute freckles to offset the warrior vibe, any girl would blush. She'd especially blush with history crackling between them. "S-sure," she stammered. "Sure. I'm sure I've got something to keep you busy."

Luke smiled, showing white teeth. "I'll be out first thing in the morning, then." He turned to Jake. "You've got quite the family. I envy you, sir, and hope someday I'm blessed with children just like yours." Luke shook his hand. "I'll be out tomorrow."

Jake's eyes shone. Corrie proceeded to follow the rest of her family out the door, but Luke's warm hand on her arm stopped her. The memory of that hand sizzled her insides. But they weren't in high school anymore, and he was no longer the football team captain. And she certainly wasn't the straight-A band geek he'd wooed and then torn apart. By fate's cruel practical joke, the one man she swore she would never speak to again was now her pastor. *Go figure.* Finding out that Luke Tuttle was the pastor of Grace Community Church had made her question her decision to return and take over the family farm. In the end, she'd quit her whining and sat every Sunday staring at the man who had stolen more than her heart. Her hand roamed to her belly. His gaze followed it. She snatched it back to her side, clenching it to keep it from trembling.

Now they were both adults. People changed. Luke obviously more so than others. That didn't make it easier to forget past wrongs, and she relived every one of them when she saw him. His eyes snapped to hers, piercing her. His hand stayed on her arm for breathless seconds before dropping to his side.

"How are things really going?"

She sucked in a shaky breath. "Not so good. Dad gets a little better some days, but then he'll have a relapse and get worse. Then he'll get better again for a while." She chewed on her bottom lip. Luke had always listened to her ramblings, and even though every part of her screamed to keep her emotions zipped and locked away from him, her mouth rebelled. "We're all on this roller-coaster ride we never wanted to get on. Every time it stops and we try to get off, the ride starts all over again. I guess I just feel powerless. Everyone, including my mom, looks to me for support, and I honestly don't know if I have enough to get myself through this." She snapped her disobedient mouth shut. Ducking her head, she studied her pink high heels.

"I'm sorry." His apology drew her gaze to him. "I'm sorry you're going through this. The one person in the world I don't want to see suffer is you, Corrie."

She stifled a building snort. *Yeah, right.* "You don't have to be sorry. When life hands you lemons, you make lemonade, right?" Her voice ended with the squeak of looming tears. She ran out of the church as fast as her heels could carry her.

AFTER Sunday dinner dishes had been stacked in the dishwasher and the floor had been swept, Corrie headed to her favorite spot, the tire swing her father had put up twenty-two years ago for her third birthday. It swayed in the warm afternoon breeze. Even with frayed edges and a sun-bleached surface, the tire still stood as a firm reminder of easier and more carefree times.

Smiling, she eased into the tire swing, and the tree branch sank slightly. She walked back on her tiptoes and, when she was standing straight, lifted her feet.

The swinging motion soothed her confusion. Having Luke touch her today had launched long-hidden emotions into orbit. Why, after months of seeing him every Sunday, were these suddenly exploding? And more confusing: Why was she reliving this after seven years? They hadn't spoken since their high school graduation night, when he'd committed the ultimate betrayal. She'd healed, body and soul—moved on, gone to college, dated other men, and gotten over the pain and ultimate rejection. Today, she felt like she'd stepped back in time. Tilting her body back so she lay parallel to the ground, she gazed at the sunlight ricocheting off the weeping willow leaves. Her hair undulating underneath her, she swung into a perfectly calm daze where nothing mattered but the green leaves and warm breeze. The rhythmic motion hypnotized her into the past, nine years ago.

"Corrie, come with me."

Corrie gazed into Luke's eyes, drowning in the green tropical waters shimmering from their depths. "Where?" she whispered, afraid to break the nightly spell the moon anointed on them.

"The windmill. Let's see if we can touch the moon again." His hot, minty breath feathered her cheek as he murmured into her ear, "Come with me." He grabbed her hand, and before she could utter a surprised cry, he ran with her to the base of the windmill and hauled her up to the first metal step, rusted and weathered by generations of rain and snow.

She held her breath as she took each step. The metal groaned and creaked, but she scarcely heard it over the thumping of her heart. Luke's movements rattled below her, and she feared the whole ladder would buckle and sag, sending her to her death. Finally, the glow of the full moon outlined the top. Its narrow ledge wouldn't offer her safety, and she shivered at the thought. Missing blades, the windmill looked toothless as the remaining rusted steel propellers grinned back at her.

Going as far as she could, she held on with clenched fists to the top ladder rung. The cool summer night breeze ruffled her hair, and she tried to angle her lips in a way that allowed her to blow away her long bangs dangling in her eyes.

"Here we are," he whispered as he came up behind her, enveloping her chilled body with his. "Turn around." His breath tickled the back of her neck.

"Are you crazy?" she hissed, her teeth clenched.

"Trust me. I've got you."

With stomach roiling, she eased herself around, her arms hooked on the ladder behind her. "This is crazy." Her nose bumped his as he brought himself closer and hooked the ends of a harness onto each side of the ladder. "Where'd you get that from?"

His teeth flashed white in the moonlight. "I stole it from Caleb when he wasn't looking." Luke let go of the ladder and leaned back. He laughed at her gasp. "We aren't going anywhere."

Her anger melted. Was it Luke's daring disregard for safety that turned her on? She wasn't sure, but her sixteen-year-old heart didn't know what to think. And she didn't think any more that evening as he pulled himself toward her and kissed her like she'd never been kissed before.

"Corrie?"

She moaned against Luke's lips.

"Corrie?" A deep voice disturbed her peace.

She lunged up and placed her hand on her chest to ensure her heart and forbidden memories remained in their proper place. She locked eyes with the handsome stranger. "Yes?"

He shuffled his feet. "You don't recognize me, do you?"

His muscular body towered over her in the swing. Mahogany hair glinted in the sun and fell slightly over his ears and forehead, rather shaggy and in need of a haircut. His green eyes looked strangely familiar but as if they should be looking out of another man's face.

His Romanesque nose and sharp cheekbones reminded her of someone she used to know. The dimple in his chin stood out under a couple of days of dark stubble mixed with specks of gray.

He grinned, revealing deep dimples in both cheeks. Her memory clicked.

"Aaron!" She wrestled out of the tire swing and outstretched her hand. "What brings you here? It's been a while."

"I was just in visiting with your father. I heard about the accident right away, but this is the first I've been home in a long time." Aaron's smile didn't quite reach his eyes as he shook her hand. "He was a good guy to me when I was growing up."

She remembered Aaron, Luke's older brother and a good ten years her senior, coming to help on the farm when he wasn't needed at home. Her memories of him were somewhat vague. He was the older brother who visited rarely and was *old*. That was all. Luke took up most of her time when she was growing up. But looking at Aaron now, Corrie did not see *old*.

"I'm glad you stopped to see him. He likes visitors. Especially ones who don't come just to snoop."

"Oh, I didn't come to snoop. I actually came to see you as well."

"Really? Let's have a seat on the porch." Swallowing against the scratchiness in her throat, she walked toward the house. "Would you like some lemonade, iced tea, pop?"

"I'm good, thanks. Your mother already hooked me up with some lemonade." He turned to her as they crossed the lawn to the house. "How is she, by the way?"

Corrie shrugged. "I don't really know. She's struggling with it all, but she doesn't talk about it much."

They ascended the porch steps and sat in adjacent wicker rocking chairs. "I can't imagine what you and your family have gone through. I'm sorry this is happening to you."

"Thanks. I'm sorry, too, about your brother. We were all shocked when we heard. Your mom comes over every day and sits with my mom for a while. I think they've bonded in their sorrow."

Aaron's brow screwed up as if in pain, and he scrubbed his face with his hands. "Sorry. It's still hard to talk about." He fiddled with the rocking chair arm. "I have a proposition for you."

"Okay." She studied his kind features. "What is it?"

"I heard from my mom that George quit on you the other day. I am here to offer my help." He raised his hands. "As unpracticed with farming as these are, I think I could get back in the swing of things pretty quickly. Dad and Luke will need me, too, but I'm sure I can handle both places without doing any damage."

Common sense killed the rush of relief flooding through her veins. "Helping your dad and then me? That's too much. I can't ask that of you."

"You didn't." He studied the farmyard. "You'll have your hands full when Nikki and Nathan start school again."

"The pay sucks. Just ask George."

"George is a no-load. And I don't care about the pay."

"I'm a tough taskmaster."

"Good." Aaron winked. "I like tough women."

Her insides warmed. Aaron Tuttle had just winked at her. He had probably forgotten she even existed until now. How she wished he would wink at her again. *Whoa! Where did that idea come from?* She scrubbed her hands over her face to mask the blush she felt blooming on her cheeks.

"I'll need someone full-time once school starts."

"I'll talk to Dad. We'll work something out. I'm sure Luke would be willing to help out too."

She felt the color drain from her face. "Oh, he offered to come out tomorrow and help. I think he wants to talk to my dad, but he said he's ready for some farm work. We'll see if he offers again after I'm done with him."

"I thought you guys didn't talk?"

Her heart pounded in her chest. "We don't... didn't... I mean we haven't." *Ugh.* She frowned. "He offered today in church. I thought it would be rude to turn him down, that's all." Corrie peeked at his profile. *How much of my past relationship with Luke does he know?*

"So, do you accept my offer?"

She gazed out at her farm. There would be no way for her to keep this property in tip-top shape without help. But seeing Aaron every day would remind her of Luke every day, and she'd done everything in her power to wipe those memories away. Her shoulders stooped. She had no choice—a running theme throughout her life. Her lack of options kept piling up.

"Sure. It's a deal."

His warm and calloused hand enveloped hers in a handshake. She wanted to hold on to that hand, take comfort in it, but all too soon, he released her. Plastering a smile on her face, she waved as he drove out of the farmyard, bringing her hand to rest over her thundering heart.

CORRIE bit off a curse. In front of her, seeming to quiver in fear, the combine header looked forlorn and guilty.

"Serves you right, you piece of junk. Rocks are not good to eat." The long sickle bar with its serrated triangle sections grimaced in a fragmented grin. Several sections were busted and broken off, but the extent of the damage lay in the feeder house. As she chewed on her bottom lip, Corrie's palms began to sweat, and her stomach roiled. She had no idea how to fix the problem in the feeder house. If

George were here, he could've handled it. Anger rekindled, scorching the part of her heart where forgiveness resided.

Refusing to cry, she waited for a miracle. Nikki was sniveling in her shirt. Nathan stood shock-still. And their cousin Joey sat on the combine ladder, munching on a Twinkie. Nope. No miracles were even close to happening.

Corrie whipped out her cell phone. One bar stood green and proud on her screen. Even though the piggy bank was on life support and there was no chance of resuscitation just yet, she had to dial the Sandy County John Deere Implement Dealer.

A diesel pickup rumbling into the field stilled her fingers.

"Who on earth...?" She shielded her eyes from the sun and stared at the familiar pickup. Luke's pickup. Jamming her cell phone into her back jeans pocket, she kept her hands locked in the denim prison to keep their twitching from betraying her stew of emotions. That Luke still had an effect on her was obvious. And she hated every piece of her heart that still pined for the boy who used to be. She wanted to carve those pieces out.

Luke shut off the engine and trotted over to the incapacitated combine. Gone were the suit and tie she was used to seeing him in. Today, he sported well-worn jeans with rips and old grease stains and a faded 7Up T-shirt. A Twins baseball cap snugged to his head shaded his well-chiseled face. His sneakered feet plowed through the chaff and stubble. He looked like his older brother. She blinked in surprise at the likeness and peered around him to see if he'd brought Aaron with him, ignoring the tinge of disappointment she felt upon finding only a solitary Tuttle brother. *Must be heartburn.*

Luke's gaze swept past a weeping Nikki, terrified Nathan, and Twinkie-eating Joey. His right foot stepped back when he made eye contact with Corrie. Her seething frame apparently kept him at a distance. "Troubles?"

She bit off a rather unpleasant remark. "Nope. Just having a nice picnic. Care for a Twinkie?"

Luke rubbed his chin. "Sorry. Stupid question. I wasn't meaning to be sarcastic."

"Sorry, Pastor, I shouldn't have spoken to you like that. And yes, we are having massive problems today."

"First of all, don't call me Pastor. It weirds me out. Secondly, I can probably help." He pretended to roll up long sleeves. "What's the issue?"

"Well, the combine accidentally ate a rock. I have broken sections and some bigger issues in the feeder house." She gestured to the long rectangular shape jutting out of the front of the combine. "I have no idea how to fix it. I was about to call the dealership for assistance."

"It's a good thing you didn't. Be right back." He jogged to his truck, his long and confident stride eating up the ground.

Corrie was staring. She whipped around, stole a still-wrapped Twinkie from Joey's hands, and scarfed it down.

"Hey!" At Joey's indignant cry, everyone started laughing. "What did I ever do to you, you... you Twinkie thief!"

Corrie licked her fingers. "If you and Nathan had done a better job this spring picking rocks off this field, we wouldn't be standing here in the first place."

Joey sulked on the bottom rung of the combine ladder.

She playfully punched his arm. "You know a day can't go by where I don't give you grief, Joey. I'll make it up to you and buy you a whole pack of Twinkies when I get to town, okay?"

He waved her offer away. "Nah. Don't bother. I'm thinking of moving on to Little Debbie's Hostess Cakes, anyway."

She studied his skinny little frame. *Where does he keep it all?* She stepped back as Luke returned with a toolbox. "Are you telling me you know how to fix this?"

Luke shrugged. "Let me put it this way. I'll try not to break it more." He squatted in front of the feeder house, its cylinder and chains glinting like braces. The combine without its header looked naked.

Trusting Luke to know what he was doing, she trudged to the header and began removing the broken serrated triangle sickles. A half hour and an assortment of muffled swear words and cuts here and there later, she finished her job, and the header grinned with new dental work.

"Bust another tooth eating rocks, and I'll take you to the rock pile and burn you," she warned. "I mean it."

"You talk to your equipment too?" Luke's voice purred near her ear. She jumped away from it and from the memories of years past when she'd leaned into that same voice.

"Guilty as charged." After staring at his helping hand, she grabbed it. He hauled her to her feet. She pulled her hand from his and brushed off her jeans. "How are things going on your end?"

"Good. It'll take me another hour, probably, and I have to go back to the farm to get some things. Why don't you go ahead and take a break or something?"

Corrie scoffed. "You've forgotten some essential things about me, haven't you?"

He gazed into her eyes. "Not the important things. I remember how much you love to read. Why don't you go home for an hour, put your feet up, and reread *Pride and Prejudice*?"

She fidgeted under his tender gaze. "Trust me, I'd love to, but I was about to leave with the truck when the combine broke. Jane Austen will have to be a luxury I take part in later."

"You need to take time for yourself, Corrie. Don't push yourself too hard. I don't want to see you hurt..." His face turned crimson, and his eyes looked at everything but her. His Adam's apple bobbed up and down before he croaked, "Any more than you already are."

"Don't worry about me. I can take care of myself." She stalked off toward the semi. Time to get back to work. And she certainly didn't need the advice of Luke Tuttle.

THE house was dark and quiet when Corrie trudged through the front door. She'd sent Nikki and Nathan home early. *No need to run them into the ground.* She had just opened the fridge door when a noise down the hall caught her attention. Her eyebrows shot up, and she followed the sounds to the spare bedroom door. After a moment's hesitation, she knocked on the door.

"Come in."

Corrie entered and paused in the doorway. Her mother stood folding socks and underwear and stacking them neatly in the bureau reserved for guests' clothes.

Cynthia closed the top drawer. "Hi, Corrie. You don't look so good. Are you okay?" She walked over and felt Corrie's forehead with the back of her hand.

"I'm fine, Mom." Corrie stepped back. "What are you doing?"

Cynthia stuck her hands in the pockets of her pastel-green robe. "Your father keeps such strange hours now, and I decided it'd be easier if I moved in here. Until things get better, of course."

Corrie pretended to believe her. "Do you need help?"

"No. Thanks, though. This is something I need to do on my own." Cynthia tilted her head. "I saw Pastor Tuttle come by today. He said you had some issues in the field. Are things fixed?"

"The feeder house is fixed, and the one-eighty behind Wilfred's cow pasture is done." Corrie gave a wobbly smile. "You know, Mom, you aren't alone in this, right? You've got all of us behind you."

Tears welled up in her mother's eyes. "I know, dear. I really do know that, but some battles are meant to be fought alone. Sadly, this battle is one of those." After planting a kiss on Corrie's cheek, Cynthia hung up her colorfully patterned work scrubs. She caressed one with a kaleidoscope of bright-blue begonias. "You know, I never thought I'd hang these up for good." A soft chuckle escaped her lips. "Just the other day, I took some goodies to the residents, and Tilly told me she missed me." Tears balanced on her bottom lids. "But your father needs me. He can't... I can't leave..." Her breathing hitched, and she wiped away a tear that dared to fall. "Don't mind me. I'll be just fine. Um, there's lasagna in the fridge for you and left-over lemon meringue pie. I put the threat of death on Nathan if he touched the last piece."

Corrie pulled her into a hug and clung to her. She wanted to feel her mother's comforting hand on her head. She wanted her mother back. Something in the far reaches of her mind told her the roles had reversed. "Thanks, Mom. Good night."

"Good night, dear." Cynthia tore herself from the hug and returned to putting into the guest closet her belongings that had once called the marital bedroom home.

Corrie closed the door and leaned against the wall. Metal hangers scraped against the rack, and soft sobs came from her mother.

Corrie walked to the dim kitchen, where she found her father. By the paltry glow of the stove light, he was making a peanut butter and banana sandwich. He glanced at her when she entered.

"Hi."

"Hi, Dad. Did you want me to get you something else?"

He shook his head. "Used to like these?"

She nodded, and her stomach clutched in anticipation as he carefully sliced a banana on his peanut butter–covered bread. After he'd gotten home from the hospital, she'd made him a sandwich that he'd thrown across the room. Closing her eyes against the memory, she sent a silent prayer to heaven as he bit into the sandwich. His face lit up. His doctor said traumatic brain injuries were finicky little suckers and could either last a lifetime, worsen with time, or improve within days or over years. He offered no hard-core answers or cures. This one small bite, though, meant the world to her.

"Good." He smiled at her and gulped down the rest of the sandwich. Within minutes, he made two other sandwiches. He handed one to her, and by the light of the kitchen stove, they ate peanut butter and banana sandwiches.

She chewed, not even tasting the sticky concoction. Her eyes never left her father's face, looking for the old spark that had lit his eyes. Her heart skipped a beat when it flickered like a dying fluorescent bulb. It was enough, though. It was a flicker of hope. A flicker of promise.

Chapter Three

Aaron showed up promptly at seven o'clock the next morning. With the hot, dry wind whistling over the land, the wheat was ready to go much earlier than in humid summers. Brown grass crunched under his work-worn cowboy boots. He glanced at the Lancaster house. No sign of Corrie.

He would never forget how she'd looked on Sunday, swinging endlessly in the tire swing he'd helped put up years ago. He'd felt like a teenage boy again, squeaky voice and all. It had been sixteen years since he'd left his teenage years behind him.

If given the choice, he would watch her swaying long brown hair or her tanned legs reaching up to touch the darting dots of sunlight all day. It had been forever since he'd seen her. Seven years, in fact. Then, she'd been a graduating high school senior and his younger brother's girlfriend, not a full-fledged woman. He swallowed. In church, her hair, her eyes, her smile, her pert upturned nose had made paying attention to the sermon difficult. She was definitely not the pigtailed girl running around the farmyard and chasing chickens with Luke anymore.

Aaron wiped sweaty palms on his jeans. He'd been gone a long time. Coming back wasn't the easiest decision, but after his older brother's death in Afghanistan, he had to help out with the farm. He swallowed the rising tears. Caleb. If he closed his eyes, he could still see Caleb's face and hear his rumbling voice. Knowing that his father struggled with the pain and loss of Caleb and that Luke needed time to fulfill his pastoral duties, Aaron had resigned from his teaching job. *No more history lessons for this old teacher.*

Bacon, the family's dog, came to sniff out the new scent. "You know me, ole boy," Aaron crooned as he stooped to scratch Bacon's floppy ears. "I was here Sunday. Don't you remember?"

Bacon licked Aaron's face. "I'll take that as a yes."

"He seems to like you." Corrie stood over him with a smile on her face and dark aviators covering her mocha eyes. "Actually, Bacon loves everybody, and therefore, everybody loves Bacon. He makes a horrible watchdog." She paused as her mother pulled up beside her in a blue Yukon. Jake sat alert in the passenger seat, studying the domain he'd once commanded. "When will you be back tomorrow?"

Cynthia shrugged. "I hope to be back by late afternoon. Your father has a morning appointment tomorrow also, but hopefully, it's a quick one and will be over soon."

Corrie leaned in, gave her mother a peck on the cheek, then moved to the passenger side and repeated the action on her father. "Love you guys. Drive safely."

The Yukon turned right at the end of the drive and disappeared in a dust cloud.

"Another doctor's appointment?"

"Yeah." Corrie nodded. "Sioux Falls is a long way from here, but Dad has to go at least once every two weeks. His therapy seems to be helping. We hope that with continued therapy, he'll get better."

"Not healed, though?" Aaron studied her in the morning sunlight and had the urge to take her ponytail out and let her chestnut-brown hair tumble down her back. He blinked and looked away to study some sparrows chasing a hawk. He sympathized with the hawk.

"That's the frustrating part. We don't really know. We keep praying for a miracle."

"I'll add my prayers too." He stashed his hands in his pockets so they wouldn't betray his need to free her hair.

Her lips quivered in a lopsided frown. "Thanks. We can use all the help we can get."

"That's why I'm here. What do you have for me today?"

"Nikki and Nathan both have sport camps today. I swear they start practice earlier and earlier every year. They may as well start in July. Not that it would do our team any good. School doesn't start for another two weeks. Two weeks! I mean, I'm not the only one who needs help on the farm this time of year, especially with the bumper crop we've been having."

Aaron grinned. "Tell me how you really feel."

"Sorry. Don't mean to vent. It's just, there's a lot of wheat left and not much time before school starts. I'd like to get the rest of the crop in first." She took a deep breath. "So one of us has to operate the combine. Would you rather do that or drive the truck?"

"What would you rather do?"

She pouted. "Not the truck. Anything but the truck."

Aaron ignored the urge to taste her pouting lips. "Not a fan of the truck, are we?"

She scrunched up her nose. "Nope. Not one bit. I'd rather go around in mindless circles than drive that thing today or the next couple of days, actually." She headed for the barn. "I'll go out to the field and start servicing the combine. If you want, you can ride along with me and then take the truck into the elevator."

She climbed into old Bertie and waited until Aaron scooted into the passenger side. She jammed the old pickup into reverse and pulled away from the barn. A breeze wisped through the open windows, catching Corrie's scent and taunting his nose with the smell of honeysuckle.

"How many more acres do you have?"

"Well, around fifteen hundred." At his low whistle, she grimaced. "Yeah, I know. We had a family powwow last night and agreed to have some of it custom combined. We just can't do it. Not with camps and practice and then school."

"But you hired Superman, remember?" He winked. *What am I doing?* Flirting with his little brother's ex-girlfriend certainly broke some rule. Besides, winking at a woman ten years his junior was creepy. *Right?* Feeling shaky and stupid, he snapped his mouth shut and gazed out the window.

A thrill skittered up Corrie's backbone at Aaron's wink. Not finding any words, she concentrated on driving. The familiar surroundings never failed to awaken her love of the land that had raised her. Across the gravel road from her farm, a field of sunflowers just beginning to bloom shimmered in the sun's morning rays. Tall and dense evergreens, planted by her ancestors, shaded the driveway from the dawning light. Every gopher hole, every dip in the road, every utility pole had long since etched itself into her memory.

She turned left onto the paved county highway and shifted old Bertie into overdrive. The warm morning air rushed through the windows and played with her ponytail. They passed the pond and the old bridge that had served as a wonderful fishing spot in her younger years. She itched for a chance to go fishing with her father. Maybe she would take him when he and her mother got back from Sioux Falls.

"Remember the old windmill?" Aaron interrupted her thoughts.

Over across a golden-ripe wheat field, the rusting metal skeleton stretched into the azure sky. Subconsciously, she licked her lips. *Remember? How could I not?* She tried to drive down both the highway and memory lane. A night nine years ago overtook her. The muggy dampness. The crickets. The luminous moon. The night a football quarterback stole a kiss from a bookworm and changed her life.

"Do you remember it?"

Corrie snapped out of her daydream. "What? Oh yeah. The windmill... yeah... everybody knows the windmill." She stopped mid-stammer. "Why?"

He chuckled. "I thought you'd remember the time you and your little sidekick decided it'd be a good adventure to trek to the windmill and climb it."

"Oh, my! I'd forgotten all about that." She downshifted to pull into the field approach. "That was very traumatic, by the way. We thought we'd be stuck up there forever. It's amazing our little legs could even climb as far as they did."

"Yeah, I think everybody was pretty surprised you two little ones not only had the guts but the initiative to try it." He reached for the door handle as Old Bertie jerked to a stop. "Whose idea was it, anyway?"

She stared at him. "Really? You have to ask?" Clicking her tongue, she hopped out. "It was your brother's harebrained idea. He thought we could touch the moon if we climbed high enough." Her mind instantly reverted to the night years after their childhood adventure when Luke proved they could indeed touch the moon. Heat moved up her face.

"That does not surprise me at all." Aaron turned and walked to the semi.

She smoothed her ponytail, adjusted her sunglasses, and marched toward the waiting combine. She needed some good, honest work to keep her mind off forbidden memories.

AN AFTERNOON OF HONEST work morphed into days that slowly ate their way into a week.

Corrie jumped from bed early Monday morning and reached for her standard field attire of ripped jeans that her mother used to wear and an old high school Mustangs T-shirt. Then she thought of Aaron. She'd never dreaded fieldwork, but knowing he would be there with a morning gift of a Pepsi, a Milky Way, and a smile complete with matching dimples, she yearned for time to speed up and get with the program.

Ditching the mom jeans on the floor, she dug through her drawer of jeans and selected a pair that had a rip at the knee but had never failed her in the backside department. Instead of a ratty T-shirt that should have been a barn rag, she pulled over her head a tank top spattered with pineapples. Nothing she could do about her hair. A ponytail would have to do, but she back-combed her hair first, forcing some volume into her 'do. In her quick trip to the bathroom, she dug around for her makeup kit, which saw the light of day only on Sundays, swiped blush on each cheek, and perked up her eyelashes with a dose of black mascara. For the mouth, tinted ChapStick would have to do. She smacked her lips and skipped down the steps.

"Well, you look nice."

"Mom, you can wipe that smile off your face. Nothing wrong with me looking nice, right?"

Cynthia pulled her in for a hug. "Nothing wrong at all." She pulled back and cupped Corrie's face. "I'm glad you have a reason to."

Corrie thought so too. With a smile, she packed a lunch and drove to the field, hungry to see a certain Tuttle boy.

She groaned as she downshifted into the field approach. Wrong pickup. Wrong Tuttle boy. Luke sauntered over as she parked her truck and stepped out. He eyed her tank top. "Looking rather tropical today."

Shove a pineapple where the sun— She forced a smile. "What brings you here, Pastor?"

His grin slipped. "Please, Corrie, we covered this already. Don't call me that. Aren't we friends?"

"Sure."

He gestured to the half-harvested field. "Need help today?"

"Nope. Have all the help I need right now."

As if on cue, Aaron's pickup rumbled into the field. Luke's shoulders squared off as Aaron joined them, a plastic bag swaying from one hand.

"Good morning, Luke. Corrie." Aaron's twin dimples winked at her. "You should have told me you were wearing a pineapple shirt. I have one myself." At her quirked eyebrow, he held up his right hand, his first three fingers saluting. "Scout's honor. I have to wear it sometimes. Mom bought it when she and Dad went to Hawaii."

Luke snorted but said nothing. Aaron shot him a look. "What brings you here this morning? I thought Dad had some things for you to work on."

"Just checking on Corrie. Making sure she's okay." He pointed at the bag. "What's that?"

Corrie grinned and showed off her treats.

"Pepsi and Milky Way, huh? Good to know." Luke tapped his temple. "Well, I've got to run. Corrie, let me know if you need anything." He took her hand. "Anything."

His touch burned and, just like at church, stirred memories she wanted nothing to do with. She tore her hand from his and rested it on her stomach. "Yeah. Thanks."

Luke stalked off. Aaron flicked a look at her hand. "Are you okay?"

She jerked her hand to her side. "Yeah."

He cocked his head to the side.

"I'm fine. Promise. Thank you. For this." She brandished the goodies.

"My pleasure." He tipped his hat. "I'll take the truck in. Need anything else?"

A hug, another one of your smiles, an escape from bad memories. "Nope. I'm good." She traipsed toward the combine.

"Corrie?" Aaron called after her. "I really do like those pineapples. Feels like I'm on vacation."

She returned his grin. "Just wait until I wear my sunglasses-wearing flamingos tomorrow."

"I can't wait."

Neither can I.

Another week flew by full of candy bars, tropical shirts—including the promised Hawaiian tourist trap button-up—and stolen smiles. Perfect harvest weather was great for work but not conducive to flirting. They could spend hours in the same field and never see each other. She had come to yearn for even his voice over the CB radio. And on the occasions where he pulled up next to her in the tractor so he could empty the combine's hopper into the grain cart, her heart would do a little flip. She scolded it whenever it did. She had no right to him. After he found out what she had done, the true history between her and Luke, he would walk away. She blamed her overactive butterflies on exhaustion. Her weary body and extra-weary soul needed a rest.

TINY bullets of rain pelted the office window. Not exactly the rest she needed. Corrie pressed her forehead against the cool glass as lightning forked across the dark sky. Three seconds. Thunder ricocheted through the farmyard, answering the lightning's electrifying call. A little less than a mile away, the core of the storm, the angry swirling center, aimed straight for the farm. Another flash scorched the night sky, leaving a millisecond of burnt air in its wake. Two seconds. Bang. The house vibrated, and the windows rattled in their casings. She stepped back from the window and headed toward the living room, where her family huddled in a tight group, eyes glued to the television station. They all jumped when another thunder crash echoed through the house.

"The wind's picking up." She chewed on her lip. "Are they calling for tornadoes?"

Nathan glanced at her, fear visible in his eyes. "No. Strong winds, though."

Corrie moved to the couch and sat next to him. She patted his knee. "We'll be okay. Are you sure you parked all the equipment you could away?"

He huffed. "I'm not an idiot."

"No. But you are forgetful. Remember the time you—" She screamed as an explosion ripped through the house, shaking the walls and engulfing the farmyard in a violent light. "What the—what was that?" She cowered next to her brother, not caring that his hand squished hers. Nikki trembled next to Jake, and Cynthia latched onto her husband's hand. Corrie opened and closed her jaw rapidly to dispel the ringing in her ears.

"It's like someone shot a gun from in here," Nathan added, not yet letting go of Corrie's hand.

"And they stood right by my head to pull the trigger." Nikki stuck her fingers in her ears and wiggled them back and forth.

Corrie wriggled her hand from Nathan's grasp and crept toward the window, leery of every flash of lightning and roar of thunder. Peering into the inky blackness, she saw nothing until lightning lit up the sky again, illuminating what was once a proud evergreen towering above the house.

"Um, Mom? You know that tree you hate decorating at Christmas?"

"Yeah?" Cynthia laid a blanket over Nikki and Jake, who snuggled together on the overstuffed recliner.

"You don't have to worry about that in a few months. It's gone."

"What?" Cynthia darted to the window, and the next flash of light revealed a toothpick where a thirty-foot pine tree used to be. "I'll be a monkey's uncle." Cynthia clucked her tongue and stepped away from the window, looking back only once. "Nathan, that's one less thing you'll have to worry about this winter."

"I kind of actually liked that tree," he mumbled from the couch, his knees pulled up to his chin. "Whatever. This storm sucks."

A giggle formed in Corrie's throat. She tried to squelch it, kill it before it came rolling out, but it would have no such thing. It burst out of her, earning her stares from her siblings and a quirked eyebrow from her mother. "Sorry," she croaked as the giggle formed into a laugh. She bent forward, attempting to get ahold of herself. The laugh, instead, grew bigger. Through her own gut-wrenching guffaws, she heard her brother snicker from the couch. In no time, Nikki joined them with her squeaky laugh, which only made Corrie and Nathan laugh all the more.

"Nikki's on the move again with her squeaky wheel. Get the WD-40," Nathan panted through his laughter.

Through the film of tears forming on her eyes, Corrie witnessed her parents share *the* look. It'd been months since they'd done that. A ray of hope grew in Corrie's chest as she laughed with her siblings, daring the violent storm outside to squelch the one tiny footstep to victory.

THE scent of freshly washed earth made Corrie's nose tingle. Inhaling, she leaned against the porch railing and admired the millions of raindrops clinging to and dripping from disheveled trees, bruised flower petals, and the gleaming red-and-green tin of the barn and machine shed. A light breeze breathed upon the mud puddles, sending miniscule ripples across the two-foot-wide, rain-made lakes. She almost felt the land sigh with pleasure after weeks of dryness. Sighing in harmony, she stepped off the porch and picked her way past and over the puddles to the evergreen sheared by the lightning bolt. It looked like a tree war zone. Fragments and pieces of the boughs lay scattered and strewn, muddied and scorched. Half the trunk, split down the middle, still stood, its jagged top peaked into a tiny pinnacle where a bead of rain glistened in the morning sunrise.

A pickup smearing its way up the driveway caught Corrie's attention. Her heart sank. George. Anger coursed through her. Chauvinist pig. She puffed out a breath. It was a relief not to have that man around anymore. Not caring about the mud or puddles, she darted across the yard, intercepting his squishy frame.

"What do you want, George?" She smiled through gritted teeth.

"Oh, I think you know what I want." He moved closer, closing the gap until only a mud puddle separated them. "I can run this farm better than you. We both know—"

"Let's get one thing straight. There is no way on God's green earth that that little fantasy swimming around in your head will ever come true. I'll never sell this farm, especially to the likes of you." She waved a hand in front of his face. "Hey, my eyes are up here. The last time I checked, my chest didn't have eyes."

George's face turned as red as a cherry. It was actually quite fascinating how the color crept up in blotches from the hair sticking out of his T-shirt to his receding hairline. "Why, you little..."

"Having trouble thinking of insults for me? I could help you out, but then you wouldn't be learning. I suggest you go home, Google some words, and come back when you're prepared." She crossed her arms over her chest. "Until then, I further suggest you get off this property and leave me and my family alone."

"You owe me money for my last week," he growled.

She swallowed her pride. "Yes, I do. I'll get that written out today and sent in the mail. As for stepping foot on this farm again, I'd advise you not to." She glared at him until he moved, sloshing through the puddles toward his truck. As he drove out of the yard, another truck pulled in—Aaron's silver Ford pickup. Her heart skipped a beat. Shaking her head at the sudden movement in her chest, she wondered if skipping breakfast caused heart issues.

"Good morning." She waved as he hopped out of the truck and dodged the mud puddles.

"Hey." He grinned when he reached her. "Did you guys come out okay last night? We heard a large explosion and figured it hit pretty close."

"You could say it hit close to home. Literally." She pointed back at the house, where the jagged toothpick stood alone among its fallen comrades.

"Oh, man. That must've scared the crap out of you all."

"I believe Nathan and Nikki needed a change of pants. I, however, was as calm and collected as a cucumber."

"You mean 'as cool as,' right?" Aaron's lips pulled back into a smile.

A tightness pinched her chest. She needed to eat breakfast and soon before her heart just decided to up and quit. "That too."

"I'm sure you didn't flinch."

"Are you calling me a liar?" She teased back, accepting his hand to help her dodge the puddle mines. His touch zinged right to her core. "Are you hungry? Because I'm telling you, I need to eat something."

"I just ate, but don't let that stop you from eating." Once they made it to the porch, he released her hand.

She grinned brightly in an attempt to dissipate the sudden feeling of loneliness. "I'm sure my mom would be heartbroken if you didn't at least have one of her caramel rolls. It's Saturday. It's tradition."

"Well, I'd hate to buck tradition. I suppose I'll have to have one."

She laughed at his pouty face. "Now, where did you learn to do that?"

"I was born with this talent, lady. I was an expert at birth on getting what I want when I want it."

"I'm sure it hasn't worked every time."

At his side-glance and grin, she felt tingles skitter up and down her spine.

"So, um... yeah. Breakfast." She opened the door, and hoping to escape from the funny feelings surrounding her in Aaron's presence, she all but mall-walked to the kitchen and the aroma of freshly baked rolls. "It smells like heaven in here." She gave her mom a side hug and scooted in between Nathan and Nikki at the table. "Slow down, Nathan. Mom always makes plenty."

Nathan shoved a huge piece in his mouth. Caramel dripped from his fingers as he reached for a napkin. "I've already called three of them."

"Three! They're as big as your head." Corrie glanced at her brother's athletic frame. "Are you sure you don't have a hollow leg?"

"It's not my fault I have a magnificent metabolism." Nathan licked his fingers, clearly forgetting about the napkin right next to him.

"Congratulations, Mom. You gave birth to a Neanderthal." Corrie grinned as he glared at Aaron's hand reaching for a roll. "See, proof." She lightly backhanded Nathan's head. "Be nice."

Cynthia walked over with a steaming plate full of gooey, caramelly goodness. "Here you go, Aaron. Ignore the caveman. He doesn't usually bite."

Aaron thanked her and sat across from Corrie. When his foot accidentally bumped hers, her heart raced, and she wished he would accidentally bump her foot again. Afraid her thoughts would give voice to themselves, she chewed viciously on a roll, forgetting even to taste it.

"Hi, Aaron." Jake entered the kitchen, still dressed in his Vikings pajama pants and NRA T-shirt. His eyes, clear and sharp, zeroed in on Aaron. "Thank you."

Aaron stood up and shook Jake's hand. "There's no need to thank me, sir. It's a pleasure to help out."

Jake's eyes, serious, glanced over at Corrie. She squirmed under his gaze. "Too stubborn to ask for help."

Wishing a sinkhole could suck her into its depths, she kept chewing and rolled her eyes at Aaron's reply and, at Nathan's snicker, jabbed an elbow into his ribs. "Shush and keep eating," she whispered.

Nathan whispered back, "But it's true. You never ask for help. You are stubborn."

She glowered over her breakfast. After Aaron sat down, she didn't look at him. Her heart didn't need any more interference.

"So, what was George doing here this morning?" Aaron asked. The sharp sound of a metal spatula hitting the tile floor preceded the silence stifling the room. He paused from taking the first bite of his roll and scanned the Lancaster family. "Sorry. I didn't mean... I mean I didn't think..." He gave up and hung his head. "I'm sorry for bringing up George's name. I just saw him leave your place when I pulled in."

Corrie melted. "No worries. George is kind of a swear word around here."

"Yeah. I got that." Aaron frowned at Cynthia, who was busy rinsing off the spatula that had tumbled from her hand. "Sorry, Mrs. Lancaster."

She smiled. "As Corrie said, no worries." She pointed toward the table groaning with food. "Eat!"

Nathan chewed for a while. "No, really, why was he here?"

"He wanted to be paid for the last week he worked."

"He's a creep," Nikki piped up.

"And a crook," Nathan joined in.

"Probably." Corrie hated sticking up for the man, but there was no getting around it. "But we do owe him money."

She glanced at her father, worried this conversation would put him back into the fog he usually lived in. But there he sat, perched in his chair, his eyes alert. "I made it clear he was not welcome on this farm again." She inwardly preened under her father's accepting gaze. At least she was doing some things right. "Speaking of which, I should go write the check out and get it in the mail before the mailman comes." Licking her fingers, she caught Aaron's gaze and blushed. She grabbed Nathan's unused napkin and wiped her fingers on it. "Thanks for breakfast, Mom. It was delicious."

AARON gulped down the last of his roll, pushed back from the table, and thanked Cynthia for breakfast. "I need to go speak with Corrie about something. Thanks again for breakfast." He shook Jake's hand and nodded to Nathan and Nikki, who were each eyeing the last roll. He walked down the hall toward the office and knocked lightly on the doorjamb.

Corrie glanced up from where she sat in the leather desk chair. When she smiled, his heart tripped over itself.

Swallowing against the nervousness clawing at his throat, he prayed his voice would sound calmer than he felt. "Did you need me around for anything? My dad would like me to fix some fencing and do some odds and ends around the farm."

"Please help your dad." She crossed the *T* in her signature. "That's why you came home, anyway. Not to help me. I feel badly the way it is. You working here and for your dad. You must be exhausted."

"I really don't mind." That wasn't the whole truth. When he was around her, his tiredness evaporated. "I'm just glad I can help."

"Thanks." She stood and came around the desk then leaned her hip against the wooden surface. Sunlight filtering through the window played on her face, bringing out her eyes. "I won't need you for a while. We got a good two inches last night, and they're calling for more in a couple of days. I can pitter around here doing chores that fell to the bottom of the to-do list."

Aaron shuffled his feet. He should go. He would look stupid if he tried to stay. "Rain helped the beans, though."

"Yeah. I'm sure they loved the shower." Her eyes darted to the door.

His ego shrank. *Silly old man,* his age taunted, *thinking Corrie Lancaster would want the likes of you.* "I'll go now. If you need me, please don't hesitate to ask."

"Wait." She stepped closer to him. If he were brave enough, he could reach out and smooth a stray strand of hair behind her ear. "I, uh, was wondering if you'd like to come back tonight. For supper. And stuff. We'll grill some steaks."

If "stuff" meant kissing the bottom lip she traced with her tongue, he was all in. "Should I bring my world-famous potato salad?"

"You mean your mother's famous potato salad?"

"Potato, po-tah-to." Before he could stop himself, he smoothed her hair back behind her ear, his heart racing at her quick inhale. He made his escape before he did something worse, like kiss her, wishing she didn't make his heart want to gallop out of his chest.

Nine hours and one potato salad later, Aaron found himself surrounded by Nikki and Nathan, cards flying at him with deadly speed.

"Hold up, bucko." He flicked his gaze at Nathan as the kid sliced an eight of spades in his direction.

"Speed is the name of the game, old man. Can't play with the big dogs?"

Corrie scolded him from across the table. "Nathan, we don't speak to our guests that way, especially *much* older ones."

Aaron's breath caught in his throat at her wink, and he nearly missed her hand plunging for a spoon in the middle of the kitchen table. Even with his old-man status of thirty-five, his reflexes bested those of Nikki, who sat openmouthed, her hand clutching nothing but air.

"Ha, you suck so bad." Nathan pumped his fisted spoon in victory.

"Shut up." Nikki pouted.

"Good, Nikki, now you can help me peel potatoes." Cynthia turned from the farm-style kitchen sink, peeler brandished like a torch. Rain dripped from the windows, changing steak plans into meatloaf-and-mashed-potato plans. As long as it involved Corrie smiling at him from across the table, Aaron didn't mind. For too many days, he'd been forced to share a field with her and see her only through dirty windows and chaff clouds.

Nikki gave an indignant snort, two spoons were set in the middle of the table, and Corrie dealt four cards. Corrie scooted to Nikki's abandoned chair, her knee brushing against Aaron's. His heart stopped.

"Get ready to lose, suckers," Nathan quipped as he pelted the cards to Aaron at top speed.

Corrie nudged Aaron's knee and grinned. "Let's show him how it's done."

Within seconds, Nathan had joined Cynthia at the counter, slicing the potatoes Nikki peeled. Nathan gave an occasional grumble, accompanied by an added chore from his mother.

Aaron bit his inner cheek to keep from laughing. Corrie obviously felt no such compulsion, which earned her a death glare from her little brother.

"Never mind him." Corrie dealt the cards and set one spoon in between them. "Ready to lose, old-timer?"

"I don't know, *squirt*. Are you ready to shake the hand of the winner?"

"Funny. I've never shaken my own hand before." She gave an impish grin. "First time for everything."

He tore his gaze away from her lips and glanced at the four cards in his hand. Three of a kind. All he needed was one more five. "Ladies first."

She grabbed a card, glanced at it, and slapped it on the table. He picked it up. A three. Another and another. A king, queen, three. Five! He made a grab for the spoon, their hands colliding with force.

Corrie hissed, cradling her hand.

"I'm so sorry." Aaron caressed his thumb over a red mark marring her skin. "Are you okay?"

She didn't pull away from his grasp. "It's the name of the game. You should see us at family gatherings. One time, my dad crawled across the table and tackled Joey for the spoon."

He hated that he'd marked her. Wanted to make it better. Without thinking, he brought her hand to his lips. Her eyes widened, her pupils dilating. It was suddenly very hard to breathe.

A throat cleared. He jumped and released her hand as if it burned. Nathan looked at them as if they'd grown three heads, Nikki looked at everything but them, and Cynthia looked like a cat that had gotten into the cream.

Aaron knew he was blushing and could feel the heat rush up his neck. "So..." He cleared his throat. "How about them Vikings? Lost again, didn't they?"

For the rest of the evening, all Aaron could think about was Corrie's skin on his lips. Her hands, work-worn and slightly chafed from manual labor, had him thinking about other parts of her that wouldn't be touched by dirt and weather. His torture finally came to an end when Corrie waved to him from the front porch, and if he wasn't mistaken, she laid the part of her he'd kissed to her cheek.

Chapter Four

Aaron tripped over a chicken. It squawked and fluttered a few feet away and clucked at him from a safe distance. "Shut up, or I'll eat you for dinner," he growled. The chicken studied him with beady little eyes. He glared back then stomped off to the machine shop.

Luke laughed. "If Mom catches you hurting her chickens, she'll turn you into dinner." He stood in the open door and rubbed greasy hands on a blue shop towel. "That part you ordered for the header is here. Did you want me to put it on this morning before I leave?"

"Nah. I can put it on. I've got some time before I need to be in the field for Corrie, anyway. With the rain last night, it'll be pretty late before we can start combining." Aaron spun around at a low clucking sound. "What in the world, chicken? Scat or I will have you for my next meal." The chicken, undeterred, inched closer. Aaron looked at Luke. "What am I supposed to do with this bird?"

"Eat it."

Aaron stomped at the bird and made a run for it. The chicken squawked and ran to its coop. "There. If I see that stupid animal again, there will be chicken on the menu tonight."

"So, what's eatin' you?" Luke tossed the soiled towel on the workbench.

The smell of machine, grease, and dirt suffused the shop. Aaron breathed deeply. There was no other scent like it—well, except for one. Honeysuckle. And that scent belonged to someone he could never have. "Nothing."

"I've never seen you lose your temper with any critter, much less one of Mom's chickens. Something's up. I bet it's a woman."

"Yeah, right. What woman around here do you think has got me all hot under the collar?"

"I don't know. But you've been testy for the past two weeks, and trust me, I know the frustration a woman can cause. Still don't know why we need them. They are infernal creatures." Luke grabbed his hat and headed for the door. "I've got a sermon to prepare. See you later."

Aaron waved to his brother and refocused on the header on the cement floor. "Just you and me for a while, huh?" As he picked up a crescent wrench, the phone rang. Frustrated, he greeted the caller rather gruffly.

"Aaron?" Corrie's voice sailed through the phone and caressed his ear.

"Yeah. Sorry about the rude hello. I was about to dissect a header."

"That's okay. I just called to let you know I did a test cut, and the wheat is still way too wet to cut today. With that big rain last week and then the other shot of rain last night, it's not going to dry off anytime soon."

Last night. The social faux pas of kissing her hand. *I am an idiot.* He fiddled with the phone cord, wrapping it around his index finger. "Got anything special planned for a free day?"

"Yeah, actually. Nathan, Nikki, and I are taking Dad fishing. They start school on Monday, so this is their last hurrah of the summer." She paused then asked, "Did you want to come along? There's room for one more."

As much as he wanted to say yes, he shouldn't. He didn't know if he could be around her and not commit buffoonery. She was as off limits to him as the queen of England. "No, thanks. I've got a header to fix." He looked out the door at the stalking chicken. "And a chicken to fry up. Hopefully, I'll see you tomorrow in the field."

"Tomorrow is Sunday." She chuckled. "I'll see you in church. Oh, and enjoy your chicken."

He said goodbye and hung up the phone. Ignoring the nagging sense of emptiness stalking him with chicken-like stubbornness, he went back to work. He had nothing to offer Corrie. She deserved so much better than a thirty-five-year-old history teacher turned farmer. But for the past two weeks, he'd found himself listening for her laugh when he lay in bed or mistaking the fragrant breeze from his mother's garden for Corrie's scent. He picked up a wrench and began loosening a bolt. His shoulders tensed. She seemed unaffected by his presence. He just was... *twist*... the older brother... *twist, twist*... with graying hair. She would think him creepy if he tried to change the status quo.

"Hey, son."

Aaron tilted his head to look at his father and schooled his features not to wince over the stoop of his father's once-broad shoulders. "Hey, Dad."

Gerome squatted next to him. "Corrie need you today?"

"No. It's too wet to combine. I'm all yours today, then." Aaron tried to smile at the prospect of another Corrie-free day—gray and empty. "After I fix the header, what else would you like me to work on?"

He shifted away from his father's piercing gaze. Eyes that reminded him too much of Caleb. Only years of laugh lines and eons of sadness framed the eyes studying him now. His father's calloused hand, permanently stained from years of hard work, landed on his shoulder. Hands that had held him as a baby, hands that had smacked his backside, hands that had congratulated him, hands that had trembled at the side of the six-foot hole. Aaron wanted to shrug off the enormity of those hands.

"Your mother's worried about you. She thinks you're coming down with something." Gerome chuckled. "I told her what you have can't be fixed with a trip to the clinic."

Aaron kept his head down and started wrenching on the header. "Mom's always worried. And I'm not down with anything."

"Son, I was born at night, but it sure as shooting wasn't last night."

Aaron gritted his teeth and placed the homeless bolt on the floor. "I'll be fine."

Gerome patted Aaron's shoulder and smiled. "Yeah. I said that, too, once. And now she's making spaghetti in the kitchen."

Gerome shuffled out of the barn and toward the house.

Weird. Aaron tapped the wrench against his knee as his mother, a squat, plump little lady, met his father with a kiss on the porch. Her soft appearance masked an iron will that kept all the men in her life in line. Not that his father ever complained. Shaking his head, Aaron got back to work and tried to forget what ailed him.

CORRIE lay on her back as cumulus clouds formed shapes in the sky. Having her dad next to her sweetened the moment. How many hours had they spent during her childhood watching the clouds, arguing over whether one resembled a dolphin or a dinosaur with an amputated tail?

Shading her eyes against the penetrating brightness, she studied him. He seemed lost in his own world. He hadn't said anything since they'd brought him to the bridge. His face conveyed his excitement, but not a word escaped his lips. Now, studying his avid face and eyes scouring the skies, she longed to reach inside his brain and restart his engines... something... anything...

"Do you think that cloud looks like a very large woman eating a doughnut or a very fat penguin eating a Hula-Hoop?" she asked.

He chuckled but didn't answer. Feeling the chasm slowly opening to suck her and her father apart, she reached for his hand and clutched it. When he squeezed hers in return, the opening to the abyss closed again. If only she could keep it that way. Feeling his eyes study her, she met his gaze. He held on tighter to her hand.

"Penguin," he said and then concentrated on the pulsating clouds once more.

Penguin. She hid her amazement by giggling. "You're right, Dad. How could I have thought otherwise?"

"I caught one!" Nathan's delighted exclamation broke into the afternoon quiet. "It's a whopper too."

She untangled her fingers from her father's hand and went to see Nathan's catch. "Um, you call that a whopper?" She tousled his hair. "That's more like a minnow." The poor fish wriggled and squirmed on the fishhook. Its mouth, gaping and red, seemed to plead for sweet release. *Poor creature.* "Unless you plan on cleaning it yourself, you should put it back."

He groaned but removed the hook and placed the fish in the water. It didn't waste any time and swam off at top speed. "Are you happy now? My prize fish is gone."

She patted his head. "If you catch a fish that looks like a daddy fish and not one of his children, I'll let you keep it. I'll even clean the dumb thing."

Nathan's frown immediately morphed into a toothy grin, and he dropped down to put another worm on his hook. After Nathan's nice cast, Corrie checked on her father, who had fallen asleep. Then she sauntered over to her sister.

"Hey, Nikki. What's the matter?"

Nikki hid her face, blotchy from crying, away from Corrie's inquisitive gaze. "Nothing."

"Is it Dad?"

"No."

Corrie's heart sank. If it wasn't Dad, it must be a boy. And boys were dumb. All except... she laid the back of her hand to her cheek, her insides warming at the memory of Aaron's lips touching her. She had hoped he'd come along, witness her fishing skills, maybe accidentally kiss her hand again. She stilled those thoughts and sat next to Nikki on the cement bridge embankment. She picked up a stone and plopped it in the water. The rings expanded and eventually faded into nothingness. "Who is it?"

"Nobody." Nikki crossed her arms over her chest. Nikki had changed two weeks ago when volleyball and football practice began.

Corrie knew from personal experience that the paths of the two teams would often cross before or after practice, and school crushes had a habit of forming. "I'm not dumb. I was once your age and very starstruck. What happened?"

A fat tear slid down Nikki's face and plopped to the cement. "Xavier Palinski."

Xavier? Palinski? "Is he Polish by any chance?" When Nikki shot her a glare, Corrie wiped the smirk from her face. *Good grief! Remind me not to have any girls!* She put an arm around Nikki's shoulders and gave her a squeeze. "Tell me what happened."

The waterworks began. With tears streaming down her face, Nikki launched in. "Well, it all happened so fast, you know? He's so cute, and he's the quarterback, and—"

"Stop!" Corrie flashed back to a similar story with a different boy. "You're not—"

"No!" Nikki pushed away from Corrie's arm. "No! Never mind. If you're going to jump to conclusions, then I'm just going to—"

"I'm sorry! I really am," Corrie pleaded. "Please, continue. I won't say another word till you're finished."

After a series of huffs and eye rolls, Nikki continued, "Well, he told me he really liked me and asked if I wanted to go to the homecoming dance with him." She peered at Corrie through red-rimmed eyes. "But I saw him with Carly this morning when I went to the store for Mom."

"Maybe they were just talking about the weather?"

"They were talking with their tongues down each other's throats, then." A fresh sob tore from Nikki's throat, and the waterworks were on full for the next five minutes.

Corrie gently rubbed her sister's back and murmured supportive words. After several minutes, she dared to speak. "Are you going to talk to Carly about this? She is your best friend. I wouldn't want a boy to come between you two."

Nikki's mouth turned into a giant *O*, and her eyebrows touched her bangs. Corrie felt like an enemy spy. "She *was* my best friend. And Xavier is not just a boy. He's *the* boy!" Nikki jumped to her feet. "You really don't know anything about boys, do you?" With an extra huff for emphasis, she stomped off toward the pickup.

Exhausted, Corrie didn't bother running after her. She laid her head on her knees as the stream swirled under her. If only her sister were right. If only she really knew nothing about boys. She sighed, picked herself up off the concrete, and went to gather her family. Nikki flung herself into the back seat of the pickup.

This was going to be a very long year.

THE Sunday sun dipped lower in the sky, and bands of orange and crimson kissed the golden horizon. A light breeze played with Corrie's hair as she carried a bowl of potato salad to the already-groaning picnic table. After church that morning, her mom had ended up inviting all the neighbors within a ten-mile radius to lunch, and everyone seemed to have accepted the invitation. Including Aaron. And Luke. She gritted her teeth. Luke had shown up at the field almost every morning for a week after his first field crashing. It mostly ended in a silent showdown between the two brothers. She guarded the part of her heart still easily swayed by Luke's easy smile. Too easy.

He had yet to apologize for abandoning her in her darkest hour. He'd hinted at it, spouting things like "I don't want to see you struggle" and other yada yadaing. He seemed to think he could march back into her life all easy-peasy-lemon-squeezy. She stuck out her tongue and waggled her head at an imaginary Luke.

"Need help?"

She placed the fruit salad bowl Nathan handed her on the table. "No. If Mom says it's okay, you can go off with your friends. Stay out of trouble and don't climb the large grain bin. The ladder's still broken."

He grinned and loped off on gangly legs to join an assortment of cousins and buddies. "When is that boy going to grow into his feet?" she asked herself aloud.

"Before you know it." Luke chuckled behind her. "Don't you remember me growing up?"

Corrie whirled around at his voice, hating the way her heart still leapt in her throat. *Stupid question!* Of course she remembered him. She'd lost herself in his green eyes and shaggy hair and doodled *Corrie Tuttle* in the back of her math notebook during class. She hadn't noticed the awkward-boy stage at all.

"Yeah," she lied. "You were pretty awkward, weren't you?"

"Hey, now." He took her hand. "You didn't have to agree with me." He tilted his head. "Would you care to go for a walk?"

Surprised at his touch and the thought of being alone with him, she panicked and stumbled for the right answer. *Why now?* she wanted to scream at him. He'd been playing the part of caring pastor on Sundays for months. That she could deal with. This new Luke with a fire in his eyes, she couldn't.

"Maybe later?" She ripped her hand from his grasp and ran into the house, away from him and the dredged-up past.

"If the wheat prices stay where they are, we'll be slaves to the government again. If my granddad were alive to see this, he'd raise hell. That's for sure!"

When Baxter took off his good DeKalb cap and slapped it against his knee, Aaron chuckled along with the rest of the men encircled around the grill. The smell of flame-broiled steaks, the hopsy taste of his favorite beer, and the good-natured bantering soothed his nerves. He'd yet to see Corrie, and he prayed when he did, no one would notice that he no longer thought of her as Luke's ex-girlfriend.

When Jake opened the sliding glass door and walked onto the patio, all the men stopped talking and laughing. His face, uncertain and hesitant, scanned the crowd. An awkward silence filled the humid air, and surely the humidity jumped a few percentage points.

Baxter was the first to break the humming silence. "Come on over here, Jake. We were just discussing how Big Brother thinks us farmers need takin' care of. Want a beer?"

Jake's eyes twinkled. The men exhaled a collective sigh and took refreshing gulps of their beverages. Baxter handed Jake a beer and commenced his tirade against any government bigger than a city council. Aaron leaned against the porch railing and studied Jake Lancaster. At times, the man's eyes were bright and focused, but within seconds, those eyes could turn cloudy and confused. The enormity of the situation lay heavy on Aaron's mind. *What's Corrie going to do? Can she do it on her own?* He took a swig of beer. No, she couldn't. She would try. She would die trying, and that was the problem. That girl was going to run herself into the ground for a farm her father might or might not even want anymore.

"Those steaks done yet, boys?" Her voice broke into his thoughts. She stood inside the sliding glass doorframe and rested her hip against it. Her short spaghetti strap sundress accentuated her long, lean legs and highlighted arm muscles cultivated over months of hard work. He didn't know or care what material her pastel-pink dress was made of, but it sure reminded him of pink lemonade. And all he wanted right now was a long, cool drink. "We've got starving women and children, and all you boys can do is gossip like a bunch of old ladies."

The men heckled back, but she waved a dismissive hand. "When you boys are done with your ladies' aid meeting, we'll be under the tent in the yard, waiting for some steaks."

When Corrie closed the glass door, Baxter slapped Jake on the back. "I tell you what, Jake. You sure raised a little firecracker, didn't ya?"

Jake's lips pulled back into a crooked grin, and he spoke for the first time since joining them. "You betcha!"

The men took steaks off the grill and poured off the porch, headed for the tables of food. That left Aaron to ponder his future and what he was going to do about the woman he couldn't have.

Hours later and after the sun had set with a pink farewell, he chuckled as the children pillaged the stash of marshmallows and created flaming balls of goo. His laugh stuck in his throat when he noticed Corrie sitting across the fire from him. Her face, bathed in sorrow, pinched his heart. What he wouldn't do to make her smile. Following her gaze, he studied her focus: her parents. Without saying a word to anyone, she got up and walked off. Not knowing what else to do, he snuck away amid the dancing embers and children with their gooey wooden sticks. He knew exactly where she would be.

He found her much like he did two weeks ago. Only this time she looked ethereal. Moonbeams and starlight cascaded upon her, and shadows danced around her as the tire swing swirled and circled. Her hair swished beneath her as her body lay parallel to the ground. The tips of her hair swept the grass and collected the late-evening moisture. He could watch her forever. That was the problem. With a quick change of mind, he turned to leave, but a cracking stick under his boots thwarted his clandestine escape.

She sat up in the swing and placed her hand to her heaving chest. "You scared me half to death."

"Sorry. I-I didn't mean to disturb you," he stammered. "I thought I'd come check on you. Make sure you're okay."

"I'm fine. Thank you for asking. I just needed some quiet time."

"I'll leave you alone, then. I'll see you tomorrow morning?"

"Yeah." She chewed her bottom lip. As if making up her mind, she got out of the swing and stood before him.

The smell of campfire and a whiff of honeysuckle assaulted his senses. Her white teeth nibbled her red lips, and he sucked in a quick breath. *Yup. I should never have come.*

"Were you ever afraid of your parents getting a divorce?"

He blinked. "Divorce? Um, no. Not really. They had their arguments, and some days were better than others, but divorce was never a concern." He studied her. "Why do you ask?"

She dipped her head and drew imaginary circles in the lawn with her bare toe. "I think my parents might be getting one." Tears cascaded down her tanned face. "I can barely handle things now. What am I going to do if they decide to quit? I just don't know what to do."

Her shoulders began to shake, and he looked around helplessly. Finding nothing but an inquisitive squirrel and a few croaking bullfrogs, he hesitantly cupped a hand on her shoulder. When she didn't shrug off his hand, he inwardly rejoiced. He hadn't screwed up—yet. But she cut his victory dance short when she barreled into him. He stumbled backward and barely kept his balance. She burrowed her head into his chest and continued sobbing. Scared spitless, he patted her back and repeated "It'll be okay" over and over again.

He tried not noticing her body touching his. He tried not counting the staccato beats of her heart. He tried not enjoying the warmth of her ragged breaths against his shirt. He tried thinking of the Minnesota Twins or the Vikings and their inevitable losing season. Nothing.

He switched his thoughts to the stalker chicken he didn't have the heart to kill. Failure. He finally gave up, stuck with the torture of thinking about and holding a woman who probably only looked at him as the older brother. The guy who was never around and came back with the beginnings of gray hair. After what felt like hours, her breathing regulated. A mixture of relief and regret bombarded him when she removed herself from his arms.

Her warm fingers roughly and hesitantly patted at the pool of saliva on his shirt. "Sorry. I don't know what came over me."

He gritted his teeth and prayed the infernal woman would quit caressing him. Okay, she was awkwardly petting him, but he chose to ignore that important detail. "It's okay. You're under a lot of stress. I wouldn't be able to do what you're doing right now." He gazed into her watery eyes. "Do you know how many people in this community praise you for what you are doing with this farm? Anyone would be willing to help. You just have to ask if it gets to be too much for you. No one is going to think less of you."

She shrugged. "It is true. I'm just a stubborn old cow, I guess." Her lips played seesaw for several seconds before she seemed to give up on smiling. "But you're right. I need to get over my pride and ask."

He cleared his throat and began fidgeting. "Well... um... I should probably go. I'll see you tomorrow?"

"Bright and early. Just meet me at Goose Landing. I'll take the truck and grain cart back if you want to combine for a while."

"Whatever you don't want, I'll take." He savored one last moment of being with her in the moonlight, surrounded by whispering trees and singing crickets. He walked away, but her hand on his arm stopped him.

"Thank you. For tonight and for the past weeks. I don't think I've enjoyed harvest more. I—" She looked past him and heaved a sigh. "Thank you. You don't know how much I appreciate you."

He swallowed. "Just being neighborly."

"Neighborly? Just that?" Her fingers loosened on his arm, but her hand remained, tentative.

Say it! Kiss her! "That's what we do around here. Right?"

"Yeah." Corrie frowned, her fingers treading down his arm as she released her hold on him. She went back to her tire swing. "Good night, Aaron."

As he walked away, he could have sworn he heard her soft hair stroking the grass beneath her. It wasn't until he was driving away that he caught the whiff of campfire and honeysuckle emanating off his shirt. He sighed. Torn between wanting to wash it immediately and wanting never to wash it again, he headed toward the yard lights of home and cranked up a George Strait song to mute Corrie's breathing still echoing in his ears.

Chapter Five

Monday was uneventful, although Corrie found Aaron's behavior strange. There was a tension between them she hadn't felt before. She didn't like it. Tuesday melted away, and he returned to his normal bantering self. Wednesday ended with no difficulties. Her biggest accomplishment on Thursday was stopping to eat a cheese button from Mabel's.

The Friday morning sun crept along the cement floor in the machine shed and under a jacked-up Old Bertie. Corrie lay on her back next to Baxter under her beloved pickup and wished he hadn't bathed in Old Spice.

"Now, you see this here, Corrie?" He pointed at something remarkably like everything else on the truck's underbelly. She wanted to shake her head, but she was dying a slow death from claustrophobia and suffocation. And she couldn't help staring at the swatch of stubble he'd missed while shaving.

"Sure do." Just a small twinge of guilt for lying. All in self-preservation.

"Well..." He scratched at the piece of rogue facial hair. "Let's just say this old girl has seen her last days."

Ridiculous tears sprang to Corrie's eyes. She wanted to believe they came from the scent cloud she'd been subjected to but knew it was plain old sentimentality.

"There, there, Corrie." He patted her arm. "I once had a 1958 Chevy Impala I had to put down. I cried like a baby when I saw her towed away. Don't feel bad about mourning Old Bertie. She's lived a full life."

Corrie wiggled out from under the truck and offered Baxter a helping hand. He swatted it away. "I'm old, little lady, but I'm not that old. The day I can't get out from under a truck, get my gun, take me out to the pasture, and shoot me."

She chuckled and swiped at the stray tears trickling down her face. Then she ran a hand over Bertie's hood and allowed fond memories to play in her mind. "Thank you so much for coming out to the farm to look at her. She's been a good girl to us. I don't know how we will ever replace her."

He took off his cap, brushed it against his leg, and slapped it back on his head. "Yup, I know the feeling. I have yet to get a car to replace my girl, Lavender Blue."

She wiped her hands on a shop towel. "Lavender Blue? Where'd you get that name?"

Baxter's face turned red. She'd never seen the old man blush. His grizzled appearance faded, and in the old man's place stood a shy teenager watching his feet create circles in the dirt.

"You know the song 'Lavender Blue'?" When Corrie scrunched her face up and lifted her hands, Baxter stammered on, "Well, it's about how this guy would be a king if only the girl he loved married him and became his queen. And, well, this is the song where I finally asked a pretty girl to dance with me at a school dance. She later made me a king by agreeing to be my queen."

"Oh, Baxter!" Corrie gave him a big hug and pretended not to notice the tears rolling down his wrinkled cheeks. "Annie's a queen in heaven now. And sure as I'm standing here, she's got a seat next to her just for you." Corrie reached up on tiptoe and kissed his wet cheek.

He laid his greasy hand on her head. "Be a good girl and don't mention this to the guys at the elevator. The only ones to know the name of my car are myself and Annie, of course. I'd lose my credibility, you see?"

"Your secret is safe with me. Thanks again for helping me with Bertie. Now I just have to wait for Aaron to show up. All that rain put us back by quite a bit. I hate to complain because my beans need rain, too, but... Anyway, it's strange he's not here yet. He's never..."

Aaron's Ford pulled up in front of the machine shed, a female passenger peering out the window. An emotion dangerously close to jealousy raised her blood pressure.

"Who's the woman with him?"

"Don't rightly know. Guess we'll find out soon enough." Baxter released a low whistle as the woman stepped out of the pickup. "I don't think she's from around here."

Corrie kept her thoughts to herself. The woman's jeans looked as if someone had painted them on her body, and her tank top left nothing to the imagination. Her collarbone and cheekbones protruded from her body, and Corrie felt tempted to offer her a cheeseburger. The woman's thighs were probably smaller than Corrie's wrists. A slightly distended stomach offset her skinny frame. Before Corrie could finalize her assumptions, Aaron emerged from the truck, said something to the woman, and both walked toward them.

"Hey, guys." Aaron waved. "On my way over here, I ran into this young lady. Can she use your phone, Corrie?"

Corrie smiled. "Sure." She held out her hand to the woman shuffling her sneakered feet next to him. "Come with me, please." When the stranger didn't shake her hand, Corrie gestured for the woman to go first. When she still didn't move, Corrie walked to the house, hoping the stranger would follow.

Feet shuffled behind Corrie. She glanced over her shoulder. "I'm Corrie Lancaster. Are you from around here?"

The woman shook her head, sending her bobbed, curled purple tresses dancing.

"What's your name?"

She froze, and her face whitened under orange-tinted self-tanner. Empty eyes pierced right through Corrie. Finally, the woman blinked and whispered, "Violet."

"That's a very pretty name." Corrie opened the front door and led her to the kitchen. Jake scrunched his face in obvious confusion, and Cynthia raised her eyebrows. "Mom and Dad, this is Violet. She needs to use the phone." Her mother gestured to the phone, and Corrie patted a chair. "Please have a seat. Would you like something to drink?"

Violet nodded and fell into the kitchen chair. Violet snatched the glass of water Corrie offered her and guzzled it down. After two more glasses, she slowed long enough to take short sips from the fourth glass. Corrie wished her mother would say something. It was awkward to carry on a conversation with someone as elusive and quiet as a coyote.

Phone in hand, she settled across from Violet. "So, who did you need to call?"

"Tow truck. My car's in the ditch miles back, and my cell phone battery's dead."

Her dead voice deflated Corrie's spirits. "What happened? Are you hurt?" She reached over to pat Violet's folded hands, but Violet pulled them out of reach.

"No. I'm fine. I just need a tow truck."

Cynthia tapped her fingernails on the table. "We could pull the car out with the tractor. I'm sure Aaron wouldn't mind."

Violet quit fiddling with her jagged cuticles. "I don't want to be any trouble."

Corrie inwardly sighed. The sooner this strange woman left her family's house, the better. Ignoring her guilt over thinking such a thing, Corrie forced a smile she didn't feel. "Just doing the neighborly thing. Let's go see about your car." She couldn't ignore the stab of pain at repeating Aaron's words from the other night. *Neighborly?*

Give me a break. She ignored the sassy part of her brain that reminded her she hadn't said anything too romantic either.

Twenty minutes later, Corrie stood on the shoulder of the road with Violet while Aaron and Baxter examined the rusted-out Ford Escort lying sideways in the ditch. Corrie cast a side-glance at Violet, and a wave of pity overcame her. Violet met her gaze. The distrust radiating from those empty gray eyes invoked a rush of goose bumps. Corrie shivered and tuned back into the men.

Aaron hooked a chain to the car and signaled Baxter, who'd climbed into the cab of the 4640 John Deere, to begin the process of inching Violet's car from the ditch. Corrie caught Aaron's eye and blushed when he gave her a friendly wink, all the nonromantic wrongs forgiven. She rolled her eyes in return and was about to make some offhand comment about men to Violet when a look of longing and despair flashed across Violet's face.

Right then, God smacked Corrie upside the head. *No, no, no! I'm not taking on another thing,* she yelled silently, still feeling the sting of his hand against her soul. *This woman has trouble written all over her. She could be a serial killer for all I know.*

It was no use. She wasn't sure how God was going to pull it off, but somehow, this strange, scrawny woman would be a fixture in her life for quite some time.

"What?" Corrie's grasp on her cell phone tightened. "What do you mean 'totaled'?" She pulled the combine's joystick back, bringing the machine to a rocking halt. She listened, dazed, to her former high school classmate turned mechanic. "Weeks? I don't know. I just met her. Yeah. All right, I'll bring a load of wheat in later this afternoon and stop by. Thanks, Derek. I appreciate it. Bye."

"Crap!" She slammed her cell onto the buddy seat next to her and exhaled the pent-up breath she'd been holding. "Well, Lord, you certainly know how to make a girl's day, don't you?" With a grunt, she shifted as dust motes shimmered in the sun-filled cab. Beyond the window, a small lake formed by flooding years ago bordered the field's eastern edge. Its smooth surface mirrored the azure sky. White fluffy clouds seemed to pause right over it, taking time to admire themselves. But the morning's beauty meant nothing as a flock of ducks paddled off and took to their wings, shattering the still water.

Not willing to wait for a full truckload, Corrie drove to the end of the field, hopped in the truck, and barreled down the highway toward an answer she didn't want to hear.

She parked the truck alongside Main Street by the elevator and trudged down the sidewalk. The grease and oil smell assaulted her when she entered Derek's shop. Unlike most mechanic shops, he kept his spit-shine clean. Not a speck of dirt or dust dared make a home anywhere, and bugs of all sorts had gotten the memo long ago and seemed to pass on by his establishment. An old Coke machine hummed by the front door. She inserted three quarters, selected an Orange Crush, and opened the glass to retrieve her ice-cold beverage.

Derek entered through a pair of swinging wooden bar doors. He wiped his hands on a blue shop towel. "Hey there, Corrie. What's up?"

"The ceiling." She sat on a revolving barstool at the counter. "You know, if you don't swing it as a mechanic, you've got a good setup to make this into a bar."

His chuckle rumbled deep in his barreled chest. "Some days, I'm tempted." He pulled a candy dish out from under the counter. "Smartie?"

She fished out a cellophane tube of the pastel candy and proceeded to pop two pieces in her mouth. Derek had been the reigning wrestling champ in high school and, from the rumors, could still pin any opponent who dared challenge him. In spite of his formidable bulldog appearance, she trusted him implicitly. "So, what's the damage?"

His smile dimmed, giving his fleshy jowls a punished-puppy look. "I don't know where you met this woman, but I don't think the car was much before it rolled. It isn't going anywhere without a total overhaul, and if she has no money for a replacement, she's not going anywhere either."

Corrie inwardly cursed her fate. As of right now, a strange woman with a bad fake tan, purple hair, and a surly disposition was camping out in her family's living room. Corrie felt a pang of pain for her mom and dad, but nothing would entice her to have Violet tagging along in the field. She'd better pick up more peanut butter for her father and order a large bouquet of roses and some wine for her mother as compensation.

"Corrie?"

She blinked. "Sorry. I got lost in my thoughts there for a second." She scooted off the stool and grabbed the rest of her Smarties and pop. "Just send me the bill when you're finished with Violet's car. I'll let you know more when I know more."

"Sounds good. Good luck." He gave her a supportive cuff to the shoulder before exiting to the back workshop.

She stood as the swinging doors swayed on their hinges. A grinder eating away at metal jarred her trance. She shoved the rest of the candy in her mouth and walked into the afternoon heat and down Main Street.

Corrie knew to the yard how long Main Street was. She'd run it hundreds of times during track season. As she meandered down the cracked sidewalk, the church's white steeple poked through the oak and maple trees to her right. One of those trees bore the mark "L+C=4ever." If she allowed herself the luxury, she was convinced she could still taste the root beer Luke had drunk the night they'd carved their names into town history. Instead of shaking off the forbidden memory, she high-tailed it to the tree grove, searching for the initials. They had grown with the tree, and she had to stretch to reach them. After digging through her jeans, she pulled out a little Swiss Army knife she kept with her and scratched through the initials, erasing them from history. *Suck it!* Not feeling any better, she shoved the pocketknife back in her pocket and trudged through the tree groves, wishing money would replace the leaves that scattered the sunlight before her.

If money did indeed grow on trees, Sandy would be canopied in it. She had work to do, but first she had to figure out what Violet was made of. And she really hoped it was cash.

CORRIE ENTERED HER house to the sound of someone puking and a soft voice crooning words of comfort. With quick movements, Corrie checked the living room. Empty. She ran to her parents' bedroom and found her father fast asleep. Relief poured into her, but retching echoed down the hallway. She followed the sounds to the bathroom and knocked. "Mom?"

"Corrie!" Relief flooded her mother's voice.

Corrie opened up the door and froze. Her mother's hand was caressing the long black hair of a strangely familiar woman. The woman's small features shone garish against the white bathroom tiles. The woman peered up at Corrie with bloodshot eyes.

"Violet?" Corrie knelt next to her. "What's wrong?"

Violet moaned and rested her head on the floor with her left arm wrapped protectively around her slightly bulging abdomen. Corrie gazed into her mother's eyes for some answers.

Cynthia patted Violet's head. "I'll be right back. Don't worry. It'll be okay."

Corrie closed the bathroom door and grabbed her mother before sinking to the floor. Then she sat next to her mother and rubbed her back. "What's going on?"

Cynthia brought her knees to her chest and laid her head on them. Her piercing gaze lifted Corrie's arm hair on end. "She's pregnant."

"Pregnant?" Corrie deflated.

"Mm-hm." Cynthia closed her eyes. "She says she's six months along. That's all I know."

Corrie bit her tongue against a foul curse word. "I talked to Derek earlier. He says her car is totaled."

Cynthia shrank deeper into her sitting fetal position. "What are we going to do?"

Corrie leaned her head on her mother's shoulder and sighed. Her mother's familiar perfume offered little comfort. "Did she give any indication about what she does or where she's from? Does she have family we can call?"

"All I got today were taciturn replies to those exact questions." Cynthia wrapped an arm around Corrie. "On the bright side, she's really good with your father. She even got out the old Operation game. Let's just say there was a lot of buzzing. But he laughed—a good sign."

A sharp cry from the bathroom cut off Corrie's reply. Cynthia hopped up and within seconds was holding Violet's hair as she emptied the contents of her stomach into the toilet. Corrie stood in the doorway, hoping she wouldn't toss her cookies too. She reached for the vanity for support from the tan marble. All she found was a curly purple wig. Yanking her hand back, she poked at the hairpiece, afraid it might move.

"Corrie!"

She jolted and spun to her mother. Blood pooled around Violet, and Corrie went weak in the knees.

"Call 9-1-1. Quick."

She didn't have to be asked twice. She whipped out her cell, placed the call, and sat next to Violet. Cynthia handed her towel after towel, and Corrie packed them as tightly as possible in between Violet's blood-smeared thighs. Corrie clenched her teeth against a yelp of pain as Violet's chewed-up nails bit into her wrist, and she placed a restraining hand on Violet's shoulders when she tried to get up.

Her gray eyes burned into Corrie's. "I can't lose this baby too. Please!"

"You need to relax. The ambulance will be here soon. You need to breathe, Violet." Violet's crazed and pleading stare sent compassion flooding through Corrie. Twisting, Corrie situated herself so Violet's head rested on Corrie's thighs. Cynthia handed her a warm washcloth, and Corrie swabbed Violet's tearstained face.

Violet's broken body shuddered with tears. Corrie kept stroking her hair and wondered about her statement that she didn't want to lose this baby *too*. Had there been others? Corrie placed a hand over her own abdomen. She remembered what it was like to have life created inside her and hated herself for having hated its presence. Her heart wept in solidarity with Violet's loss. Her ruminations screeched to a halt when the paramedics arrived and loaded Violet on a stretcher and into the ambulance.

Corrie's mind fluttered with activity as she followed the ambulance to the nearest town big enough to support a hospital. She chewed her bottom lip. Sweetwater was another twenty minutes away, and even though she didn't know the woman hemorrhaging to death in the back of the lighted-up vehicle before her, Corrie couldn't stop the terror skimming up and down her spine. Violet's repeated mumblings about not losing another baby replayed over and over, conjuring up a night seven years ago. There had been so much blood. More than any period Corrie'd ever had. Scared and ashamed, she'd wept at the loss, screamed when the little life passed from her and into the toilet. She had fainted and woken up in her mother's arms. It was then that her mother knew, but there had been no scoldings or looks of disappointment. Just her mother's arms around her and words of love whispered in her ear.

Her cell phone rang, jarring her from her past. She swiped at the hot tears streaming down her face and hit the green button. "Hello?"

"Corrie? What's going on? I got your message about Violet. Is everything okay?"

Aaron's voice soothed her nerves instantly, and it hit her: she'd been needing to hear from him. She had waited for his call, to hear his voice. She breathed deeply. "I don't know. She's bleeding really badly. She might lose the baby."

"Baby?"

If the moment weren't so tragic, she might have laughed at the teenage-boy squeak. "Yeah. She told my mom she was six months along."

"How are you with all this? Do you need me to come with?"

Yes! She wanted to melt into him, share her fears, her past. "No. I'll be fine. I need you in the field. Remember, Nathan's first game is tonight, so he won't be there to help. I already called Nikki. She's skipping volleyball practice. She should be in the field shortly. Put her in the combine."

"Do you want me to check on your mom?"

"No. She was good when I left. I'll give you updates as I get them."

"Okay. Corrie?"

"Yeah."

"I'm praying for Violet... and for you."

She smiled despite the butterflies in her stomach and the despair for the young woman suddenly thrust into her life. "Thanks."

She ended the call, wishing time would fast-forward, and followed the ambulance into town.

LIKE A PENDULUM, THE tire swing went back and forth in the darkness, circling and revolving, never stopping. Corrie's thoughts did much the same as she let the motion rock her. She couldn't forget the image of Violet's eyes, and she couldn't erase the young woman's pleas for the doctor to save her baby. *Has it really only been one day?* She shook her head. Just this morning, she'd thought Baxter's cologne was enough to finish her off. Now a destitute woman was fighting for her life and the life of her unborn child.

Closing her eyes, she inhaled the humid evening air. She opened them and gazed into the starry sky. *Lord, where do I fit in all this? What do you want from me?* Stars winked in their cold silence. She would get no verbal answers. Still, she swung back and forth, waiting for the answer God would give in his time.

A car crunched gravel in the driveway. Nathan was finally home. She squeezed out of the swing and met him on the front steps.

"Hey, buddy, how'd it go?" She slung her arm around his shoulders. "Hey, when did you get muscles?"

He smiled. "That's what Avery asked tonight. After we won the game!"

"First of all, that's great." She squeezed him in a half hug. "And secondly, who's this Avery chick? Would I approve of her?"

He ducked his head. "Yeah. She's nice."

She ruffled her brother's hair. "I'm sorry I couldn't come to your game tonight. Today was pretty hectic and weird."

"Don't worry about it. We smoked 'em, anyway." He eyed the door warily. "Is she here?"

"Who?"

"That lady you called about. Is she in the house?"

Corrie sighed and pulled Nathan into one of the wicker rocking chairs. "She's in the hospital in Sweetwater."

His suspicion melted into wide-eyed concern. "Is she going to be okay?"

"I don't know. I really don't." She studied him. "You want to know something?" She placed her hand on his cheek and marveled at the fine sprouting facial hairs. "Mom needs to buy you some razors, doesn't she?" Now his face sprouted red splotches. "Sorry. Anyway, I'm proud of you. You work your butt off for me. You take on so much and never complain, and you have the most amazing heart of anyone I know. You are an incredible young man."

He cleared his throat, mumbling something incoherent. She tugged him into a hug and released him when he squirmed.

"Dad's still up watching some game show. Nikki's in bed, and Mom's at the hospital with Violet. You should go talk with Dad. He's got something for you."

"I think I'll just go to bed." Nathan's face darkened.

"Nathan," she whispered, "just try. Please."

He grumbled but walked into the house and paused at the living room doorway. The furniture-cleaner smell announced the Friday cleaning, and the flickering television screen cast shadows about the darkened room.

"Go." She gave him a gentle nudge, and he approached their father's recliner, his muscles rippling with anxiety. *Poor kid.* A matching quiver vibrated her heart as he knelt next to Jake.

"Hi, son." Jake smiled.

"Hey, Dad."

"Got something for you." Jake reached over to the side table next to his chair and handed Nathan an envelope.

Her heart quivered faster as Nathan ripped open the envelope. She knew what was in it. She'd made them with colored construction paper and half-dried-up Elmer's glue long stashed in the junk drawer.

"Whoa!" Nathan blinked as he looked at the pieces of colorful paper. "Tickets? To my games? All of them? You're going to come to all my games?"

Unshed tears glittered in Jake's eyes. "My boy."

Corrie fought her own tears as Nathan rested his head on the armrest of his father's chair. She gave up when Jake cupped his hand on top of Nathan's blond hair.

THE next few days whizzed by in a blur of activity, worry, and hope. Corrie felt split in two as she divided her time between fieldwork and switching places with her mother to sit with Violet in the hospital. She imagined herself running mindlessly on a hamster's wheel, never knowing when the contraption would stop. *Maybe it won't.* She drove into the field approach with her new used red Dodge Ram pickup with questionable shock absorbers and unquestionable rust spots and parked next to the semi, glad to be out of the cramped hospital room and equally cramped memories until the next day. A cloud of dust and chaff billowed in the distance. *Good. Aaron must have gotten my message.* Her thoughts froze, however, when she spotted two other clouds on the far side of the field. Corrie climbed into the truck and pushed the button down on the side of the receiver.

"Aaron?"

"Hey." His simple salutation made her smile.

"Straw."

"Touché. I hope you don't mind, but I found reinforcements."

Mind? She bit her lip. *I could kiss—*

She schooled her smiling lips into a straight line. Her smile refused to stay where she'd told it to. Instead, it slid upward until her cheeks hurt. *Could I really kiss Aaron? Do I want to? Um, yes!* Freaked out by her rebellious thoughts, she turned her attention to the three green machines making their way in her direction down the field. She couldn't tell which combine contained Aaron. But he was in one of them, and the thought alone sent her stomach flip-flopping. His kindness, playful banter, and occasional touches over the past weeks flooded her mind. And it finally hit her: she hadn't thought of Luke in a positive light at all these past days. In fact, ever since his older brother walked into her life, she hadn't thought of him much at all, for better or for worse.

"Corrie? Are you there?"

Aaron's voice startled her, and she flung the radio receiver out of her hand. As it bobbed up and down on its cord, she scrambled to catch it. "Yeah. Sorry. I really don't know how to thank you."

"You just did."

Corrie held on to the small black object, hoping he would say something else. But the radio remained quiet, and the three combines containing Aaron, his dad, and Baxter cut their way past the semi. Each waved and smiled, but Aaron's washed her heart with a warmth she'd never known. Doubt soon began shooting darts at her happiness. What would a man want with her, a woman who had once carried his brother's child?

"But I'm more than that!" she exclaimed to the nothingness in the cab. "It was a mistake. A stupid mistake."

But surely Aaron wouldn't see it that way. Once he found out, he would reject her, and that dampened her spirits for the rest of the day. How could he ever forgive her and get over the fact that he wouldn't be her first, that his brother had taken something she couldn't give again?

Chapter Six

"Will you be okay?" Aaron studied Violet. Her brow dripped with perspiration, and her skin looked nearly translucent. He glanced at his brother, who'd helped carry her into the house. Luke's face mirrored Aaron's concern.

Cynthia bustled in with an extra comforter and a glass of water tinkling with ice cubes. When she met Aaron's eyes, she stopped in the doorway.

"What's wrong?" She walked over to the bed, placed the glass on the bedside table, and leaned over Violet before using the back of her hand on Violet's damp forehead to check for a fever.

Aaron relaxed. If anyone could nurse this helpless creature back to health, it was Cynthia.

She glanced at him then Luke. "She doesn't have a temp." She concentrated on Violet, murmuring words of comfort Aaron didn't catch.

Feeling itchy, he cleared his throat. "I think we'll be going now if you'll be okay. My mom said she'd be coming over in an hour or so with a casserole and to help you with Violet."

Cynthia lifted tired eyes to Aaron. "Thank you." She held her hand out for each of the men to grasp. "Really. You two have been a blessing to me and my family. I don't know how I can ever repay your kindness."

"Mrs. Lancaster"—Luke patted the hand that clung to his—"it's our pleasure. Anytime, day or night, call us if you need anything."

Aaron squeezed Cynthia's hand and exited the room, glancing back in time to witness her pull up a rocking chair and begin singing to her patient.

"Do you think she'll be okay?"

Aaron squinted at his brother as they left the house and stood on the front porch. "Who?"

"Violet. She seems so lost and small."

"She must have the constitution of a healthy horse, because she and her baby survived. A miracle, really." He slapped his brother on the back. "I think we're leaving her in good hands."

Luke jammed his fingers through his hair. "Dad needs me to finish the field behind the levy. After that, I plan on dropping by the field to talk to Corrie."

A jealous flame ignited inside Aaron's chest as he followed his brother to Luke's pickup. "What about?"

"Let's just say I've got some apologizing to do. I'm hoping after she forgives me, maybe she and I can, well, rekindle what I destroyed."

"What actually happened between you two? You were thick as thieves one moment, and the next, poof, it seemed like you hated each other."

"I never hated her." Luke yanked open the driver's door.

"Then what happened?"

"It's none of your da—darn business." Luke placed his palms on the doorframe of the truck, his knuckles whitening from his stranglehold on the metal. "Look, man, I'm sorry. I'm just nervous, you know. I should have never let her go. But hopefully, with my winning smile and apology, I can make her mine again."

Every fiber of Aaron's being wanted to punch Luke in the face. Hard. Maybe draw some blood from his spoiled younger brother. Instead, he slapped his brother on the shoulder. "I wish you the best of luck! See you later." He trotted off to his pickup, hoping that even if Corrie did forgive Luke, she wouldn't fall in love with him again. Aaron wasn't convinced he could give her up without a fight.

CORRIE wiggled in the combine seat and prayed for the wheat spewing out of the auger to hurry up. She should have peed at the end of the field, but by then, Aaron had been there with the tractor and was all lined up to perform the harvesting dance between combine and grain cart. She cursed his efficiency in running the grain cart. Maybe she would keep him around. Maybe... goose bumps popped on her arms. And while she was at it, she allowed herself the luxury of wondering what his lips would feel like on hers. *Good grief.* But seriously, how could she prove she wasn't just another flighty girl in her twenties? How could she impress a man ten years her senior enough to make him believe she was truly worth his time and energy? And maybe a few kisses here and there? She skillfully kept cutting stalks of wheat and simultaneously dumping bushels of wheat kernels. She needed to get a serious handle on herself or she wouldn't be impressing anybody anytime soon.

With a small wave, she let him know the combine hopper was empty. He gave a thumbs-up from the tractor cab and sped back to the semi. With this load finishing off the trailer, he would be gone from the field for a while. As soon as the grain cart was out of sight, she stopped the combine, shut off the header, throttled down the machine, and descended the steps, using the grimy handrails for balance.

The heat of the early afternoon sun baked her chilled skin. The dryness refreshed her, and the earlier goose bumps disappeared. After she finished using the big tire as a screen from the outside world, she headed to the back of the machine and checked for stray kernels. Everything was going great. The combine kept cutting along nicely, Violet was safely tucked in bed, and her baby still grew inside her. Corrie tilted her head back and sent a prayer of thanks to the heavens.

A tractor's low rumble growled just over the hill. *What now?* She placed a hand on her hip. Aaron wasn't driving the tractor. *Crap! What is he doing here?* She should have knocked on wood earlier. Everything was *not* great.

The tractor jerked to a halt. Luke waved from the seat and shut the tractor off.

She cringed. This wasn't a quick visit, then. Plastering a smile on her face, she welcomed him as he approached. "Hi, Pas—Luke. What can I do for you today?"

"Nothing." He beamed. "I just thought you could use the company. Besides, I brought you a present." From behind his back, he proffered a Milky Way candy bar and a bottle of Pepsi.

She stared at the gift. *How dare he!* He couldn't even come up with something original. He had to steal from his brother. She couldn't squelch the thought that years ago, Old Luke had stolen something that belonged to Future Aaron. Something she'd already given and paid for. A blush heated her body at the thought. Aaron hadn't even kissed her yet. "Thanks," she mumbled. "I appreciate this. But I don't need the company. I know you're a busy man." She hoped he would take her hint, but alas, he chuckled.

"My sermon's all done, and I need to talk to you." His green eyes gazed into hers, and she heard herself relent to his request.

Bad idea, Corrie. Very, very bad idea. I must be going crazy! She decided she was indeed insane as she climbed into the combine cab, took a seat, and throttled up the machine.

Luke settled into the buddy seat to the left of the driver's seat. His eyes fixated on her as she maneuvered the combine and began cutting again. For a few blissful moments, thousands of golden wheat stalks bowed slightly before being sliced from their roots and methodically scooted into the feeder house to be pulverized and separated. The mechanical engineering inside the machine she operated never ceased to amaze her. The efficiency. The businesslike manner in which the machine did its job.

"So, how've you been doing lately?"

His voice cut into her thoughts. She ground her teeth. He had no right to invade her personal space or private time. He'd essentially cornered her. And like a wounded animal, she was ready to strike or stop the combine, flee, and let him finish the field. She allowed the thought to skitter through her head before she answered.

"Well, considering the circumstances, I'm doing fine." She lifted the header, turned the combine at the end of the field, lowered the header, and resumed cutting up the field. The whoosh of air from the air conditioner kept the silence from being unbearable. Still, she almost reached to turn on the radio to fill the silence pounding in her eardrums.

She glanced at Luke. His normally tanned skin looked pale, and his gaze skipped nervously around the cab. She cleared her throat and grabbed the Pepsi behind the buddy seat. Her hand accidentally brushed against his shoulder blade, and he jumped.

"Sorry," she murmured. "I was just reaching for my pop." She studied him. "You okay?"

He took in a shuddering breath. "No. I'm a horrible, cowardly man who is too long in asking for your forgiveness."

If only she could shut his mouth with duct tape. She didn't want to relive that night. Didn't want to hash it out. Not right now. Not ever. And she certainly didn't want to have to forgive Luke Tuttle.

He snaked a hand through his hair and pulled. Then he pivoted toward her until their knees touched. Through her peripheral vision, she watched him study her. She refused to smooth down her hair or rid herself of the dust clinging to her skin.

"Can you stop the combine for a second? Please."

She huffed but did as he asked. She lifted and switched off the header and throttled down the machine.

Luke gave her a shaky smile. "When you walked back into my life, I thought I could handle it. I convinced myself seeing you every Sunday and around town wouldn't do damage to my heart. Turns out, I was wrong." He shifted toward her more, and his kneecap bit into her left thigh.

Stuck between a kneecap and combine console, she couldn't go anywhere. Tension tingled up her spine. Every drop of moisture in her mouth evaporated.

"I am a dumb man, Corrie, and I was an even stupider boy. Not a day goes by where I don't think about that night, where I don't see your scared face, where I don't see myself walking out on you. No matter how many times I've asked forgiveness from God, I can't forgive myself for what I did to you." He dipped his head and studied his hands. Hands she knew all too well. Hands that reminded her of someone else's. Although Aaron's would be different. More confident. More gentle. More possessive. More safe. Maybe. She tossed those thoughts from her head. They were nothing but a pipe dream, anyway.

"Please, Luke, I really don't want—"

"I'm sorry." He clasped her hand and held it tightly. "I'm sorry for using you and then throwing you away when you needed me the most. You were far too good for me then, and you're still far too good for me now."

She opened her mouth but snapped it shut again. She had nothing to say. Not anymore. She couldn't forgive him. Not yet. Nothing felt as if it would be okay again. If she only knew how she felt about the man sitting next to her. He was not the same boy who'd coaxed her into showing him physically how much she loved him. He was not the same boy who'd left her crying and frantic in a semitruck bed in her parents' farmyard.

Her ears still rang with the careless words he'd tossed at her that night. "There's an abortion clinic in Fargo." She wanted to take her hands off the steering wheel and plug her ears against the echo. "No, Luke, I don't want to get an abortion. We can do this. You and I. I thought you loved me!" Her reply still sounded as hoarse and terrified as it did so long ago. The conversation, set in the granite of memory, glared at her from the past. The words he'd hurled at her. The tearful pleas she'd begged. And then the pain of losing the baby the day after she'd resolved to keep it and be a mom. The blood. The realization that a human life had slipped from her, tiny and lifeless.

She dared a peek at him. This man had clearly turned his life around. She entrusted her soul to him every Sunday, but she could not, would not entrust her heart to him.

"I don't know what to say right now," she whispered. Afraid of her own voice, Corrie looked out the windshield. A hawk perused the wheat field for mice spooked out of their hidey-holes. Feeling like an unhoused mouse, she kept her voice low. "I appreciate your apology"—*Seven years later!*—"and I will think about it. That's the best I can do right now." The swooping predator lifted high again, and she faced Luke. "I'd appreciate some quiet time."

If he was disappointed in her response, he didn't show any sign of it. With a stolid face, he smiled. "Sure. Thanks for letting me talk." He got out, gave a slight wave through the glass door, and disappeared down the ladder. Then he ambled toward the tractor.

With a sigh, she throttled up the combine and began cutting again. This time, the silence grew unbearable. She flicked on the radio. Something about bleeding love. With a grunt, she hit the seek button. "A Cheating Heart" crooned at her through the speakers. With a tiny scream, she tuned in talk radio only to hear Rush Limbaugh discussing the fated relationship between two high-profile movie stars. She punched the power button with her finger and allowed the silence to drift around her, a mist of unsaid things echoing in her ears.

THE volleyball whizzed through the air and landed with a thud just outside the line. Corrie groaned as Nikki dipped her head and slapped her thigh. Her sister was off her game, and as Nikki glanced into the stands, Corrie spotted the reason. Xavier Palinski. His long blond hair hung over his shoulders in golden waves. Even though he wore the same canary-yellow Go Mustangs shirt as the rest of his comrades, all eyes were on Xavier. He seemed to have a magnetizing charisma that drew both young and old. And right now, either his charm or his hair was seriously damaging her sister's game. Corrie wanted so desperately to pull a Delilah on his hair. Anything to take away the mysterious power he had over her sister and half the crowd in the school gym.

Knowing she would give a small kingdom for a pair of scissors, she shuffled out of the bleachers and headed to the concession stand. Maybe a Pepsi and some nachos would soothe her boiling mind. If only Nikki's boy issues were Corrie's only problems concerning the opposite sex.

The smells of nacho cheese, candy, and Axe body spray assailed her nose as she ambled into the school cafeteria. Yellow banners and posters with various war cries of victory plastered the cafeteria's oatmeal-colored cinder block walls. Memories of her innumerable days eating in this place, trying to choke down the food, mooning over Luke, and enduring the endless years of drama flicked through her head like the movie projectors her ancient science teacher used to drag out on special occasions.

Part of her smiled, and part of her cringed. She felt sorry for the teenagers who packed the room. If only they knew high school was just a blip on the radar, and in the full scheme of life, prom, games, and tests really didn't matter. She nodded to a couple of men across the cafeteria, whom she ran into regularly at the elevator. *Yup, pretty sad social life!*

With her nachos and Pepsi, she excused her way back to her spot next to her mom and dad and sucked in a quick breath when she spotted Aaron sitting next to her father, chatting away about something. Aaron waved at her and continued talking with Jake. Aaron was wearing the same shirt that he had that infamous Sunday night—the shirt she'd cried into. She closed her eyes, remembering what his chest felt like under that shirt, smelling his cologne as he comforted her, savoring the pressure of his hands on her back as he held her while she wept. Butterflies twirled and swirled inside her stomach. She was slammed with an intense longing to feel his arms around her again, for his heartbeat to race under her fingertips. Stuffing those thoughts and desires in the dusty closets of her mind, she leaned over and whispered to her mom, "What are they talking about?"

Cynthia rolled her eyes and smiled. "What most men around here talk about, farming."

Corrie chewed on her fingernails. "Do you think Violet's okay? I really hate leaving her."

"Mary will take good care of her." Cynthia chuckled. "Mary has taken on Violet as a pet project. She likes being needed. I think this gives her mind a rest from thinking about Caleb. Oh"—she dug her phone from her purse and swiped at the screen—"and get a look at this."

Corrie stared. "Is that Luke?" She peered closer to the picture to answer her own question. Luke sat next to Violet, who was tucked into a recliner, and had a book in his hand. A smile was on both their faces.

Cynthia beamed at her. "According to Mary, he's been reading to her for over an hour. They seem to have connected over Louis L'Amour books."

The image of Violet snuggled up under the sunny yellow comforter—her head barely peeping over the embroidered edge, her eyes wide and owlish peering at her surroundings—struck at Corrie's heart. Corrie wanted to know how she had come to be such a hardened and frightened young woman and prayed that Luke could nurture her out of her shell.

She refocused on the game. Everything rode on this last set. If the Sandy Mustangs won, they won the whole thing. And things were not looking up. Finally, her sister stepped up to serve again, and Corrie's heart beat faster. She silently prayed for God to block the rays of awesomeness leaking out of Mr. Palinski.

With a boom, the volleyball flew over the net and hit within millimeters inside the line. The line judge signaled the ball was good, and yellow-clad fans jumped to their feet with a resounding victory roar. A sea of spectators flooded out of the gymnasium. The two volleyball teams gave half-hearted good-game handshakes and headed to the locker rooms.

"It was good seeing you tonight, Corrie."

She looked up into Aaron's eyes. For some reason, she couldn't quite swallow. "Ditto." She squelched the desire to slap her palm on her forehead. *Ditto?*

Laugh lines crinkled around Aaron's eyes. "I'll see you tomorrow." His fingers brushed her hand. And off he went, helping her dad down the bleachers. He sauntered across the gym, talking animatedly. Then he settled Jake on a chair in the lobby and glanced back at her before walking out the door.

She blushed. He had caught her staring. Wincing, she stood, stretched, and stopped short. In a covert corner on the far side of the gym, Nikki ripped her arm out of Xavier's grasp. Sisterly protection reared its warrior head, and only her mother's staying hand kept Corrie standing on the wooden bleachers, as if she were the meerkat assigned to sentry duty for the family—although she wasn't exactly sure who the predator was. Xavier, golden hair flicking side to side as he emphatically shook his head to a question Nikki must have asked, tried grasping for her hand. She stomped her sneakered feet, wagged her finger in his face, and gestured toward the locker room. Corrie could only assume Carly's name had come up in the argument.

Finally, Nikki smacked Xavier across the face and stalked off to the locker room. Corrie winced and started down the bleachers in search of her sister.

Cynthia caught Corrie's arm. "Leave her. She won't be ready to talk to you. Not yet. Give her time."

"So I should let her stew and get all broody? You know what she's like when she's pouting. The doors in the house will never forgive you, Mom. Besides, I'm sure the issue between those two is just a misunderstanding. A silly mistake. All teenagers make them." She ended on a sigh, her own mistake haunting her. If Corrie could save her sister from just a tenth of what she'd suffered, she would.

"Mistakes are a part of life. The important thing is that we learn from those mistakes and forgive those whose mistakes affect us."

Corrie wrinkled her nose, and she and her mother made their way down the empty bleachers. Jake was already at the door, waiting patiently. "Somehow, I don't think you're talking about Nikki anymore."

"I'm talking about both of you." Cynthia stopped Corrie with a touch to the arm. The harsh fluorescent lighting made her mother look ten years older. Her once-luscious blond hair now hung in thin rivulets over her shoulders. Dark circles surrounded her tired brown eyes, and no amount of concealer could hide the wrinkles cracking under them. "What Luke did to you is abominable. But you have to remember it's not all his fault. You are partly to blame for what happened." When Corrie began to speak, Cynthia held up a hand. "But he is a changed man, just as you are a changed woman. Can't you begin to forgive him? You need to for your sake as well as his." Cynthia reached out and gently touched Corrie's cheek. "I want to see you happy, and you're not."

Corrie pulled away from her mother's touch. Anger coursed through her. How dare her mother talk to her about forgiving the man who—Corrie took a deep breath. "I know, Mom. But when's the last time you were happy? You seem to be angry at Dad for something that wasn't his fault."

The blood drained from her mother's face. Remorse smacked Corrie upside the head, but pride kept her silent.

"I know you don't understand the situation, dear, but I'm trying. I really am. It's hard, though. He's not the same man I married. And even though it shouldn't be important, it is. Very important." Cynthia dabbed at her eyes. "He's more my patient than my husband. He doesn't even look at me like he used to." She stopped short. "Sorry. This is not something you need to be hearing."

Corrie clutched her mother's shaking hand and held it tightly as they walked across the gym floor. She studied her father's face as they drew nearer to the door where he was waiting. Her mother was right. There was nothing. The light that had once fired up in his eyes at the sight of his wife did not ignite. Corrie held on tighter to her mother's hand, longing to instill some hope that someday, maybe, her mother's husband would come back to her.

AFTER last night's volleyball game, the last thing Corrie needed was more stress, but here she was, watching her little brother get pummeled by a guy twice his size. Wanting to tell the referee a thing or two, she instead bit on the straw sticking up from her Pepsi. She sucked in a breath when the Mustangs snapped the ball. The quarterback, Xavier Palinski, threw the ball down the field toward Nathan. Catching it and tucking it into his arm, Nathan ran for a touchdown, making it across the end zone before one of the big dudes in red crushed him to bits.

She leapt up and cheered. Pride overwhelmed her, and tears pricked at her eyes. Brushing away the rogue tears, she clapped along with the school song, remembering her days in the pep band and cheering for the quarterback at the time. Of course, every girl had had a crush on Luke Tuttle, but he'd been hers. He'd become her identity. She quit being Corrie Lancaster and became Luke Tuttle's girlfriend.

Looking back, she could see how the toxicity of the relationship caused such tragic events. She erased the thoughts. They did no good. Across the stands, her dad sat with Gerome and Mary Tuttle. Across the field, Luke leaned against the chain-link fence, talking with other spectators. Corrie craned her neck but didn't see Aaron anywhere. Mary rose and made her way over to her. Hopefully, Luke wouldn't invite himself over as well. He was the last person she wanted to sit next to.

"Hello, dearie," Mary huffed as she squeezed in between Corrie and another spectator. "Excuse me... sorry..." Mary shimmied her backside onto the cold aluminum stands. Once settled, she turned to Corrie. "Your dad seems to be doing better over there. It's not so loud or rambunctious."

"Good."

"They've mainly been talking farming, but I can tell he's proud of Nathan, especially the last touchdown. I almost saw the old Jake come out." Mary patted Corrie's knee. "So, how are things on the Lancaster farm?"

"Let's just say it's going." She played the chewed-up straw over her lips. "Aaron has been such a godsend."

Mary patted Corrie's knee. "Yes, that he is. After Caleb passed, just his being home helped more than I think he knows. Helped

Gerome out especially." She took a quick breath and shook herself. "Sorry, I'm just an old lady getting emotional."

Corrie wrapped an arm around Mary and gave her a squeeze. Not knowing what to say, she settled in to watch the game, oohing and aahing or creating inventive kid-friendly swear words for the referee.

"Are we still on for tomorrow, then?" Mary asked after the whistle called a time out.

"Yeah. Mom and Dad leave early in the morning, so I'll need someone to watch over Violet."

"That girl's got some baggage. You can see it in her eyes. After I met her, I told Gerome she looked as if she was carrying the weight of all the sin in the world. I bribed Luke with some of my fried chicken if he'd go spend some time with Violet, read to her, teach her how to play pinochle, and other nonsense like that." A mischievous glint lit her eyes. "But I don't think I have to bribe him anymore. I think he's taking a liking to her. Or maybe it's pity. Whatever it is, maybe he can help get rid of some of her ghosts."

Corrie stood and stretched her legs. "She's haunted by something. That's for sure." Taking one last look around, she ventured to ask, "Where's Aaron tonight? It's not like him to miss a football game."

"He had a headache, although I'm starting to think his recent ailments aren't so much of the body." Another twinkle lit the older woman's eyes.

"Well," Corrie blushed and stammered, "I-I best be getting Dad home. I told Nathan we'd try with half games first and see how they went."

"But he's having fun. Look."

Across the stands, her father chattered and smiled, and a half-eaten Snickers bar melted in his hand.

"If you need to go, go. Gerome and I can bring your dad home." While Corrie wavered, Mary said, "You look tired yourself. Go home, get some rest, and I'll make sure your dad gets back safe and sound."

Corrie finally agreed and walked over to Jake. "Hey, Dad. Is it okay if I go? Mary said she'd take you home."

She thought he would demand to be taken home to his game shows. But the whistle blew, and she followed his gaze while Nathan took to the field. "I want to stay."

"Good." She kissed her father's cheek, thanked Gerome and Mary again, and walked to the gate.

"Corrie! Wait." Nikki caught up to her, panting and holding her sides. "You're quick for an old lady."

"And you're out of shape for a spry young athlete. Maybe I should tell your coach you need more cardio."

"Don't! I'm sorry about the old lady comment. You're not *that* old." Nikki darted away from Corrie's swat. "May I go out with Xavier after the game?"

Corrie blinked. "I thought you were never going to speak to him again as long as you live, especially after that slap heard halfway 'round the world."

"I've changed my mind." Nikki twirled her hair. "Can I?"

"Did you ask Mom?"

"No. There's no service here. I can't even send a text. Can you tell her?"

"So, you're going for the whole it's-easier-to-ask-for-forgiveness-than-permission bit, huh?"

"Something like that. Please?" Nikki clutched Corrie's hand. "You know what it's like being my age."

"If you want my permission, that's not a solid argument to use with me. But in spite of that, you may. Just be careful and don't do anything stupid."

Nikki took off before Corrie had put the *d* on *stupid*.

"And be home by midnight," she yelled to her sister's retreating form. She rolled her eyes as Nikki bounded to the stands and took her place among the cheering fans. Exhausted, Corrie trudged to the pickup and drove home, looking forward to a hot shower and a chapter in *Pride and Prejudice*.

Chapter Seven

"Violet?" Corrie whispered in the artificial darkness of the room Violet had called home for over a week. Soft breathing from the bed answered her query. Corrie turned on a bedside lamp and pulled up an old rocking chair. "Violet?"

Violet stirred under the covers and brought her head out in the open, blinking against the soft light. "Yeah."

"I was wondering if you'd like to get up and come outside. It's a beautiful morning. You could sit in a chair on the back porch."

Violet licked her cracked lips and cast her gaze around the room as if looking for a hidden enemy. "I don't—"

"It'll be good for you. As you're not a vampire, I don't think the sunshine will harm you."

A small smile threatened the corners of her mouth. "I don't want to be a bother to anybody. You've done more than you should already."

"Nonsense. You're no trouble at all." Corrie reached to help Violet out of bed. "Do you need help getting dressed?"

"I think I can manage. Nikki gave me some of her gym shorts and bigger T-shirts. I haven't thanked her yet."

"I'm sure she knows you're grateful. If you need any help, just holler. I'll be in the hall."

Violet opened her mouth, but no sound came out. After several seconds, she attempted to speak again. "Do you have a phone charger I could use? Mine doesn't work."

"Sure. It's in my room. Use it anytime." Corrie closed the door behind her and leaned against the wall. Seeing Violet weak and vulnerable tugged at Corrie's heart. She crossed her arms and tipped up her chin. No matter what, she would care for this woman and her unborn baby. Do for Violet what Corrie had never gotten a chance to do—help bring a baby into this world and love it.

The door opened, and Violet, dressed in day-glow orange running shorts and an oversized Mustangs T-shirt, stepped into the hall. Her dark hair, pulled into a tight ponytail, accentuated the shadows setting up house under her lackluster eyes.

Corrie wrapped her arm around Violet's bony shoulders and led her to the back porch. Pink and white geraniums bobbed their pretty heads, and a light breeze played with the tendrils escaping Corrie's quick, messy bun. Tucking them behind her ear, she led Violet to the porch swing.

"I've been meaning to ask if you have any family we should be calling." She settled herself next to Violet on the swing. A tenseness seemed to creep along Violet's body. "I'm sure they're worried about you."

Violet massaged the basketball bump sprouting from her stomach. "I don't have any family."

"I'm sorry." Corrie reached out a hand to squeeze Violet's, but Violet moved her hand away, rejecting Corrie's offer of support. Corrie cleared her throat. "Do you have any friends we can call?"

A harsh laugh erupted from Violet. She clasped a hand over her mouth and gave Corrie an apologetic look. "Sorry. No. There's no one to call."

"How far have you and Luke got in *The Lonesome Gods*?" Corrie had seen the book on the side table in the living room just that morning, an old Tractor Supply gift card used as a bookmark sticking out from the pages of her father's favorite western.

For the first time since Violet's arrival, Corrie saw the woman relax. A phantom of a smile touched Violet's lips. "Pastor Luke is too kind. He has better things to do than babysit me."

"Trust me, if Luke doesn't want to do something, he won't. And if you'd rather not read L'Amour, I have some other books you can borrow."

"No. Thank you, but I like Johannes Verne. He has every reason to hate, to want revenge, but he chooses a different path. I haven't had much experience with men like that."

Unable to sit anymore, Corrie pushed off the swing and began pacing. Before she could delve deeper into the mysterious woman, a vehicle barreled down the driveway. Her heart stopped. George.

The mud-covered pickup lurched to a stop, and George jumped out and stomped across the yard. His ample belly swung side to side as his harsh strides ate up distance between them.

Corrie crossed her arms over her chest. "George. How nice to see you."

He bit off a curse. "Don't play games with me. You know why I'm here."

"I haven't the slightest. Enlighten me."

"I need compensation for the damage done to my truck while working for you."

She couldn't help laughing. "You bring this up now? You quit more than two weeks ago. Or did you forget? I don't owe you anything. It's not my fault you ripped through my fields like a prepubescent teenage boy. The damage you did to your truck is your fault and your fault alone. And if you think you can barge onto my property and make wild accusations, I suggest you get your head examined. Now shoo. I'm done with you." She turned on her heels to walk away.

A meaty hand to her upper arm stopped her. "I'll get the sheriff involved with this, Corrie."

She glared at his hand, wishing for laser vision. She would burn a hole right through the disgusting appendage. "Get your hand off me." When he released her, she faced him. "No one, including Sheriff Steve, is going to believe your accusations. Especially because it's been a couple of weeks since you've worked for me. Now, get off my property before I—"

George was no longer looking at her but at something behind her.

"My, my, look at what we have here." He brushed past Corrie, checking her in the shoulder.

Corrie spun. Panic exploded on Violet's face. George was a jerk, but he was mainly harmless. However, Violet's expression froze Corrie's blood.

"So, you're the pretty little thing that's been stranded." His eyes roved over Violet, stopping at her protruding belly. He spit a stream of brown tobacco juice at her feet.

"That's enough, George. Leave her alone and leave my farm. I won't ask you again."

"Now, I'm just trying to make friends. Nothing's wrong with that."

She wished they weren't alone. No parents. No siblings. No Aaron. Just her and Violet. Not much against a bear of a man. George took a step closer to Violet, and Corrie's mama bear instincts kicked in. She steadied herself, planted her right foot in front of her, and said George's name. As he circled around, she slammed her fist directly on his nose. The snap of nose cartilage crackled against her knuckles. George howled and cradled his bloody nose.

"Get off my property. Now."

He shuffled to his truck, yelling epithets her way. As he sped off, the tires spit rocks in every direction, and the rush of adrenaline left her body in a tsunami. She sank to the porch's floor, tucking her aching and throbbing hand under her armpit.

"Corrie!" Violet hustled toward her, sank down next to her, and wrapped Corrie in a tentative one-armed embrace. "Are you okay?"

"I should be the one asking you. I'm so sorry about George. He's a donkey's patoot."

Violet shook her head. Her hand, lifeless and limp in Corrie's, became clammy. "It's not the first time I've—"

"Violet?" Corrie waited until Violet looked her in the eyes. "Where are you from, honey? You seem haunted by something. Can I help you?"

"You and your family have shown me more kindness than anyone I've ever met." A sad smile spread across Violet's lips. "And no. You can't help me. The damage has already been done. Can't slap a Band-Aid on a bullet wound, can you?"

Violet tugged her hand out of Corrie's grasp and made her way back into the house. Corrie's heart broke for the young woman who seemed entirely lost in her own shadow, but another approaching vehicle grabbed her attention. Her nerves danced, and her hands balled into fists. She relaxed them as soon as she saw the pink VW Bug soar into the yard. Mary Tuttle managed to get all of herself out of the car and waved excitedly at Corrie.

"Good morning, my dear. I hope I'm not late. I needed to lock Gerome in his office until he took care of the piles of paperwork he needed to do. Men." An equal dose of love and annoyance infused the last word. The tone was one that Corrie's mother used to take with her father when he was well and himself and a typical man. Corrie missed that tone.

"Don't worry, Mrs. Tuttle."

Mary's eyes twinkled out of her pudgy and kind face. "I believe there's a certain gentleman waiting for you." Corrie felt her face droop. Mary chuckled. "Anyway, my dear, I'm ready to nurse this little bird back to health. I think Luke will stop by after visiting his people at the nursing home. Is she up?"

"Yeah, however, we had a slight run-in with George." Corrie lifted her still-throbbing hand.

"Oh my!" Mary gasped. "What did he do?"

"Let's just say that he probably didn't deserve a broken nose, but he was ticking me off and scaring Violet to death. He wouldn't leave." Corrie shrugged, trying to feel guilty over unjustly assaulting someone. Didn't work.

"You should contact the sheriff." Mary clucked over Corrie's war wounds.

"No. I think I'll just wait and see. It's not like I did anything wrong, right?"

Mary's eyes lit up. "You did what everybody in a sixty-mile radius wants to do to George. I say we give you a medal."

"Thanks. I think." Corrie retrieved her hand from Mary's doctoring. "I best be going, Mrs. Tuttle. Thanks again for watching Violet today."

"No problem. You better get going before my son starts worrying about you."

Corrie jogged into the house and checked on Violet only to find her napping. She grabbed her lunch cooler and sprinted out the door, hoping—oh-so-hoping—that maybe Aaron did a lot more than just worry about her. Maybe he thought about her too.

All the way to the field, Corrie's heart hammered in her chest with that wish. When she saw him scrambling out of the combine, a Dust Buster vacuum in hand, her hammering heart stuttered a beat. The ends of his shaggy hair peeked out from under his ball cap, and Corrie's palm itched to tuck them back under. He looked so darn cute. *Wait. Can a man in his midthirties be cute?*

He tipped the brim of his ball cap to her and grinned.

Her heart melted. Yup, a man in his midthirties could most definitely be cute and adorable and hot and—

"I was getting worried. Is everything okay?" He jumped down the ladder and jogged toward her. "Is Violet all right?"

"Yes and yes. Your mom was a little late. That's all. Nothing to worry about." Guilt gnawed at her, but no way was she going to share the other part of her morning.

"Good." He dug his booted toe in the stubble. "So, um, this field is almost done."

"Yeah. Which means we're almost done with the wheat harvest."

"Yeah." He swiped off his hat, scratched his head with the brim, and slapped it back on. "The combine is all cleaned and ready for you. I did a test cut, and things look ready to go."

"Good." She smiled. "Thanks. For everything. I don't know what I'd have done without you."

A blush crept up Aaron's freshly shaven face. Maybe he liked her after all. He certainly wilted when she mentioned the ending of wheat harvest. She shook herself. Probably just her imagination playing cruel tricks on her.

"Corrie, I, ah..." He began to reach for her hand, but he quickly retreated. "Never mind. You're welcome." He pivoted on his heel and marched to the semi.

She stood for a second, dazed and off balance. *What just happened?* Shaking the cobwebs from her brain, she grasped the combine ladder rails and winced. The crush cloud she'd been floating in burst, and the morning's events rained down upon her. George. Ignoring the pain in her right hand, she continued up the ladder and slammed the door. Gripping the joystick was an issue, and by the end of the day, she would probably regret her earlier actions. But for now, she couldn't stop the mischievous grin that skipped across her lips as she remembered her fist coming in contact with George's fleshy, fat face.

"What a creep!" she exclaimed to the empty cab. "How dare he come to my house and demand compensation! The very thought of it makes me just want to—" Corrie cut herself off with a growl. "And if he ever threatens Violet again, well, when I get through with him, he'll wish he had come face-to-face with the Grim Reaper!"

Taking a couple of deep breaths, she forced herself to calm down and pay attention to the wheat and any rocks willing and able to jump into the combine. Without the anger, however, nothing shielded her from Violet's terrified face and haunted eyes. That woman had a story. Corrie's inner reporter jerked to attention. Violet must have seen a special kind of hell for it to have left such definite marks. Corrie prayed Violet's torment would quit haunting the poor woman, letting her finally live and blossom.

AARON drove the Peterbilt into the field, turned it around, and parked it. His rumbling stomach told him the time. Corrie would be starving but too stubborn to stop and eat. He'd have to take her lunch to her. After hopping out of the truck, he swung past her rusted-out Dodge, grabbed the Igloo cooler from the shade, and climbed into the John Deere tractor.

"Corrie?" He released the button on the CB receiver and waited.

"Go ahead."

"You needing to dump yet?"

"Yeah. I'm pretty full. I'm on the southwest side of the field. I'll catch you going north."

"Ten-four." He put the tractor in gear and drove as fast as the ruts allowed. As he bumped along, he tried thinking of anything but Corrie. Didn't help that he was around her all day. It didn't matter if they hardly saw each other or spoke, just being in the same field was enough to drive him crazy. And it certainly didn't help that Luke never shut up about her. As soon as the harvest was done, Aaron wouldn't have anything to do with the confounded Lancaster woman. He extinguished his fevered thoughts. He could simply be the neighbor who never borrowed a cup of sugar.

Aaron sighed. *Who am I kidding?* God himself would have to smack him over the head to keep his thoughts off her. But maybe the separation would assuage the pain of knowing he could never have her.

She probably thinks I'm some old fogey, anyway. I am *an old fogey.* He scratched at the graying stubble on his face that he hadn't bothered to shave off this morning and wondered if those coloring kits for men really worked. Like that wouldn't cause talk around the little town of Sandy. He abandoned the idea. Gray hair was supposed to be a sign of wisdom, although he felt very much like a fool at the moment.

With pulsating heart, he pushed the receiver button. "Could I ride along with you after we dump? I've got your lunch."

Maybe it was just his imagination, but the pause in the airwaves lasted an eternity. Finally, her voice broke through the CB. "Sure."

"You are an absolute idiot!" Aaron scolded himself as he lined up under the protruding combine auger. He prayed the full two minutes it took to dump. Prayed he wouldn't make a complete donkey's hind end out of himself or do something worse—like steal a kiss. She would probably find it disgusting. *Right?* At her signal that she was done, he stopped the tractor, shut it off, and hopped out. She had slowed the combine to a crawl, and he jogged to catch up with the moving machine. Carefully balancing himself and the lunch cooler, he climbed the ladder, opened the door, and plunked down in the buddy seat.

"Hi." He smiled at Corrie's profile.

"Hey." She smiled back then returned to watching the header and the various bars and numbers on the computerized screen to her left. "Thanks for bringing me lunch. I thought I'd have to start eating the candy bar I found under the seat."

He chuckled. "I wouldn't advise it. What would you like? Ham and cheese with Pepsi or ham and cheese with Pepsi?"

"You certainly give a woman a lot of choices, don't you?" She tapped her chin. "It's a difficult decision, but I'll take the ham and cheese with Pepsi, please."

He dug around in what used to be a bright-red cooler. Years of dust and field duty had stained it a dull rust color. "Ah! Look what I found. Not only do you get your entrée of choice but a side of tapioca pudding and grapes."

"My day just gets better and better."

"From what I've heard, it didn't start out that way." Under her gaze, he finally understood what a butterfly pinned to a display board must feel like. "George came into the elevator when I was buying you this." He proffered his normal gift of a Milky Way.

"Sorry for the stare-o'-death. That man just makes my skin crawl and my teeth fuzzy." She grabbed the offered chocolate and stored it on the console. "What did George have to say?"

"He had plenty to say even though none of it was worth hearing. He came in the weigh house, screeching about how you attacked him and showing everybody his black eyes and bruised nose."

"Attacked him?" She squeaked indignantly. "Me? Attack him?" She opened and snapped her mouth shut several times. "That scum. No. He's not just scum. He's the scum on the scum that feeds off the scum." She wiggled in the combine seat. "Well, maybe I did attack him, but he deserved it. He wouldn't leave, and he was scaring Violet half to death. I had to do something."

Aaron chuckled. He nabbed a sandwich from the cooler and took a bite. "That may well be, but he vowed to report you to the sheriff for assault." At her gasp, Aaron held up a hand. "We both know the possibility of George actually doing so is slim to none, and besides, do you really think Steve's going to put you away for life?"

"Might actually be a vacation," she mumbled as she accepted the ham-and-cheese sandwich he handed her. For several minutes, the thrashing of the feeder house and the constant growl of the engine created the only sounds in the combine cab. "What if George does file a complaint, and Steve does come and get me?" She took her hand off the steering wheel long enough to swat at him. "No, don't laugh! I'm serious. I don't think I could take being handcuffed."

The cab echoed with his laughter. "I'm sorry," he pleaded after her eyes filled with tears. "Oh, Corrie, don't. I'm sorry. I shouldn't have laughed. It's not funny." He reached around her and brought the combine to a stop. Kneading her shoulders, he turned her until she faced him. His heart beat in his chest as he thumbed away a rogue tear dashing down her cheek. "Let me see your hand." He cradled it and studied the bruising spreading across her knuckles and fingers. "George deserves a lot more than a fist to his nose." He risked looking into her eyes and was rewarded with what looked like admiration. But he didn't want her admiration. He brought her hand to his lips and brushed a kiss against each injured knuckle.

He tensed when her hand cupped his cheek, her thumb playing over his stubble. Blood roared through his veins and thundered in his ears, deafening him. He locked gazes with her. He didn't need to see her lips for his own to aim for them. Just a few more breaths, a few more heartbeats, and he'd be home.

"Aaron?" The CB receiver clicked on, allowing Luke's stupid voice to crackle through.

Aaron growled but didn't move. Neither did Corrie, her hand still resting on his cheek.

"Aaron? Corrie?"

Her hand slipped from his cheek then curled in her lap. Her teeth nibbled on her bottom lip.

He swallowed and reached for the receiver. "What do you need, Luke?"

"Dad couldn't reach you over your phone. Needs you home for a little bit if Corrie can spare you."

Corrie laid her hand over his. "I'm okay. You go help your dad."

He didn't want to break contact. "Are you sure?"

She nodded, and his hand sagged from hers.

"I can walk back to the tractor. You can make it one more full round." He snagged an extra sandwich, a baggie full of chips, and a can of Pepsi. "Thanks for letting me ride with you. See you in a bit." But the bit couldn't be short enough. Even seconds without her seemed like hours. He was in big trouble.

A startled grumble jolted Corrie from her dream of Middle Earth. She sat up in bed and squinted at the red numbers on the clock. Two a.m. She shook her head, dispelling the dream that she was the elf princess, Arwen. Aragorn had looked mysteriously like Aaron. Gimli had had the face of Luke. She pressed her knuckles to her cheek, savoring the memory of Aaron's lips on her skin, and strained to listen. It wasn't an animal. It was too mechanical.

She sprang out of bed, flung her feet into a pair of flip-flops, and ran down the steps and out the front door.

There in the middle of the yard, the combine grumbled and growled its discontent at being woken up after a long day of work. With its back end facing her, she had no idea who was disrupting the night's peace. She crept around to the ladder and climbed, afraid of who might be in there. Relief and pain warred in her when she saw who was sitting in the operator's seat.

She opened the door and sat in the buddy seat. "Dad?"

He didn't look at her. He kept staring out the windshield, his head turning side to side as if combining an actual wheat field. His right hand formed around the joystick, and every once in a while, the header moved up and down.

"Dad? Talk to me." She touched his shoulders.

He turned his head, his eyes glistening. "Forgot how to combine."

She took his left hand and placed it against her cheek. She allowed the tears to come. To splatter on his callus-free hand. "No, Dad, you didn't. It's in your heart. Not your head. Remember what Grandma used to say? That you were a farmer the minute you were born. That gift is a gift God won't take from you. You'll learn again. I promise."

His thumb caressed her wet cheek. "My baby girl."

"Always and forever." She smiled through the sadness and gently placed his hand back on the steering wheel. "Shall we start?"

He nodded, and for the next thirty minutes, she walked her father through the important elements of the combine. Everything from the throttle to the buttons and controlling the header and engine speed. It wasn't long ago that he had spent days teaching her how to run the same combine. His patience and belief in her ability to operate the expensive machine still brought a wave of adoration for her father. Now, she was the teacher, and he the student. His hand, once work-worn and huge, used to swallow up the joystick. Now, it looked weak and small, its muscles struggling to remember what once had come so naturally.

"George?"

She jumped and attempted to hide her hand. "What about him?"

The look her father gave her made her smile. She hadn't seen that cut-the-crap look in so long. His gaze flitted from her face to her hand.

"I sort of punched him in the face. How did you know?"

One side of his lips twitched. He cupped his hand over hers. "Violet."

"Yeah." Corrie sighed. "He was scaring her. He's a butt."

Her father's lips twitched, but he said nothing. Turning and looking at the console, he flipped the switch and turned the header off. The noise deflated, leaving just the engine's whirring. "I'm tired."

She nodded. "Yeah. Combining at two in the morning will do that. Here, let's park this baby away, shall we? You want to drive, or should I?"

He stepped on the release button on the floor next to the steering column. The steering wheel went up, and he stood and slid out.

She squeezed in and maneuvered the combine into the machine shed. After shutting the engine down, she patted the steering wheel. "Well, old girl, another wheat harvest done. You did well, my friend. You did well." She stole a look at her father and met his gaze. "Dad—"

"Proud of my baby girl." His eyes shone with the love she knew he couldn't quite express.

"Thanks, Dad. I love you too." She kissed his stubbly cheek. "You get yourself to bed. I'll be following in a bit."

He shuffled out of the machine shed, across the lawn, and into the house. Exhaustion crept up her legs, wrapped around her torso, and leaked into her brain. She sank to the gravel and lay on her back while the stars performed their nightly dance. So far away, so remote and cold to her plight. *God, where are you? What do you want from me? Why are you so far away?* She fought the tears pricking the backs of her eyes. *Show me what you want me to be. I feel like such a failure. I don't know if I can handle this. I need you.*

A comforting presence surrounded her, calming her racing thoughts and soothing her fevered soul. She sighed and embraced the peace washing over her. She staggered to her feet and started walking toward the house. A flicker of light from the semitruck cab caught her attention. Stopping, she stared at the cab, waiting for the flicker again. Seconds passed. *Now what?* She trudged to the truck to investigate. Her precious night's sleep was dwindling away, and she wanted nothing more than to slip back into bed and return to her dream of hobbits and the strange Aaron-and-Aragorn mix.

She ripped open the driver's side door and gasped. "Nikki!"

Her teenage sister squealed and ejected herself from Xavier Palinski's arms, yanking her shirt back over her head. "Corrie! We were, we were, just... um... talking." Nikki looked down at her hands twirling around in her lap.

Rage bubbled under the surface of Corrie's skin. She pinned the young man with an icy stare, and a smirk teased the side of her mouth when he shrank and wilted like her mother's houseplants. "You, Mr. Palinski, button up your pants, put on your shirt, and come with me. Now."

As soon as his feet touched the ground, she grabbed one of his earlobes and dragged him away from the truck. Under the yard light's glow, he squirmed, his gaze darting to and fro.

"Make a run for it. Please. Give me an excuse to beat the living daylights out of you." She released his ear and swatted at the bugs flitting and fluttering around her head. "Are you prepared to marry my sister? Do you love her? Or are you just looking to peruse the buffet before you buy the meal?"

Xavier's mouth opened then shut. "No. Yes. Um... what?"

"I'm sure Pastor Luke would be up for a late-night pastoral visit. We could call him right now. You could marry my sister and then bring your plan to fruition."

"I, um..." Xavier's mouth kept making motions, but no sound emanated from his chapped lips.

"That's what I thought." She took a step closer. "Here's the plan. You are going to leave immediately. I honestly don't trust myself not to punch you in your pretty-boy face. However, you will be here tomorrow afternoon. Two o'clock sharp. If you are as much as a second late, I'll make sure your parents know all about this. You understand me?"

Xavier turned and ran down the drive, apparently to retrieve his vehicle hiding in the tree line.

She took a few deep breaths, trying to regain the inner peace God had given her moments before. She stomped back to the truck, where Nikki sat sniveling on the grass.

"I'm so sorry, Corrie. I just—He said he liked me. He wanted to apologize for kissing Carly." Tears plopped into her lap, drowning her skinny jeans. "I don't want you to be angry. Please. I don't know if I could handle you being angry at me." Her body started shaking.

Corrie sank down beside her sister and scooted Nikki's quaking body close to her own. She lowered Nikki's head to her shoulder and caressed her hair.

After several moments, Nikki's sobs diminished into hiccups. She lifted her head. "I'm a terrible person, aren't I?"

Corrie brushed a stray tear from Nikki's nose. "No. You are a child of God. You are a princess of heaven. You are beloved by Christ."

"But I was doing something bad." Nikki looked down at her soaked jeans and whispered, "I don't think I would have stopped if you hadn't found us."

Memories seared Corrie's mind. She blocked those and concentrated on the present. "Look at me." She searched her sister's eyes. "I know exactly what you're going through. I wasn't always as boring and lame as I am now." She rolled her eyes when Nikki's lips twitched. "You have something so special inside you. Please be careful who you give it to. I don't want to see you hurt."

"Can you ever forgive me?"

Corrie tucked a stray hair behind Nikki's ear. "Already done." She got to her feet and helped Nikki off the ground.

Fresh tears sprang to Nikki's eyes as she catapulted into Corrie's arms. "Thank you." She pulled back and asked, "Why didn't you kill Xavier?"

"He's a stupid boy. Killing him would be unfair. I have a worse punishment in store for the young man."

Nikki reached for her, and they walked hand in hand to the house. "Like what? Please don't scar him for life."

"Tempting, but no. I don't *plan* on a lifetime of scars. Counseling, maybe, but scars, no."

Before they entered the house, Nikki stopped. "I suppose you'll tell Mom."

Corrie ruffled Nikki's hair. "Yeah, but Mom's been down this road before. Trust me, you aren't her first wayward daughter."

"You mean." Nikki stammered. "You did...?"

"And regretted it ever since. Some things, you don't forget. I don't wish that fate upon you."

"Who did you, well, you know?"

"That, my dear sister, is none of your business. Now go to bed."

Corrie followed her sister up the steps, made sure Nikki settled securely in her room, and then fell into her bed, succumbing to sleep and hoping her own mistakes wouldn't haunt her dreams.

Chapter Eight

Aaron eyed the chocolate chip cookies riding shotgun in his truck. The smell tantalized his nose, and his fingers twitched. No one would notice one missing cookie, but before his hand could swoop in for the kill, guilt clutched his stomach. His mother had baked them for Corrie and given orders that the baker's dozen not decrease by one.

He likened his mother to a love shark. She smelled pheromones in the water, especially after she'd caught him staring at Corrie in church this morning. So here he was, sent off like Little Red Riding Hood with baked goodies. He hoped his budding attraction for the recipient wouldn't be eaten alive by Corrie's indifference.

He shook his head as he turned in to the Lancasters' long driveway. He'd never had so much trouble with women. Before he could come up with any answers, he pulled up next to Luke's truck and a car he'd never seen. Jealousy reared its ugly head and started spitting venomous thoughts through his mind.

"Get a grip," he growled through gritted teeth. "If Corrie chooses to give Luke a second chance, then... then..." Aaron gave up and gripped the door handle, yanking it open. He grabbed the baked goods, closed the truck door, and forced himself to amble up the steps when all he wanted to do was stomp up, yank open the door, and taste Corrie's lips.

"Aaron!" Cynthia exclaimed when she opened the door. "Come on in. Luke's here too."

"Yeah, I saw his truck." Aaron hoped his steady voice didn't come off as fake as it felt. "Is he here to see—"

"Corrie," Cynthia interrupted. "We've had a busy morning. Come and join the madness."

She led him into the kitchen. The well-lit kitchen didn't dispel the humming tones of disharmony. At the kitchen table, Corrie sat with a young man he recognized from sporting events. Some kid with a funny name. From the look on the kid's face, Aaron could only assume he would rather be washing his teammates' jock straps than sitting across from Corrie. Aaron's gaze didn't last long on the squirming teen. Corrie's gaze drew him, captured him. A smile spread his lips. His heart pounded as he took in her face, her eyes, her ponytailed hair. He knew what it looked like loose, swaying in the wind, brushing the dewy grass beneath it. Needing something to do with his hands, he placed the cookies on the table in front of her and stuck his hands in his front pockets.

"Hi," he breathed.

"Hi." Her frown faded, and she smiled back and motioned to the cookies. "I didn't know you could bake. Is there anything you can't do with your hands?"

His throat closed. Her innocent statement twisted in his mind, and for a second, he allowed himself a mental picture of what he couldn't do, but really wanted to, with his hands. *Dear Lord, you're going to have to help me. I can't think of her this way. She's not mine, but oh, how I really want her to be.*

Cynthia snatched a cookie, squeezed Aaron's arm, and headed out of the kitchen. "Xavier, follow me. Pastor Luke might be able to work a miracle."

The boy stumbled out of the kitchen and followed Cynthia through the sliding glass doors off the kitchen and to the porch.

Aaron raised his eyebrow. "You look a little stressed."

She sighed, got up, poured two glasses of milk, and sat down. "Better sit. It's a long story."

He settled across from her and watched more than listened as she retold the tale of two young lovers. Her hand, calloused with fingernails bitten to the quick, waved back and forth as she grew agitated. The mesmerizing dimple in her cheek winked every now and then. He never wanted to take his gaze off her animated eyes.

"...and so I told the little brat that if he wanted to be involved with my sister, he would do it the right way. He'd court her."

Aaron choked on the cookie he'd pilfered from the platter. After taking a sip of milk, he cleared his throat. "*Courting?*"

"Yeah, you know. Old-fashioned stuff." Corrie bit a cookie in half and waved the remainder in her hand around the kitchen. "He certainly is not a gentleman now, but by the time I get done with him, he will be the Mr. Darcy of Sandy, South Dakota. Minus the sideburns. He's too pretty-boyish for such masculinity."

Aaron couldn't help laughing. "You are the most amazing woman I've ever met." He clamped his mouth shut.

A blush crept from her exposed, sharp collarbone to the roots of her hair. "So... yeah." She shredded the napkin in front of her. After moments of silence, she looked up, her eyes serious. "Thanks. That means a lot. But I think you're pretty amazing too. Without you, I really don't know what we would've done."

His heart thudded. "Corrie, I—"

"Aaron, what are you doing here?" Luke opened the sliding glass door and beamed at him, Violet at his side. It was a wonder the woman didn't run into the doorjamb as her eyes were cemented on Luke's ear.

Aaron gritted his teeth. "Cookie delivery." He slapped his brother's hand when Luke dove for one. "They're for Corrie."

"That's all right." She proffered a cookie to Luke. Her fingers brushed his. Luke's face brightened, a stupid grin playing on his face. Violet's face fell, and she shook her head when Corrie offered her a cookie.

Aaron clenched and unclenched his fist. Feeling itchy, he stood to leave. "I should get going. Good luck with the whole courting thing."

"Wait, Aaron." Corrie jumped out of her chair. "I still owe you a check. Why don't you follow me to the office?"

His stomach sank to his feet as if he were cresting the highest point of a roller coaster. He knew what it felt like to be in her presence, smell her scent, drink in her smile. Wanting to experience the rest of the ride, he followed her down the hall to the office, his heart thundering in his chest. He'd been in the room many times when Jake commanded the farm. Aaron chuckled to himself. Nothing had changed except the scent. Instead of leather, grease, and Old Spice, honeysuckle hovered just above the surface, tantalizing him, taunting him.

Corrie opened a desk drawer that held several tractor-pull trophies and various farm magazines. "I really can't tell you 'thank you' enough." She sighed and bent over the desk as she read a figure off a piece of paper.

Tearing his eyes away from her lithe body, he studied the unseeing glass eyes of a deer head on the wall. He needed to get away. Fast. Before he could formulate a game plan, she stood in front of him, holding out her hand, check quivering slightly. His mind rewound to the night she'd cried into his chest. She'd felt so good. The moment in the combine, when he'd been a breath away from her lips, had him gazing down at her makeup-free face. He wanted to explore every line, every crevice, and even the occasional scar.

"Aaron?"

He heard her whisper his name. Smelled chocolate chip cookie on her breath. Felt heat radiate off her body. Watched her tongue dart out and lick her lips.

Murmuring her name, he pulled her to him and captured her lips. She squeaked in surprise but matched his fervor with her own.

Firm and slightly chapped, her lips played against his. A moan escaped her lips, wafting against his cheeks. He pressed his hands against her back, drawing her close. His stomach dropped to his knees. Heat coursed through his veins. He wanted to devour the woman in his arms.

"Hey, Aar—"

He tensed at Luke's strangled growl. Corrie jerked out of his arms, and Aaron whirled around, smacking into his little brother's chest.

"What do you think you're doing?" Luke jabbed his finger into Aaron's chest. "She is not yours."

"Well"—Aaron clenched his fist—"she's not yours either, is she? You kind of screwed that up a long time ago, bud."

Luke's face drained of color, and his eyes studied the carpet.

Anger drained from Aaron, leaving him weak and speechless.

Corrie cleared her throat. "I think it's time both of you get out of my house."

Aaron dared a glance and wished he hadn't. Her eyes gleamed with unshed tears. Her voice lashed his heart. "And just to clear things up, gentlemen, I'm not sure I want to be either of yours." She spun on her heels and marched out of the room.

Her words rekindled Aaron's anger. He glared at Luke. "Moron."

Luke scoffed as he headed toward the door. He paused and turned, a sneer on his lips. "You don't have a chance with her, *grandpa*."

Aaron froze as his brother stormed out of the study. With a groan, he planted his hands on the smooth wood of the desk and hung his head. For several minutes, he remained amid the fragrance that was Corrie. He forced himself to leave the room and trudged down the hall to the front door, where he met up with the young man who'd sat traumatized at the kitchen table earlier. He still looked as if he'd swallowed a watermelon whole. Aaron felt his pain.

"What's your name, kid?"

"Xavier. Xavier Palinski."

Aaron clasped the young teen on the shoulder. "She's scary. But she's true. Remember that."

Xavier swallowed hard, his Adam's apple bobbing up and down. He nodded, tracing the grouting between the tiles with his boot toe. "She didn't kill me."

Aaron couldn't keep back the chuckle. He opened the door, allowing Xavier to go through first. "Yeah, she didn't kill me either." He waved away Xavier's incredulous look. "Never mind. Let's just hope she doesn't have another reason to kill us. Oh, about this courting thing? Any tips you can give me?"

WELL, this sucks! Corrie slammed her bedroom door and refused to throw herself across her bed. Only children and fictional heroines did such foolish things. *But I am a fool.*

"No, strike that. I'm an idiot," she mumbled as she paced her room. She licked her lips and still tasted Aaron's ChapStick. Her insides warmed, and her lips tingled at the memory of his kiss. "Yup. An absolute idiot!" She wanted nothing more than to hunt that man down and plant another kiss on him and apologize for kicking him out when she should have told Luke to go pound sand.

She eyed her bed, wanting to bury herself under the comforter for hours. Before she could launch herself into its pillowy depths, a knock interrupted her.

"Corrie?" Violet asked through the door. "There's someone here to see you."

"Who is it?" *Please be Aaron, please be Aaron, please be Aa—*

"The sheriff."

Her breathing stopped, and her heart tumbled into her stomach. *That sorry good-for-nothing George turned me in.* Attempting to stem the tide of panic threatening to swamp her, she opened the door, smiled brightly at Violet, and descended the steps.

"Hi, Corrie." Sheriff Steve stood up from the kitchen chair where he'd been munching on a cookie. One of her cookies. From Aaron.

"Hey, Sheriff. What can I do for you?"

"You know I don't like when you call me that, Corrie. It makes me feel old."

She studied him. He hadn't gained a pound since high school, but his shaved head didn't retain any evidence that his hair had been the envy of most of the girls. The military had not only knocked the bad attitude out of him but knocked out his hair as well. It was rumored he'd actually cried as the razor cut swath after swath of chestnut-brown locks from his head.

She stuck her chin out a little higher under his gaze. His eyes, one blue and one green, missed nothing. She wouldn't give him reason to think she needed to be cuffed and locked up for life.

She scanned the empty kitchen. "Where is everybody?"

"They're in the garden, I believe." He sat. "Have a seat, please."

She slid into the nearest kitchen chair and placed her hands on the table, folding them, hoping her fingers wouldn't betray their shaking. "Is this about George?"

"Yes. He came to me a couple of days ago. I admit, I've been reluctant to come see you about this. But I have to. I hope you don't mind me coming on a Sunday. But I know you're busy, and I didn't want to inconvenience you too much. So tell me about your incident with him."

She swallowed the saliva pooled in her mouth and filled him in on everything that had happened. She played with a hangnail on her thumb. "You should have seen her. She was terrified. He wouldn't stop even after I asked him to. When he started walking toward her,

I resorted to punching him in the face. It was the only way I knew how to stop him." Corrie took a deep breath and looked at the sheriff, surprised to find his lips twitching into a smile.

"I figured as much. George has a bad habit of shooting off his mouth. He told one too many renditions of the story. In fact, by the end of it, you had run to the barn, grabbed a crowbar, and threatened to castrate him right there in your driveway." His smile disappeared. "If George bothers you again, please let me know. He's got it out for you for some reason. Don't underestimate him." He rose and motioned for her to remain seated. "No need to walk me out. And please, call. Even if you think you're being paranoid, just call. It doesn't even have to be me. Aaron said he'd watch out for you as well."

A blush worked up her neck. "That's not necessary. To bother Aaron, I mean. I can take care of myself."

Steve cocked his eyebrow. "That mindset has gotten a lot of people in trouble who didn't have to be."

Giving a final nod, he walked out and left her to her thoughts—which currently weren't too comforting. With a sigh, Corrie pushed away from the table and ambled into the garden before joining her mother in the tomato patch, where she plucked off a sucker and played with the baby green vine between her fingers.

"Corrie"—Cynthia clutched at her arm—"why was Steve here?"

Violet looked up from pulling a weed, panic flickering on her face.

Corrie frowned and refocused on her mother. "Just asking me some questions about a tiff that happened between a couple of people last week. Nothing serious."

Cynthia eyed her but remained silent and retreated to her tomato plants. Corrie locked eyes with her father sitting in an Adirondack chair next to the tomato patch. Ever since his accident, being away from his wife caused him unnecessary anxiety, and if sitting in a chair fiddling with an Operation game eased his mind, no one dared question the odd setup. He'd seen through her lie. If only she could tell him her problems. She missed the days of years gone by when she would snuggle against his side and share her day. Granted, the story of her elementary days was less dramatic than the story of a man with a grudge, but it would've been nice to sit at his feet and hear his wisdom. He always knew what to do.

She kissed his cheek and whispered, "It'll be okay. I promise." Her vow stuck in her throat. His hand wrapped around her wrist as she moved away. His touch soothed her, and his look of confidence bolstered her confidence.

"Corrie?" Violet tentatively placed a hand on Corrie's shoulder. "Can I talk to you, please?"

Corrie squeezed her father's hand and followed Violet to the tire swing. Violet, too, seemed to gravitate to the swing in times of trouble. Corrie leaned against the tree and studied Violet as she situated herself in the tire. Her belly bump grew more pronounced every day. Corrie chewed her lip. A baby would certainly change the dynamics of an already-crazy household.

"I've been living a lie here, and I can't do it anymore." Violet's eyes shimmered. "You and your family have been so kind to me. I don't deserve any of it."

Corrie slid to the ground. "If we all got what we deserved, we'd be in a world of hurt." She smiled at Violet. "You don't need to worry about anything. You are more than welcome to stay."

Violet held up a hand. "Please, let me say what I need to say. Then I promise I'll pack my bags and leave. Trust me, you won't want me after you know the truth."

"Please don't talk like that. I don't know what you've done, but it can't be bad enough where—"

"I ran away from my fiancé. He's the father of my baby." Violet's body quivered, and tears streamed down her face. "This baby inside me will have no father." She slipped out of the tire swing and rocked herself back and forth on the ground.

"Violet," she whispered, afraid to speak for fear of making Violet run. When she got no response, Corrie inched closer. As if approaching a wounded animal, she reached out slowly and enfolded Violet's hand in hers. Violet jerked but didn't run as Corrie predicted. Instead, Violet sat motionless for several moments before crumpling into Corrie. Corrie wrapped her arms around the sobbing woman and rocked her back and forth.

Questions swarmed in Corrie's mind. She recalled the day Violet landed on her farm, disheveled, wigged, and with the worry of the world stooping her shoulders. *What hell has this woman seen?*

"Violet?" Corrie smoothed back Violet's sweaty hair from her pale forehead. "It'll be okay."

Violet pushed away and wiped at her tears as if they stung. "Don't you understand? I've failed everybody, including the little person inside me. I've forever doomed it. I've forever doomed myself," she ended with a whisper. Her emotion dissipated, leaving a shell of a woman defeated by life and circumstances. "I'm doomed."

The whispered condemnation broke Corrie's heart.

Violet's sobs decreased into erratic sniffles. "I'm sorry. I didn't mean to slobber all over you."

"This is nothing. You should see me after my sister uses my shoulder."

She studied Corrie, her nose scrunching and her eyebrows puckering in bewilderment. "You don't hate me?"

"No. I don't hate you. Why would I?"

"Because of what I've done."

Corrie situated herself so she faced Violet. Placing her index finger under Violet's quivering chin, she tilted Violet's face up so their eyes met. "I don't know your circumstances. It really is none of my business, but I will gladly be a shoulder to cry on when you wish to talk about it. You must have an excellent reason for leaving him. The baby inside you will have a family. Us. It's as simple as that. Trust me, Mom has been itching for grandchildren for a very long time."

"But you don't really know me, what I've done. What if you change your mind?"

"Have you seen us stubborn Lancasters? Not a chance of us changing our minds on anything." Corrie tamped down the nagging questions about Violet's circumstances. Something or someone had made Violet run with nothing but the clothes on her back. Violet's reaction to George, her quiet yet defensive demeanor, prodded at Corrie's reporter antennae. Violet must have escaped an abusive relationship. Anger sharpened Corrie's need to make things right, to bring justice to a woman who had probably never seen it. Nothing would make her give up Violet and her unborn babe.

"Have you changed your mind on Pastor Luke?" Violet hiccupped and swiped at a rogue tear. Ever since Luke had started reading to Violet, her yearning gaze had followed him whenever he was around. Corrie wanted to warn her away, but from what, she wasn't sure.

Corrie's chest felt heavy. "That's pretty complicated. A lot of history, you know." She ignored the churning in her stomach and the stinging questions. Trying for a levity she didn't feel, she offered her hand to Violet. "How about some ice cream? I don't know about you, but my day has certainly been a Jonah day."

For the first time since her arrival, Violet's eyes twinkled. For real. "Is it cookie dough?"

"Is there any other kind?" Corrie laughed as she helped Violet to her feet. "Come on. Let's raid the freezer." They walked to the house to the melody of birds, the buzzer from the Operation game, and Jake's frequent outbursts of "Ah, come on!"

AARON lay awake, tossing and turning. It had been a week since he'd laid eyes on Corrie, and he felt itchy. Unable to lie in bed any longer, he stretched to his full length, plopped his bare feet on the floor, pushed off his bed, and shuffled to the window. He scratched at his week-old gray-flecked beard and turned his eyes in the direction of the Lancaster farm. He stood motionless while a distant fire licked the moonless night with tongues of yellow and red too big to be a firepit. A curse word slipped through his tightly clenched teeth, and the sound propelled him into action. He whipped on a pair of jeans and an old flannel shirt then stormed out of his room and knocked on his parents' bedroom door.

His dad opened the door. "Aaron? What is it?"

"Corrie. The farm. It's on fire!"

Gerome placed a hand on Aaron's shoulder. "You go. I'll call 911. I'll be right there."

Aaron raced down the steps, threw on his boots, and ran out the door. Gravel skittered from under the truck as he gunned the engine. The scant miles between their farms stretched on forever as he swerved down the gravel road. A combination of swear words and prayers shared his airspace.

He forced himself to calm down. He'd be of no use if hysteria controlled him. Pulling into the driveway, he got a better look at what was burning: the machine shed. Where the lifeblood of the farm awaited the fall harvest. After screeching to a halt, he sprinted to the house and pounded on the door. He waited and pounded again, this time louder. Finally, from inside the house, an annoyed voice told the visitor to "keep your pants on."

"Corrie, it's me. Open up!" he yelled at the door.

The door whipped open, revealing an angry Corrie clad in pajama shorts and a tank top. "What do you—"

"The machine shed!"

The seething look melted into terror as she stepped outside and saw the scene behind him. In the distance, wailing fire trucks barreled up the highway. He caught her before she crumpled to the porch floor. He held on to her, afraid she might fall to pieces, but she soon squirmed from his grasp and made a dash toward the machine shed. He ran after her, clutching at her hand.

"Stop, Corrie."

She wrenched away and sprinted to the conflagration. He followed on her heels and captured her heaving body in his arms.

"Dear Lord," Corrie wailed, looking up to the heavens. "Why?"

"I'll fix this. We'll fix this." He held her tighter.

"How?" She beat his chest with her fist.

Fire trucks screamed down the driveway, cutting off his answer. Firefighters scrambled out and hooked up hoses to the pump truck. Spewing water and hissing flames soon joined the chaotic dance between man and fire. Her family joined them, creating a unified front against the roar of the flames.

Aaron eased her from his arms, put her in her father's arms, and jogged over to his parents and Luke, who had just arrived.

"What happened?" Gerome asked, his arm protectively around Mary's shoulders. "Do you know what caused it?"

"I suppose it's too early to tell. A lot of things could have caused the fire."

Mary spat on the ground. Reflections of the fire danced in her eyes. "I know exactly how this fire started. George."

"Mom." Luke shook his head. "You can't just say those things."

"Watch me! That man has had Corrie in his crosshairs for far too long. I wouldn't put it past him to set fire to the shed. He wants to destroy her, and he knows this is the one thing to do it."

Gerome tucked his wife farther into his side. "There, there, Mary. It's not right to judge. Luke is right. We can't accuse someone without having the facts. We'll just have to wait and see."

She rolled her eyes. "Wait and see." With that, she pulled herself from Gerome's arms and waddled over to Cynthia, then she held the weeping woman in her arms. Luke joined her, his head bent in prayer, his hand tucked in Violet's.

Aaron leaned against his dad's truck, his heart breaking while the Lancaster family witnessed the demise of their livelihood. He'd promised he would fix it. Problem was, he didn't know how. *But I will. Somehow.*

Chapter Nine

Corrie picked through the warped and twisted tin sheeting scalded black by last night's flames. The rancid smell of burned metal, wet ash, and hot oil settled at the back of her throat, inducing a gag every time she breathed. But she had to see it. Her combine squatted before her, a shadow of its shiny green self. Black and broken, it sat on melted tires, still oozing its innards on the charred cement floor.

Tears trickled down her face as she took in her baby. The tractor hunkered next to the combine, its right side burnt to a crisp from the flames bursting out of the combine. Soot and ash covered the tractor's left, and less damaged, side. The fire inspector was right. The fire originated in the combine. *But how?* She threw this question around in her head as she stumbled out of the broken shell of the shed.

She had been meticulous about blowing the combine off after wheat harvest. She'd even pressure washed it. Nothing in the combine or on the combine could make it suddenly go *poof.* Closing her eyes, she attempted to shut her brain off then trudged into the house. The cheery atmosphere of late had disappeared. In its place hovered uncertainty and fear. Eerily quiet, the house echoed every prayer and plea of its occupants. She hated it.

She searched for her father and found him sleeping in his favorite chair. She gently kissed the top of his graying head. He needed the rest. She walked into the empty kitchen. Looking for her mother, she glanced out the patio door.

Cynthia knelt among her beloved tomato plants. Not wanting to disturb her, Corrie journeyed through the house, ignoring the silence. No music burst from Nathan's room, and when she cracked the door, she found him fast asleep on his bed, curled up with Mr. Wiggles, a bear he hadn't slept with since he was five. She backed out, silently shut the door, and checked on Violet. She stood at the window, looking upon the remains of the machine shed. She must have heard Corrie's muffled footsteps because she swung around, placing her cell phone behind her back. Her black hair hung stark against her pale, sharp face.

"I'm so sorry this happened," she whispered, her eyes large and panicked.

Corrie hugged her, surprised to find the young woman quivering like a leaf in wicked winter winds. "It's not your fault. You have nothing to be sorry for. We'll figure something out."

Violet wiggled out of the hug.

Corrie dropped her arms. "It takes a lot more to bring a Lancaster down. Why don't you lie down and rest for a bit? I'm going to check on Nikki." She escorted Violet to the bed, tucked her in, and as she walked out, Corrie swore she heard Violet whisper, "It is my fault."

A small skitter skipped down Corrie's spine at those ominous words. She ignored it and trudged to her room, exhausted and in need of a nap. She paused briefly at Nikki's room and heard the sound of weeping. Corrie cracked open her sister's door. Items lay strewn over every inch of a normally immaculate room. She sighed at her sister's weeping frame lying in a fetal position on her bed. Without saying a word, Corrie lay down beside her, pulled the comforter over both of them, wrapped her arm around her, and quietly sang to Nikki until the young girl's sobs stopped and her breathing shallowed and evened. Then Corrie allowed her eyes to droop and fell into a fitful sleep haunted by fire.

"Corrie!"

Corrie bolted awake, blinking from the light streaming into Nikki's bedroom. Nikki stirred awake, too, eased herself up on her elbow, and glared at the intruder.

"Nathan Jacob Lancaster, what on earth are you doing?" Nikki threw a pillow at his head. "Get out!"

He threw the pillow back at her, making sure it connected smartly with her nose. "No. You both have got to see this." When neither of them moved, he gesticulated with his arms toward the door. "Seriously. You have got to see this." He stood there, tapping his feet, his arms crossed again over his chest. "Mom sent me."

After sharing a glance, both Corrie and Nikki bolted out of the twin-sized bed and followed him down the steps. Violet rushed to them, and in an unprecedented show of emotion, hugged Corrie. "Isn't this great? I never knew people could be so kind."

Corrie shrugged at Nikki's quizzical look then patted Violet's back, perfectly aware that at any moment, a baby foot could, and probably would, kick her in the stomach. "I really have no idea what you're talking about." She released herself from Violet's grasp and looked at her parents, whose beaming faces seemed ready to burst with light. "Seriously, what's going on?"

Cynthia gestured to the kitchen window. "Look."

Corrie walked over and gasped. Pickups, loaders, and men took up the entire yard. In the late-afternoon sun, they began dismantling the ruined shell of the machine shed, piece by blackened piece. Tears pooled in her eyes as she surveyed the scene of neighborly charity and kindness. Her breath caught in her throat when she spotted Aaron, seeming to orchestrate the men as they performed certain tasks.

"Who did this?" Nikki came up beside her.

Corrie tucked an arm around her sister's waist. "I think I have a good idea." She ruffled Nikki's bedhead hair then asked Cynthia, "Mom, when did they arrive?"

"About twenty minutes ago. I was in the spare bedroom doing some cleaning when I heard an awful racket. I thought we were being invaded."

"We are." Corrie smiled. "By the good guys."

AARON grunted as he hefted a mangled tin sheet and threw it into the bucket on the loader tractor. His leather gloves protected his hands from the sharp metal, but nothing could protect his heart from the piercing ache he experienced whenever he looked at the devastation. Sighing, he bent again to retrieve another load of rubble when he heard the Lancaster family laugh and cry with the men who'd come to help them. Backs were slapped, hugs were given, and cheeks were kissed. He threw the metal into the bucket and turned right into Corrie. Her gaze dried his mouth up like the Sahara Desert.

"Hi," he breathed, pulling off his gloves. He jolted when she took his hand, and he allowed her to drag him to the back of the shed, out of what used to be the rear door, and to the tire swing swaying in the calm autumn breeze.

Corrie released his hand. "I don't know how to thank you for this."

"How did you know it was me?"

"Because you're blushing. It was a wild guess, but you just confirmed it."

He glanced at the ground, then the tire swing, then back at the mangled machine shed. "You don't have to thank me. I'm just doing what any neighbor would do."

She placed her hand against his cheek and brought his gaze back to hers. "Is that the only reason?"

He fidgeted. His toes wiggled in his boots, and his fingers scratched the insides of his palms. This was the moment. He licked his lips and studied her eyes. He saw fear and heartache, but he also saw a yearning. *For me?*

"Ah, truth is, Corrie, I did it for you. You, um, have come to mean a lot to me, and I wanted to show you how much I cared. About you." Tears formed in her eyes, and he awkwardly patted her shoulder. "Sorry. I know I'm probably the last person you wanted to hear that from bu—"

She stopped his mouth with hers. Blood warmed and raged through his veins as her lips and tongue tasted him. He pressed her to his body, her softness and curves fitting perfectly to him. Every thought in his head retreated, leaving only the sensation of her hands gliding over his shoulders, cupping the back of his neck, giving her fingers the freedom to swirl figure eights over his skin. He was barely aware of raised voices until they grew loud enough for him to recognize his brother's voice.

Not again. Aaron groaned inwardly. This time he would stand his ground and not let his brother take what wasn't Luke's any longer. He pulled his lips away from Corrie's and, still keeping her in his arms, faced his brother. Turned out, he didn't need to, for at Luke's heels was a very pregnant, very determined Violet keeping pace with Luke's long-strided strut.

Before Luke could get toe to toe with him, Violet stepped between them. "Stop it!" Everyone blinked. She had yet to speak in more than a mouse's squeak. Her voice, now commanding and authoritative, had Luke screeching to a halt. "Knock it off. Are you a child?" she asked a blushing Luke. "Well, are you?" After he shook his head, Violet pointed at Corrie. "She is not yours anymore. I don't know what you did to lose her, but you certainly didn't do a good enough job to keep her. Corrie is not your property. She is her own woman, and if she chooses your brother over you, then you will need to get over it and quit sulking like a spoiled child. There are other women in this world who would—" She choked on her own words and turned her head away. "Just leave her alone." She finished, in a weaker voice, seemingly exhausted from her speech. She cast a wobbly smile toward Corrie and puttered back to the house, her hand on her protruding belly.

Luke stood there, shuffling his feet in the dirt track left by years of feet skidding and sliding under the tire swing. He avoided eye contact with them. "Sorry. Violet's right." For a second, he met Aaron's gaze. "Take care of her." He walked away, head down, toward the half-demolished machine shed. He fired up a loader and continued to smash and load pieces of the crippled building onto awaiting trailers.

Aaron's heart broke for him, and as he looked at the woman in his arms, he understood how precious she was. "Well." He smiled. "What's next?"

"I have an idea." She curved her body into his and captured his lips with hers.

"You have a little something on your face."

Corrie swiped at her right cheek. "Did I get it?"

Nathan laughed. "Yeah. In your hair now." He athletically dodged the balled-up, oily rag she chucked at his head. "I hear Aaron likes greasy hair on a woman. Lucky for you." He gave a toothy grin.

"Who invited you, anyway?" she scolded, attempting to drag what was left of an old oil drum out of the back corner of the shed.

"Mom."

"Well, consider yourself uninvited. Go do homework or something."

"That's boring. I'd rather do this than write a stupid paper about nomadic tribes." He kicked at a pebble, sending it flying into the air only to ping against the remaining shell of the building. "Besides, all Violet and Mom do is talk about the birthing process, anyway. I can't escape it. It's safer out here."

"You could hang out with Dad. I'm sure he's watching television."

"Nope. He's gotten on board with the baby thing too. All he does is watch YouTube videos about babies before they're born, babies during birth, and then babies after birth. He actually dug out one of Nikki's dolls and was practicing putting diapers on the dumb thing."

Corrie bit back a laugh. *Poor Nathan.* "Where's Nikki? I'm sure she could be a source of entertainment for you."

"She's busy doing what you told her to do about what's-his-face Palinski."

"His name is Xavier."

"Well, whatever it is, it's a stupid name." Nathan dumped the trash can he'd been loading the entire time into the bucket of the loader. "This one's full. I'll take it to the metal pile." He hopped up into the cab and, before shutting the door, asked, "By the way, what is 'twitterpated,' and why does Xavier always carry a copy of Shakespeare's sonnets in his back pocket?"

Corrie giggled. "That's a whole other conversation for later." After Nathan had disappeared to the metal pile growing by the hour, she snuck a look toward the tire swing. Nikki perched inside the swing, gently going to and fro while listening to Xavier read from the little leather book that Corrie had provided from her own collection.

"Hey." Luke's voice resonated behind her.

She stumbled backward but regained her footing. Crossing her arms over her chest, she faced him with a bravado she didn't feel. "Yes?"

"I came to apologize for yesterday. I was a complete buffoon and only proved again that I am an absolute idiot. Can you—no, *will* you—forgive me? Please?" He took off his ball cap and scrunched it in his palms. "I know I don't deserve anything from you. I realize that now. What I did years ago totally negates everything. I really didn't get it until Violet laid into me."

Tension flowed out of Corrie's body. Relaxed, she walked toward him. "What we had wasn't real. You know that, right? It was physical. It was chemical. It was amazing. But it wasn't real." She cupped his cheek in her hand. "I can forgive you, Luke. But I'll never forget. Even though you are a changed man, I can't ever truly trust you again."

Luke laid his hand on top of hers. "I know. I'm sorry."

"Don't be. We're different people now." She slid her hand from his grasp and placed both hands in the front pockets of her pants. "You deserve someone who will trust you. With her whole heart. Let mine go, Luke. It's not yours anymore."

He bent slightly, pressed a chaste kiss on her lips, and walked out. No longer in the mood for cleaning up, Corrie trudged to the house and slid into a kitchen chair. She plopped her arms on the table and rested her forehead on them. Breathing deeply, she felt her soul stitching up old wounds, one thread at a time. It stung but felt good, felt right.

"Corrie?"

She startled when her mother's fingers played with the ends of her ponytail. "Yeah," she muttered into the crook of her arms.

"I saw Pastor Luke drive away. Did he need something?"

As soon as Cynthia sat, Corrie curled into her mother's side. "He needed to return my heart."

"Oh, honey."

"I didn't think it would feel this way. Me telling him it's over. Forever." She glanced up at her mother's face. "I didn't want it to hurt. Part of me feels like I should have tried harder." With a huff, she buried her face in her hands again. "I love Aaron. This might make for some awkward Christmases."

Her mother's chuckle soothed Corrie's nerves. "Maybe. You always were my little thinker and planner. I'll be happy if your siblings make a conscious decision about anything." She planted a kiss on Corrie's hair. "I'm proud of you. Now go round everybody up for dinner."

After shooing Nathan and Nikki to the kitchen, Corrie knocked on Violet's door and entered at the small voice bidding her to come in. "Hey, Violet. Mom sent me to get you for supper."

Violet scooted off the bed, stood, and stretched. "I've never napped so much in my life. I feel lazy and useless."

"Please don't say that. You have done so much for this family. Look at what you've done for my dad. He dotes on you, and his eyes sparkle like back before the accident." Corrie slung her arm around Violet's expanding waistline. "Besides, you figured out the Tuttle boy problem for me." She raised her eyebrows. "By the way, how *did* you figure out those dynamics?"

Violet shrugged. "It didn't take me long to deduce the little love triangle." Violet played with a frayed thread on her T-shirt. "I kind of wish Luke would look at me the way he looks at you."

Corrie clapped her hands together. "That's an amazing idea. Why didn't I think of it? I've always wanted to play matchmaker."

Violet barked out a laugh. "Yeah, right. Besides, he only pities me. Which is probably for the best. There are many things I've done that I can't even think about without wanting to crawl into a hole. What decent, God-fearing man would want a woman like me?"

"A man who knows the power of sin and the miracle of redemption. And trust me, Luke Tuttle has had a perfect measure of both." With schemes skipping through her head, Corrie walked arm in arm down the steps with Violet to join the family for supper.

"So this here model, the S680, is the top of the market right now. It's got everything to make this a lean, mean, green harvesting machine."

As the salesman's mouth moved, the huge space in his teeth and the wart on his tongue fascinated Corrie. She jerked to attention when he asked her a question.

"Ah, um..." She glanced at Aaron, who had kindly offered to go with her, hoping he would bail her out.

A glint in his eyes told her he would, but he'd expect some form of payment. She didn't mind the extortion. She looked forward to it.

"Sorry about that, Tim." Aaron placed his arm around her waist. "Corrie is just so blindsided by the tragedy that this is all so hard to take in. She loved her old combine as if it were her own child."

Tim smiled, showing off the gap in all its glory. "Don't I know that. I once had a combine I had to put down, and boy, that was pretty rough. She was my girl." He pulled up his stained jeans, which had slipped to a dangerous level of peekaboo with a Hanes logo showing. "But back to the question. Are you needing a header as well?"

Corrie pictured the farmyard. The bean header lay in the grass next to the other farm implements waiting patiently for their turn. "No. It wasn't in the fire."

"Good. Glad to hear it. Well, this machine is used, but the previous owner took real good care of it. Asking $275,000 for her."

She swallowed the lump in her throat. Grateful that Aaron stood by her side, she clutched his hand and hung on for dear life. "That's a pretty price for a used machine."

"Well, they're going over four hundred new."

She let out a breath. "Yeah, I know." She took one last glance around the lot at all the pretty, shiny green things. "Tim, I'll have to get back to you. Soon. Bean harvest is just around the corner." She shook his outstretched hand, thanked him again, and walked hand in hand with Aaron to his truck.

Once inside the cab, he turned to her, cupped her face in his calloused hand, and kissed her soundly on the lips.

She raised one eyebrow at him as he wiggled into the driver's seat. "Does haggling over combine prices turn your engine?"

"Nope. But watching you do the haggling does." He slipped on his sunglasses, winked at her over the lenses, and drove out of the parking lot. "So, I ran into Xavier yesterday at the post office. That boy's got a hitch in his stride. What'd you do to him?"

"Shakespeare."

He slid her a glance. "Care to elaborate?"

"Not really. Then you'd know the secret weapon to get into any girl's heart."

He grabbed her hand and played his fingers over hers. "There's only one heart I care about."

"In that case, I'll let you in on my little secret. Ready?" She leaned over in the seat and whispered in his ear. "Poetry."

"Really? Long-haired, hippie Palinski is reading poetry to Nikki."

"If he doesn't want to become a steer, yes."

"Poetic justice, I'd say, after what he was trying to get away with."

She sighed. "Yeah, but we've all done some pretty stupid stuff, and Xavier is proving himself the perfect gentleman. So far."

"Are you going to teach him the art of singing under a girl's window next?" Aaron made a fist and, pretending it was a microphone, took a deep breath as if to sing. Corrie slapped a hand over his mouth, giggling.

"Don't underestimate the power of showing vulnerability. Girls like guys who can shed a tear now and then."

"Does getting hit by a baseball in a very sensitive area count?"

"No!" She shifted slightly toward him, wishing she didn't believe in seat belts. Tempting as it was to snuggle up next to him, she settled on holding his hand and bringing her kneecap closer to his. "Seriously. When's the last time you cried for real?" As soon as the words hit airspace, his hand went limp in hers, and she shuddered and cursed herself. "Oh, Aaron, I'm so sorry. I didn't think. I'm an idiot. You don't have to answer that."

He veered off to the side of the road into a field approach. He killed the engine, unbuckled his seat belt and hers, and slid her over to him. "Don't apologize. I want to share this burden with you if you'll let me." He played with her ponytail, wrapping it gently around his index finger. "The last time I cried, I thought I'd never stop. Some people claim they felt something wrong before they knew a bad thing had happened. Well, that certainly didn't happen for me. I was out with some buddies, drinking a few beers, playing pool, talking about certain jerk-heads of students we had, when my phone rang." He let out a sigh. "I actually rolled my eyes when I saw Dad's name come up on my phone. Can you believe that?" He shook his head. "I answered it, anyway, thinking of ways I could cut the conversation short."

When he stopped and stared out the windshield, she snuggled deeper into his side, hoping maybe she could absorb some of the pain.

He swallowed hard and wiped at tears starting to trek down his face. "I, uh, answered the phone, and the first thing my dad said was 'He's dead.' Just like that. 'He's dead.' I don't remember much after that, to be honest. One of my buddies drove me to my apartment, where I believe I grabbed a bottle of whisky and didn't stop drinking until it was gone." He ran the back of his hand over his mouth, as if trying to wipe the alcohol taste from his lips. "It didn't hit me, Corrie, until I saw a picture of Caleb with his arms slung over mine and Luke's, his face beaming and his uniform crisp and clean. The last picture Mom ever took of us together. There will be no more."

Corrie held him as he wept. Nothing she could say would help or make things magically disappear, so she prayed. She beat down the doors of heaven for peace for the man she'd come to love. For the man she knew loved her.

Chapter Ten

Corrie bent over a tomato plant, plucking red fruit off the vine. Closing her eyes, she bit into the tomato and relished the flavor as the outer skin burst, allowing the juicy center to spill over her tongue.

Overhead, the sun's rays stretched like fingers across the farmyard, whispering a welcome to the land. The fingers of light seemed to hesitate as they drew near the machine shed, which was no longer there. There was nothing for the light to touch or caress except a charred slab of cement.

She stared at the barren spot. The evidence of the fire, deemed arson by the fire inspector, lay in heaps on the metal pile barely visible over the hillcrest on the backside of the farm. Her heart seemed to disintegrate in her chest at the thought of someone wanting to hurt her family in such a way.

Looking behind her shoulder for arsonists in the tomato patch, she swallowed the remainder of the tomato and hightailed it to the house. She stuck her head in the kitchen patio door and called for her mom. When no answer came, she entered, slipped off her muddy shoes, and searched the house. The living room was still and quiet, the television black. Her brother and sister were at school, and Violet had taken Luke up on his offer to drive her to a doctor's appointment. Corrie grinned. It hadn't hurt to send that boy a text, tugging on his heartstrings for the poor, defenseless mother-to-be. Now, if he could only see the adoration for him in Violet's eyes.

Corrie looked in the guest bedroom, expecting her mom to be rearranging drawers. No such luck. The master bedroom where her father slept alone proved empty as well. Tapping her bottom lip,

Corrie checked the last room on the main floor. As she neared the office, however, faint murmured voices wafted from the half-closed door. She crept closer and peeked through the crack. Her father sat in his leather chair, swiveling back and forth like he used to. Cynthia sat next to him at the desk, in an antique wooden chair reserved only for an equally ancient doll. The doll, abandoned to the floor, stared with button eyes at the two people deep in conversation.

"Jake, I know what this means to you. I really do, but we have to think of the future. Our children's future."

Corrie strained to hear his reply but couldn't quite catch it.

"Corrie?"

She jumped at her name and knew she'd been caught.

"Jake, think about her. Do you think Corrie wants this? Don't you see the burden she's under? She's tough, and she's stubborn. Just like you, dear. But that's the problem. She'll die trying to keep this farm afloat."

She sagged against the wall, her mother's words sinking to the depths of her soul.

"Corrie can!" Jake's voice wavered. "Farm in her blood too."

Corrie traced her veins, tributaries of blue running down her arm. But they ran deeper than that. They ran into the very soil—the same soil that beckoned her to plant something and watch it grow.

"Jake," her mother started again, speaking softly, "have you ever asked if this is what she wants?"

Silence. Corrie dared a peek through the crack again. Inside, her father shook his head. Pain and loss etched across his face. Cynthia placed her hand on his right cheek, swiveling his face so he looked at her. Corrie's heart beat in her chest at the sweet gesture. She felt out of place, but she couldn't move.

"What do you want?" Cynthia whispered, running her thumb up and down her husband's stubbly cheek. Corrie waited, breath held, for his answer. The answer, however, did not come verbally. His hand cupped his wife's cheek in a reciprocating manner. He brought her forehead to his and closed his eyes. Corrie tore herself away. She'd eavesdropped on a moment she was not privy to.

Needing fresh air, she dared enter the great outdoors once more. Sneaking into her barn, she kept an eye out for an unknown enemy. She jumped when something wet stabbed her hand. "What the—" She whirled around only to karate chop at Bacon at her feet, his tail wagging. "Oh Mylanta, Bacon, you scared the living daylights out of me."

He sniffed her hand, for she usually gave in and surrendered a treat.

"Not this time. You need to go on a diet, according to the vet."

He cocked his head to the side and stared at her. A whimper formed in his throat, and his adult-dog eyes conveniently turned into puppy-dog eyes, all round and big.

"Knock that off. You can't bribe me with your pitiful looks and begging ways." She scratched between his ears. "Do you want to go for a drive?"

His ears perked up, and he jumped in the back of the pickup.

"We'll go fishing, boy. What do you say?"

She gathered the tackle box and her fishing pole as Bacon hunkered in the back of the truck, tongue yo-yoing out of his mouth. She placed the gear in the back, scratched his head, and drove out of the yard. She switched the radio to the local country station, and the crooning cowboy soothed her soul as she pushed her parents' stolen moment out of her head. False hope was dangerous, and she didn't feel like gambling with her sanity just yet.

The sunflowers, in full bloom, dipped their yellow heads with the weight of their seeds. She felt much the same way. She had so many seeds to carry, she wasn't sure she could withstand the pressure. Could she bear it as gracefully as the sunflowers in the field, or would she crash to the ground under the slightest setback? *Well, I didn't go certifiable when the shed burned.* She shook her head, emptying her thoughts of the nagging reminder that her setbacks weren't over. And even though insurance would cover most of the cost of the combine, the idea that someone wanted to destroy it had her checking the rearview mirror for suspicious vehicles.

Refusing to think on that anymore, she turned in to the pasture approach, right next to Baxter's old, beat-up Ford Ranger. The original paint was hard to decipher, but she always guessed it used to be blue. She climbed out, retrieved her fishing pole and tackle box, whistled for Bacon, and headed to the banks of the Sandy River. Over the crest of the hill, she sighted Baxter in his bag chair, fishing pole stuck in a hole he'd made for such a purpose. Bacon ran straight for the old man.

"Hey, Baxter! Catching any today?" When he didn't turn or acknowledge Bacon with the usual scratch to the ears, she hailed him a little louder. "Baxter!" Still no response. Her walk turned into a jog. When she reached him, she found him slumped over in his chair, unresponsive and not breathing.

"Baxter!" She shook him. His head lolled even closer to his chest. "Dear Lord, help me." She eased him out of the chair and laid him on the ground. Whipping out her cell phone, she saw she had one bar. Biting back a curse word, she prayed there was enough signal strength for a text to go through and shot off a message to Aaron.

After laying her cell on the abandoned chair, she ripped at the buttons on his shirt, intertwined her fingers, placed her hands on his still-warm chest, and began performing CPR. With her first thrust, his rib cage snapped and crackled and popped. Knowing she couldn't quit, knowing Baxter wouldn't like it if she didn't try, she continued through the noise for a few more thrusts. Then the only noise was her breathing, rough and labored. To keep herself in the right rhythm, she began singing "Stayin' Alive." After thirty thrusts, she tilted his head back, put her mouth on his, and breathed into his mouth, filling his lungs with air. Within seconds, she was back to thrusting, making sure every push was even and deep enough.

"Come on, Baxter. I don't like this song enough to sing it forever. Wake up!" she cried, stopping only long enough to give him two more breaths. Sweat beaded down her face, falling in droplets on his flannel shirt. Bacon whined next to her, tilting his head back and forth, occasionally sniffing at Baxter's lifeless hand. "It'll be okay, Bacon. Baxter will be okay." She swallowed the rage bubbling inside her. "Don't you leave me, Baxter. Don't you dare leave."

Thirty. Two. Thirty. Two. Over and over. She didn't know how long she'd been at it. Five minutes or five hours. It felt the same. Her arms, rubbery and weak, wanted to quit. Her heart pounded in her chest, but because she knew his didn't, she kept going, willing her arms to continue.

Bacon barked. Never stopping the thrusts, she looked up and wept with joy.

Aaron sprinted down the knoll, skidding to a stop next to her. Without a word, he scooted her over and began the CPR thrusts.

She sank to the ground. Her entire body seemed to vibrate. She tried lifting her arms, but they refused to answer.

"Do the breaths, Corrie." At his request, she crawled to Baxter's head, and as soon as Aaron counted to thirty, she breathed into Baxter's mouth. Without losing momentum or rhythm, Aaron said, "The ambulance will be here very soon. I called them right after I got your text."

She only nodded, too stunned to do anything else. Bacon nuzzled her hand. She scratched his ear and listened for Aaron's counting. Thirty. Two breaths. They continued the pattern until they heard the sirens, and they persevered until the paramedics jogged down the hill, stretcher and gear in hand. She crumpled to the ground as they hooked Baxter up to the AED machine. She overheard them talking, but nothing computed. Her brain, overloaded and hazy, failed to translate medical jargon. She did understand the looks they gave each other over his lifeless body. One of the paramedics, a lady she recognized from the grocery store in Sweetwater, turned to her and Aaron.

"I'm sorry. There's nothing we can do for Baxter. You did the right thing, though. This wasn't your failure."

Corrie could only nod. Tears burned her eyes, and her throat felt as if it would close, suffocating her.

The paramedics placed his body on the stretcher, covered it with a blanket, and climbed the hill. Within minutes, the ambulance's back door slammed shut, and it pulled away, carrying Corrie's dear friend in its belly. With a scream, she chucked the nearest thing, Baxter's half-empty Coke can, across the stream. It pinged off the rocks and clattered into the water. Swearing, she stumbled to her feet and walked to retrieve the can. Before she made it two steps, her legs faltered, and she fell to the ground.

She swore and attempted to get up. She fell back down but this time into Aaron's arms. Wrapping her arms around his neck, she dug her face into his chest and sobbed. Deep, aching sobs threatened to rip open her rib cage.

"It'll be okay," he murmured into her hair.

She stiffened. Every moment, every life-sucking event culminated into one. The anger boiled over and burst. "No! No, it will not be okay. Nothing is okay." She jolted out of his arms, refusing his embrace when he reached for her.

"Corrie, please. I just meant things will get better. We'll get through this."

She slapped his hand away. "Leave me alone. I don't need your help." She ignored the pain on his face and stumbled up the hill, whistling for Bacon. When Bacon whined at Aaron's feet, she yelled, "Fine, Bacon, whatever. Traitor."

Ignoring Aaron's pleas for forgiveness and for her to stop, she ran up the hill, afraid he would catch up to her. *What then?* She fumbled for the keys to the truck. *What would he do then?* Refusing to stay and find out, she slammed the door, put the truck in reverse, and tore out of the approach, spitting mud and grass from the tires. Her last image in the rearview mirror was Aaron standing in the middle of the gravel road, Bacon at his side.

AS the taillights disappeared in a cloud of dust, Aaron trudged to his pickup, his footsteps as heavy as his heart. Driving to his farm, he replayed the morning in his head. He could see her working on Baxter, her tears dripping on the old man's shirt. He could hear her sobs, her pleas for Baxter to wake up. He could smell the Old Spice that Baxter insisted on bathing in. Aaron smiled sadly. "Well, Baxter, I hope God has an ample amount of that stuff for you up in heaven. I'm going to miss you." With a heavy sigh, he turned his thoughts again to Corrie and her anger.

"What did I do, Bacon?" he asked the dog holding its head out the window, windsurfing with its tongue. "You're a help, aren't you, boy?" Bacon paused long enough to bring his head inside the truck cab and sniff at Aaron's hand before using his tongue as a kite again. Aaron's fingers twisted on the steering wheel, the seed of resentment over her outburst festering and growing.

A still small voice urged him to call her. He ignored it. "Nope. Don't make me, Lord. I'm not calling that woman." Trying to push her out of his mind, he prayed for Baxter's children all the way to the farm.

"Hey, Aaron!" Gerome hailed from across the yard.

Aaron whistled for Bacon, who trotted at his heels. "I've got some bad news," he said as he and his father met. "Baxter's dead."

"What!" Gerome exclaimed, ignoring Bacon's invasive nose in his palm. "When? Where?"

Gerome shook his head as Aaron relayed the morning's tragedy. "He was a dear friend. Baxter always said he wanted to go out while in the saddle or fishing. I'm glad he got his last wish." He slung an arm across Aaron's shoulder. "I'll go tell your mother. She'll be devastated. She always had a secret crush on that old man. She thought him the Sean Connery of the Midwest. How's Corrie taking all this? I know how close she was to Baxter. He was like a grandpa to her."

Aaron's conscience smacked him across the head. "I don't know. She kind of freaked out on me. I'm not so sure she wants to talk to me right now." He frowned. "All I said was everything will be okay."

Gerome studied his son. "Is what you have with Corrie worth fighting for?"

"I thought so, but if she's willing to abandon it over something so—"

"Son, I'm not here to tell you what to do with your life. But if you think Corrie is worth it, if this is a hill you want to climb because you know the view is spectacular on the other side, then climb it."

Aaron swallowed hard around the lump in his throat. Emotions he'd kept in check threatened to take over. Seeming to sense this, Gerome patted Aaron's back and walked to the house, his shoulders stooped.

Aaron swore. He whipped out his cell and sent her a quick text. His bruised pride didn't need another face-to-face blow. *Hey, how are you doing? Worried about you.* He stared at the words on the screen. *Stupid.* That was what they were. Growling, he deleted the entire message. Typing furiously, his thick thumbs sent autocorrect constantly second-guessing his word choices. *Thinking about you. Let me know if you need anything.* He exhaled and looked down as something bumped his leg.

"Oh, hey, Kentucky. Do you have any advice for me on woman issues?"

Aaron's stalker-turned-pet-chicken clucked up at him, her beady eyes shimmering in the noon sky. She pecked at the ground.

"I know, you're hungry. Do you think that's Corrie's issue?"

Kentucky glanced up at him again, crooked her thin neck, and squawked.

"Hey, I don't like being called stupid, especially by a chicken."

He double-checked the message, gave up, and hit Send. With a short prayer, he stomped off to the barn, where he kept Kentucky's favorite snack, corn nuts. "I got you the ranch flavor this time. Thought I'd switch it up for you."

She clucked and followed at his heels.

"Yeah, someone should talk to her. Maybe Luke?" As much as the idea grated, he sent Luke a quick text. "There." He poured out some corn nuts for Kentucky. "Maybe she'll take out her anger on him instead." Leaving his newfound pet to her own devices, he grabbed the grease gun and approached the combine. Disgusted with his cowardice, he greased the combine, getting it ready for the bean harvest looming on the horizon.

"Aaron?" His mother's voice interrupted him when his entire torso was stuck up inside the machine.

"Yeah?"

"Can I talk with you?"

He grunted as he climbed out. Then he wiped his hands on the greasy rag hanging from his back pocket. "What's up, Mom?" He squirmed under her teary gaze.

"Dad told me you seemed upset. I was just coming to check on you. Make sure you're okay."

"I'm fine."

"Aaron Tyler Tuttle, I know when I'm being hoodwinked. Don't start lying to me now."

He gritted his teeth. A thousand butterflies lodged in his chest and tried to flutter out of his throat. He stared at her. "Look, Mom, I just don't want to talk about it. Okay? Thanks for your concern, but I'll get through."

She placed a hand on her ample hip, squishing the cats embroidered near the bottom of her shirt. "I know how close Baxter was to you. Is that what's bothering you?"

Aaron ran his hands through his hair. "No... yes... I don't know." He leaned up against the combine ladder. "I'm sorry about Baxter, and I'll certainly miss the old-timer. But I... it's—"

When she closed the distance between them and drew him into an embrace, he glanced down at the top of her mahogany hair laced with silver, which came to the middle of his chest. *I probably gave her all those gray hairs.*

"You're a lot like your father. You know that? Stubborn as the day is long." She squeezed his waist then let go, looking up at him. She brushed her hand over the stubble on his face. "I'm so proud of you. You sacrificed your job to come home after Caleb's passing, and you worked your butt off for your father and still found time to work even harder for Corrie." Mary smiled. "Son, you keep looking out for everyone else's heart. When are you going to extend the same courtesy to your own?"

He couldn't speak. The butterflies congesting his vocal cords wouldn't let him.

"Do you love her?" When he blinked in surprise, his mother giggled. "I'm not as naïve as you might think. If Baxter's death isn't making you walk around the farmyard talking to a chicken, there's only one other person who would put you in such a tizzy."

"Mom." He scooped off his baseball hat, scratched at his scalp with the brim, and slapped it back on. "I'm not in a tizzy, for goodness' sakes."

"If I say you're in a tizzy, you're in a tizzy." She reached up and straightened the brim. "Whatever happened by the creek is only a mistake if you let it become one. Fix it. Go talk to her. Make things right."

"But I didn't do anything wrong." He walked away from his mother. "I just told her that everything would be okay. That'd I'd help her. What's so wrong about that? She's the one blowing this whole thing out of proportion."

"You're right. She's in the wrong here, but does this attitude you have make you right, make you the good guy? No. You're being just as foolish as she is." Mary played with a string hanging from Aaron's shirtsleeve. "Look at what Corrie's had to endure the past nine months. You can't judge her in the one moment that broke her. She needs you. Go to her." She walked away, but as she neared the door, she turned around. "That's an order."

His mother waddled across the yard.

"That woman makes me feel sixteen again," he mumbled. She was right. He would go apologize and throw himself at the feet of the only woman who had the power to break his heart.

Chapter Eleven

Corrie relished the feel of the axe in her hands. The wood, worn silky smooth from years of use, caressed her palms as she hoisted the axe above her head and brought it down upon the log. The log split, two halves irrevocably torn apart. Swiping at the tears rolling down her face, she set up another log, brought the axe up again, held it there for a split second, enjoying the strain in her muscles, then slammed it down, breaking the log in two.

As Corrie grabbed another log, she recalled the shock and horror on her mother's face when Corrie told her about Baxter. Cynthia insisted on leaving right away to be with the family, and Jake went along. Corrie allowed the axe to drop. In her cowardice, she had refused to go. She couldn't face his family when she'd let Baxter die. They would hate her, knowing she'd failed.

Tears poured down her face. She counted the split logs. Not enough. It would never be enough. Nothing could alleviate the tightness in her chest, knowing Baxter would never again hop onto the step of her truck. Nothing could erase the words she'd thrown at Aaron. Nothing could quench the thirst for revenge for the fire that had destroyed her family. Nothing could bring her dad back to being the man he once was. Nothing. Nothing would ever be okay again. With a scream, she plunged the axe deep into the center of the next log.

"Corrie?"

She spun around, axe in hand, wielded like a weapon. "What?"

Luke put his hand out as if approaching a trapped animal. "I dropped Violet off at the house. She was pretty tired after her appointment and needed to lie down. Aaron texted me and wanted me to check on you."

She snorted. Sending his brother when he could have come himself. She hated the part of her that had ignored Aaron's first text. She wished she could take an axe to the dark part of her heart, chop it out, and expose it to the light. But the dark won. "I bet. So, you're doing your brother's dirty work now, huh?"

Luke cocked his head but ignored her comment. "I heard about Baxter. I'm so sorry. But I'm proud you at least tried to save him."

"Don't you dare talk to me like I'm a child, Luke."

He stopped midstep. "I wasn't. I was—" He peered at her, his eyes scrunched as if seeing her for the first time. "Corrie? Are you okay?"

"Don't. Just don't." She placed another log in front of her. "I'm not a child. I can do things all by myself. I don't need anyone." She swung down. The axe met wood, and a crack rent the air.

A strong hand whirled her around. "Corrie."

She refused to meet his gaze.

"Drop the axe." His firm command had her placing the axe on the ground. "Look at me."

"No."

His hand gripped her chin, and he tilted her face to his. "Corrie. Look at me." He gently shook her. "Quit being a baby and look at me."

She snapped her eyes open, hoping the hate in them would burn him to a crisp. "You have no right to speak to me that way. No right at all."

"I'm sorry. I really am, but we're friends now, aren't we? And friends don't let friends be stupid."

She brought her hand up to slap him. Luke preempted her move and caught her hand, stopping her open palm from making contact with his cheek. "Do you want to hit me? Then hit me. Lord knows I deserve it." He dropped her hand and stood still, facing her.

Panting, she studied him. He looked so much like Aaron, it was uncanny, really. *What would it be like to feel his lips on mine again?* She felt something inside her snap. Wanting the pain, needing the past memories to drown the recent nightmares, she threw herself into Luke's arms. She grabbed the back of his neck and pulled his head down. Spreading his lips with hers, she tasted him. Memories flooded her mind. The windmill. Under the bleachers. Her father's semitruck. Notes passed in class. Secret two a.m. phone calls. The love. The betrayal.

Luke pushed her away and stared at her, his chest heaving. "What has gotten into you?" He wiped his mouth with the back of his hand. "What about Aaron?"

"Aaron Schmaaron," she spat.

A throat cleared behind her.

Her heart, which she didn't think could possibly go any lower, slithered to her toes. *Dear Lord, what have I done?* She scrambled to say something. Anything.

"I... uh... will leave you two alone, then," Aaron stammered, his hands raking through his hair. "I dropped by to see if you were okay, Corrie. Looks like you're doing just fine." Pain and betrayal shattered Aaron's eyes. Then he turned, disappearing around the corner of the barn.

"What in the world, Corrie!" Luke stared at her. "You tell me we'll only be friends, and then you kiss me like that." He scrubbed at his face with both hands. "That was not fair. To me or Aaron, and you know it."

"Since when do you care about your brother's feelings? I thought you loved me. You should care about my feelings too!" The darkness squeezed in on her vision, pinpointing with laser accuracy her stupidity, her lunacy, but she couldn't stop it. Fighting for control, to quell the nausea churning deep within her, she took a step to escape the situation.

Luke lunged in front of her. She backed away from his shaking form and clenching fists.

"That's the problem." He scrubbed his face with his hand. "I do love you, and guess what, I probably always will. I will always regret that I threw you away. I don't deserve you. Now you have to prove you deserve my brother, which by the way, you're doing a sucky job at right now."

She bit her lip to keep from crying. "Go away!"

"No." He planted his feet. "I'm not going anywhere until we hash this out."

She sent a swear word sailing through the air.

"That's always a good start, swearing at the pastor. Do you have any others you'd like to get out of your system before we continue with an adult conversation?" At her stony glare, he put his hands out in a friendly gesture. "Please, Corrie, you have to talk to someone."

She glared back. "Well, it sure won't be you." She took a step closer. "Now get out."

Embarrassed by the pain that washed across his face, she hated herself even more. She knew that if the last ten minutes had been a war, carnage would have been splattered everywhere and she the only villain. Her shoulders sloped as he walked away, and when the rumble of his truck faded, she fell to her knees in the dying grass. Angry and exhausted, she refused to pray. She would show everybody that she didn't need anybody. She could and she would do it all. After lifting herself up, she approached the log pile, vaguely aware of the abyss opening underneath her.

MONDAY arrived in a fanfare of gold and pink cresting over the trees shivering in the cool breeze. Corrie hated it. She ignored the beauty of the leaves rustling in the wind, refused to be refreshed by the crisp morning air. Shivering in just her tattered sweatshirt, she trudged to the side of the barn and stared at the new combine, shimmering in the sun like a green god. She hated it too.

Ever since Tim had dropped it off on Saturday, it had become her albatross. It reminded her to be afraid. It reminded her someone out there wanted to burn her to the ground. Glancing at the empty cement pad across the driveway, she relived the night it went up in flames, the day Aaron showed up with an army to fix it. She sighed and fiddled with the hoodie strings. Aaron. She grabbed her cell from her sweatshirt pouch and read Aaron's text for the hundredth time. *Thinking about you. Let me know if you need anything.* Yeah, she did. A good spanking. She had been a fool. A destructive fool. At the end of the day, she'd failed to save the life of one man and broken the hearts of two others.

She should call Aaron. But the look on his face when he'd caught her kissing Luke was seared into her vision for eternity, proving she not only had burned the bridge but also was the bridge troll. Remembering the feel of Luke's lips on hers, she wiped her mouth, trying to erase his touch. The only man whose kisses she wanted for the rest of her life was the one man she'd hurt, possibly irrevocably. Defeated and embarrassed by her actions three days ago, she climbed the combine ladder, hating its grime-free feeling.

"Not for long," she crooned to the combine. "You'll have to earn your keep around here. Let me tell you about the footsteps you have to fill." Corrie continued talking to the new piece of equipment as she played with all the buttons and switches on the console. "You sure are a pretty thing, though, aren't you? But looks aren't everything."

"Do you need better company to talk to?"

She whirled in her seat at the familiar voice. Her stomach twist-ed in knots, and her heart sped out of the starting gate. "Aaron? What are you doing here?"

He studied his scuffed-up boots. "I don't know, really." He looked her in the eyes.

She longed to pull him to her, to take away the look of mistrust in those green eyes she loved to get lost in. Words failed her, and her hands stayed in her lap.

"My dad said I should come over and see if you need help. He mentioned you might start combining this morning if the beans are ready."

Corrie swallowed her disappointment. "I don't want to bother you. I can manage this morning. And then there's..." Her voice fal-tered. "There's, um, Baxter's funeral this afternoon." She picked at a speck of dust on the combine's steering wheel. "You can leave." *Say you're sorry,* her mind screamed at her. *Now!* But no words escaped her closed throat.

"Do you want me to?" His voice, a whisper, carried with it a breath, a hint of hope.

However badly she wanted to, she couldn't tear her eyes off the steering wheel. Her head wouldn't shake. Her hands wouldn't move. In an instant, he was gone. She wrenched her hands from the steer-ing wheel to wave him down, but he was already halfway down the driveway, his pickup swirling dust behind it.

Corrie rested her head on the steering wheel and let the tears come. She was an idiot. Of that, she was sure. Tears plopped on the clean black cab floor, leaving little ghosts of themselves when they evaporated. She felt the same way—only a ghost of her former self. *What happened to me?* Fire and death. The fire simply primed the pump for the crippling act to follow.

She lifted her head and stared at the empty spot on the farmyard. "I will find you," she promised the bareness. "I will hunt you down.

And when I find you, I'll... I'll..." Corrie screwed up her face and tapped her index finger to her lips. "I'll do something." She assured herself that whoever had burned her hopes would rue the day they'd messed with a crazy lady turned maniac.

Pushing back the thoughts of Aaron, the fire, and Baxter's impending funeral, she started up the machine, enjoyed the deep rumble vibrating through her body, and moved the joystick to maneuver the combine out of the yard and down the gravel road to the first soybean field.

AARON slammed his truck door and stomped into the house, past the kitty welcome sign and doorstop and right into his little brother's chest.

"You're going to want to move," Aaron growled.

"I need to talk to you." Luke moved only enough for Aaron to squeeze past him into the kitchen.

Aaron felt his brother's eyes on him as he reached for a beer.

"I didn't know you drank your breakfast. When did that start?"

He whirled on Luke. "Ever since I caught my brother with the woman I love." He shoved the beer back in the fridge and grabbed the milk instead. "How could you?"

"I'm not here to defend myself. But after you refused to speak to me the past three days, I thought I'd come clear the air. That's all." Luke situated himself in one of the kitchen chairs. "Will you at least hear me out?"

Aaron poured himself a glass of milk, squirted chocolate syrup in it, and stirred it around. "Can't hurt." He sat on the opposite side of the table, tracing the huge flowers imprinted on the tablecloth. He'd always wondered about his mother's decor choices. But he learned early that if Mary Tuttle wanted flowers everywhere and ceramic cat figurines on every square inch of surface, no one was going to tell her any different. Taking a sip of his chocolate milk, he eyed his brother.

Luke stared at the cat flower vase perfectly centered on the tablecloth. "Have you ever wondered about Mom's style of decorating?"

Aaron rolled his eyes. "Oddly enough, I was thinking the same thing."

Luke nodded and cleared his throat. His hands trembled.

Aaron felt sorry for the impending punch his little brother would feel. He was done playing Mr. Nice Guy when it came to Corrie. If he had to fight for her, he was sure going to win. That was, if she still wanted him. After she dismissed him and ignored him this morning, he might be taking up a battle not worth fighting. "So, you going to say your piece yet, or are you intent on tracing the tulip all morning?"

"I didn't kiss her, Aaron. She kissed me."

"I thought pastors weren't supposed to lie."

Luke banged his hand on the table. The kitty water vase shook. "I'm not lying." He spread out his hands toward Aaron. "I'm not lying, Aaron. I checked on her just as you asked me to. I dropped Violet off at the house and found Corrie in the barn. She was all crying and stuff. I swear I never touched her. I essentially told her to quit acting like a baby. I could tell she wanted to slap me, so I told her to. God knows she has every right." He pushed his hands through his hair. "The next thing I know, she's on me, kissing me as if her life depended on it." When he dropped his hands, they thumped to the table. "I never kissed her back. You have to believe me. And for what's it worth, I don't think she liked kissing me either. I think watching Baxter die really put her someplace dark. She kissed me out of pain, not desire."

Aaron studied his brother. Dropping his gaze, he stared at a large magenta tulip until it swirled. He blinked to clear it. Meeting Luke's gaze again, he nodded. "I believe you."

"You really love her, don't you?"

Aaron barked out a laugh. "Yeah. Love is for fools and suckers, though. Too bad I fit the bill on both counts."

"Come on. Don't talk like that." Luke pinned him with an inquisitive gaze, making Aaron squirm. "What happened this morning, anyway?"

Aaron shrugged, wishing his emotions were as easy to shrug off. "Corrie told me to go away."

"Really?"

"Yup. Hardly even looked at me." He leaned back in his chair and stared out the kitchen window at the chickens pecking at the gravel driveway. "I don't know what I did to tick her off. How can I apologize for something if I don't know what I did wrong?"

"Do you want me to talk to her again?"

Aaron raised an eyebrow at his brother. "No. I'd rather not have the fox babysit the chicken coop."

"Oh, come on!" Luke threw up his hands. "I thought you believed me."

Aaron couldn't quite make his smile touch his eyes. "It's not you I have trust issues with right now." He downed his glass of milk and got up to rinse it out and set it in the dishwasher. "You ready for Baxter's funeral?"

"No. I hate doing funerals." Luke sighed and heaved himself out of the chair. "I'll miss that old man. He was in a league of his own." He slapped Aaron's shoulder. "I'm really sorry about Corrie. May I give some unsolicited advice?"

Aaron shut the dishwasher and faced Luke. "Shoot."

"Corrie's hurting. Think of everything she's had to endure over the past months. She's stressed about the farm, terrified after the arson attack, and devastated by Baxter's passing. Don't let her go it alone. She's used to being in charge and having all her little ducks in a row, as Mom would say. Her little ducks have scattered, and she's drowning. Swallow your pride, brother, and go to her again and again and again if you have to." Luke paused and cuffed him on the shoulder. "Take it from me. She's not a woman to toss away at the first sign of trouble. Fight for her, like I wasn't prepared to years ago. I sure as heck wish I had."

Aaron grinned. "I'd like to thank you firsthand for your stupidity, by the way."

"Jerk." He gave Aaron one more shoulder slap. "See you in a few. And remember what I said. Corrie needs you. She's just too stubborn to apologize. She's worth the wait."

Aaron waved Luke away and retreated to his room, where he laid out his suit for later. He walked to his window. The blue curtains his mother made him eons ago fluttered in the breeze from the open window. "Well, Baxter," he murmured, "I hope you're having a party up in heaven right now. Say hi to Annie from all of us. I bet she was happy to see you." He turned from the window. He had hours of chores ahead of him. "But really, you old coot, you didn't have to die on Corrie. That was not very gentlemanly."

Shaking his head, he walked out the front door. Kentucky ran up to him, clucking her delight.

"You know, chicken, people are gonna start thinking I'm weird for not eating you."

Kentucky clucked low in her throat.

"I'm sorry. The truth hurts. Eventually, the crazy lady on the farm is going to fry you up." Aaron walked to the barn, chicken in tow. "However, maybe I'll put in the movie *Chicken Run* for you. Give you some ideas. Now, shoo. I have work to do."

He climbed in his dad's combine, started it up, and drove to the field Gerome wanted him to do a test cut on. Forcing Corrie out of his mind proved futile. She was all he saw as he lowered the header to the smooth ground and began cutting.

Chapter Twelve

Corrie wished for the cool temperatures and gentle breeze of the morning as she got out of her parents' vehicle. The late-September sun, usually mild this time of year, pierced the sparse clouds with intense rays that shimmered in the still air. Pulling at the pearl necklace around her throat, she grabbed Nikki's hand, and it clamped down hard on hers. Waiting for her parents and Nathan and Violet to exit the Yukon, Corrie eyed the growing crowd gathering around the gaping hole.

A sea of black, speckled with the occasional pair of dusty jeans and work boots, converged around the closed casket with a spray of cheery yellow sunflowers and golden wheat stalks. No one spoke. No one laughed. Even the children, dressed in their summer church clothes, stood aloof next to their parents. The pillar of the community, the grandfather figure of Sandy, lay inside the casket, stuffed into a suit he would have hated. She smiled softly and brushed away a tear. Baxter always said that if he were buried in a suit, he'd come back to haunt the poor soul who'd dressed him.

Jake approached and held his arm out to her. She accepted and wound her arm through her father's, keeping a tight hold on Nikki's clammy hand. Nathan followed with Cynthia on one arm and Violet tucked next to him on the other side.

Corrie's heels sank into the soft ground, leaving clumps of grass sticking to the soles of her shiny black shoes. She tried not to think about who would soon be underneath that same soft ground.

She avoided eye contact with people. She couldn't bear her irrational guilt over Baxter's death. What-ifs haunted her sleep. *What if I had shown up sooner? What if I'd done a better job performing CPR?*

157

Deep inside her soul, she knew these thoughts were destructive, but she couldn't shake them.

Drops of sweat beaded under her black dress, and she could feel every one of them roll down her body. Nikki's hand, all squishy and hot, became unbearable. Corrie wanted to go. She couldn't see Baxter's body lowered into a dank, dirty hole. She'd barely held it together during the funeral service at the church. The smells, the songs, the waxy face that looked kind of like the Baxter she used to know. Stars danced in her eyes. Darkness crept upon her in her peripheral. A strong, steady hand replaced her father's trembling one.

"I've got her, Mr. Lancaster. See to your wife."

Knowing the hand, knowing the body it belonged to, Corrie allowed herself to fall into Aaron's side. His arm slipped around her waist and held her to him. His other hand, slightly shaking, caressed her cheek before dropping to his side again.

She whispered, "Thank you."

"My pleasure," he whispered back, his lips brushing her hair next to her ear. "Lean on me. Let me help you, please."

She could only nod and let him escort her under the tent set up for shade to escape the brutal sun. Her ears rang as if someone were pounding on a gong right next to her head. Dizzy, she leaned on Aaron and watched through blurry vision the community of Sandy settling around the open gravesite. An oppressive silence hung in the heat. She counted the sweat beads dripping down her body, concentrating on each one.

Bodies shuffled, and sniffles filled the air when Luke stood at the head of the coffin. Corrie made herself look at him. She stared at his eyes, eyes that mirrored the hurt she felt clawing at her insides.

"We are gathered today to say goodbye to an excellent father, devoted husband, caring neighbor, and a dear friend. Baxter was the type of guy to hop up on the door of your semi and tell a joke while you waited for a ticket. He was the type of guy to come help you at two a.m. when a cow was having trouble calving. Baxter was the type of guy to slip a child a sucker or pay for a full meal for someone in need. He lived the Golden Rule and exhibited Christ in every way possible."

Luke's voice cracked as he struggled for composure. "Though we shed tears for him, we must remember that he is enjoying his new home. The home he yearned for and sought after. He is where he belongs, with Christ, his savior."

The ringing in Corrie's ears deafened her to the rest of Luke's message. As she stood there, his mouth opened and closed, and she counted how many times his tongue darted out to lick his dry lips. When the vision of his face began fading, she put all her weight into Aaron's side, knowing he would never let her fall.

Then she followed everybody else's lead and bowed her head for Luke's closing prayer. She tried to pray. She wanted to scream, to scold God for taking away her beloved friend, but her lips remained still and her soul unmoved. She lifted her head only when Aaron gently prodded her.

"It's time to say goodbye, Corrie."

His voice, as if echoing through a tunnel, reverberated in her head. She clutched Aaron's arm for support. Fear swept through her. Fear of fainting into the deep hole that would entomb Baxter's body. Fear of breaking down beside the coffin and ripping it open for one last glimpse of the wrinkly, friendly old face. But the wrinkly face there wouldn't quite match the one of her dear friend. The one she would never look upon again on this earth. She wanted so badly to smell his Old Spice cologne, see the missed patches of facial hair, hear his jokes.

Swallowing hard against the lump of tears threatening to suffocate her, she filed past his children, hugging each of them and whispering the niceties one whispered at a funeral. Then she came to his coffin, the color of the prairie sky on a clear, cloudless day. He would have loved that blue. She reached out a tentative hand and caressed the head of a wheat stalk, enjoying the sticky roughness of the beard.

"Take one."

She jumped at the female voice and faced Baxter's only daughter, Delilah. Her gaunt cheeks, made even more hollowed out by her red-rimmed eyes, moved up in a sad smile.

"Please, take one." Delilah plucked a wheat stalk and handed it to Corrie. "My dad talked so highly of you." Delilah tucked a stray piece of silver hair behind her left ear and nodded toward Aaron, who hovered over Corrie as if she might break into a million tiny pieces. "Aaron told us what you did for our father. That means the world to me and my brothers."

Corrie tried to find words to say but ended up nodding dumbly. When Delilah brought her in for another hug, Corrie's nose twitched at a familiar smell.

Delilah must have heard Corrie's sniffing. She chuckled and released Corrie. Holding up a man's handkerchief, Delilah shrugged. "I had to have something to get me through the day. I don't think my dad would mind a missing handkerchief and a few drops of Old Spice." She placed the damp white cloth into Corrie's hand. "Keep it." Then Delilah walked back to her brothers.

Grasping the handkerchief for dear life, Corrie put it to her nose and breathed in the scent. Aaron's arm wound around her again, leading her away from the casket, away from the hole, away from her friend.

"Do you need to sit down for a while?" Concern bled through with every word.

She lost herself in the depths of his eyes—ten different shades of green swam in the ocean of them. "Yeah. I might fall down if I don't sit down first."

When Aaron guided her to a wooden bench next to the cemetery gate, she sagged onto it and breathed a sigh of relief. She darted her tongue over her lips and yearned for a drink of water or even a cool breeze. Across the cemetery, her family paid their respects to Baxter's children and filed past his casket, her father's gait unsteady on the uneven ground, her mother clutching his arm, her face blotchy. Nathan hovered over Violet, ready with a steady arm to assist the mother-to-be. Nikki held onto her father's hand, probably more for her support than his.

Sitting next to the potted bloodred geraniums cared for by the Ladies' Aid Society, Corrie felt a wave of love wash over her from her family. They were hers. They depended on her to care for them, to keep the farm afloat. It was no longer a question of needing to stay. She wanted to. This was her world, and she would protect it and nourish it until she had no more strength left. She remembered the eavesdropped moment with her parents the morning Baxter died. She glanced at her veins, the tributaries of life flowing through her, standing out garishly against her pale skin. Somewhere, mixed in whatever kept her alive, the farming gene ran deep.

She felt Aaron's hand on hers, and she relaxed against him, leaning her head on his shoulder. Her heart melted within her as he caressed the back of her hand with his thumb. Why he still cared for her, she had no idea. She should apologize for her terrible treatment of him but not right now. The sweltering silence demanded quiet. Besides, she had no words. They had jammed in her throat.

All too soon, her family reached them. Aaron took his hand off hers, stood, and caressed her cheek. "Take care of yourself." He shook hands with Jake, gave Cynthia a hug, and walked away, his blue dress shirt sticking to the muscles coiled under the material.

Her mother's perfume tickled her nose as Cynthia sat next to her. "Do you want to go to the VFW for the meal, or do you want to go home?"

Corrie leaned on her mother's shoulder and enjoyed the strength there. "I'll go with you guys. Besides, I could use something to drink."

Nikki piped up, "I hope Mrs. Krumm made her famous slush." Her face fell. "Baxter loved those too."

"Well, then." Corrie stood up slowly. "Let's all have one for Baxter." She wound her arm through Violet's and Nikki's and began the long walk to the VFW. "Violet, you have no idea what's in store for you." Corrie chewed on her bottom lip. "Nikki, how would you describe the slush?"

"It's like frozen fruit cocktail and Sprite had a baby."

For the first time in three days, Corrie laughed. It felt good. She refused to look behind her, knowing the men who had dug the hole were filling it in. She shoved that thought to the back of her mind and proceeded to tell Violet about the delicacies awaiting them. "Just wait till you have kuchen."

"And what's that?" Violet perked up at the talk of food.

"Nikki, seeing as you did such a good job describing slush, give it a go with this one."

Nikki screwed her face up, her nose twitching slightly as if sniffing the air for a faint scent. "Let me see. Let's say a pie filled with fruit and custard married a piece of the moistest vanilla cake ever. They'd make a baby and call it kuchen."

Corrie enjoyed the light rumble in her chest as a laugh rolled out of her. She gave Nikki a side hug and kissed her sister's hair. "Thank you."

"For what?"

"For just being you."

AARON punched his pillow and laid his head back into it. Grunting, he rolled over on his back and stared at the ceiling. Light from the farmyard filtered in through the drawn curtains and created abstract shapes on the ceiling. Even with his eyes open, he could still see the look on Corrie's face as she said her final goodbye to Baxter. His heart broke for her then, and all he wanted to do was hold her in his arms until her pain subsided and she softened against him...

He rolled over, fingers playing with the sheet hem. The soft cotton felt good on his fingertips, and he couldn't help thinking about Corrie's hair under his hand and maybe someday on a pillow next to his. He blew out a frustrated huff. She'd yet to apologize, but a small flame of hope flickered within his chest. After all, she hadn't pushed him away at the funeral. Maybe he'd been nothing more than a human walking stick, only there to support her from falling lifelessly to the ground.

Aaron flopped to his other side. *Exasperating woman.* Tomorrow, he would confront her and demand some answers. He would not allow her to put him in the doghouse anymore like a disobedient puppy. Cementing this notion in his mind, he shut his eyes and prayed for sleep.

Sleep eventually did come, two hours later. Far too soon, his alarm squawked at him. He crawled out of bed, stretched his tight muscles, grunted and growled a good morning to the rising sun, and scratched at the scruff on his face. He shrugged, dismissing the idea of shaving, threw on some clothes, brushed his teeth, and headed down the steps, past the kitchen.

"Hey, Mom. I'm going to run to Corrie's for a bit. It's time that girl got a good old-fashioned spanking. I'll eat breakfast when I get back. I'm not real hungry." He started toward the front door, stepping over his father's shoes that notoriously clogged the entryway.

"There's no need to, dear. Corrie's right here." A hint of amusement peeked through his mother's voice.

He stopped midstride, his right foot hovering in the air, not sure of its next direction. Feeling a blush work its way up his neck and spread onto his face, he did an about-face and sheepishly stepped into the kitchen.

There she sat, hair down and sparkling in the rays flooding through the kitchen window. A plate of scrambled eggs with cheese and bacon bits waited untouched before her, and her hands were folded so tightly together beside it that her white knuckles glared at him.

"Hi," he breathed, afraid anything louder would cause her to crumble right at the kitchen table.

"Hi," Corrie mumbled.

Mary cleared her throat. "Well, I've got some chickens to feed." She walked by Aaron and squeezed his shoulder. As soon as the door slammed, silence settled in the kitchen, covering every surface with its presence.

"I... I came to apologize for my ridiculous behavior the past couple of days."

He walked to the table and sat next to her. He moved her plate of uneaten eggs and took her intertwined hands into his. When she looked up and her eyes met his, his heart raced. He gazed into them. Tiny flecks of green glinted from the depths of melted chocolate.

He caressed the top of her hand with his thumb. "I'm sorry, too, for saying you needed a spanking." He eyed her as a snicker escaped her lips. Lips he really wanted to kiss—right then, right there. "Did I say something wrong?"

Her snicker erupted into a giggle. She pulled her hands away from his and waved a napkin in front of her face. "No. It's just that, well, when you said spanking, my mind went..." Her voice faded into her napkin as she put it to her mouth. "Never mind." The napkin filtered her words.

His mind joined hers in the gutter. His face grew hot. "I, well," Aaron stammered. "I didn't mean..."

Corrie smiled, her top teeth biting her bottom lip. "You mean you didn't mean it in that way?"

He tried wrapping his thoughts around the rule change in the game they'd been playing. "Yes—I mean no—" He put his head in his hands. "There is no right answer to this question, is there?" He grabbed another napkin and waved it in the air. "There, I surrender. Be kind to your new captive."

She latched onto his hand and held it between hers. "In all seriousness, I am sorry. I had no right to treat you like that. I have no excuses. I was an idiot and a hurtful one at that. Please forgive me. I don't think I could stand you being mad at me."

He brought her hands up to his lips and kissed every knuckle, savoring her sharp inhale. "It's okay. You've been through more than anyone I know. If anyone had the right to snap, it was you." He scooted his chair closer to hers, cupped her face in his hands, and brought it within inches of his own. "Just remember, the only person you can kiss when you're angry is me." He captured her lips with his, creating an unbreakable bond, an unspoken promise.

STILL high on Aaron's kiss, Corrie drove home, scampered across her farmyard, and strode in the front door of her parents' house to the smell of ham and scalloped potatoes. She inhaled a whiff and walked into the kitchen. She turned the corner and halted at the sight of her parents kissing next to the stove, her mother's back pressed against the corner, a spatula dripping with sudsy water clutched in her hand. Her mother's other hand cupped the back of Jake's neck. Corrie bit off a surprised gasp.

With stealthy moves, she tiptoed backward out of the kitchen, her heart racing. Her mind struggled to grasp the sight she'd witnessed. Chewing her bottom lip, she went to the office, where she plunked down in the dark leather chair. She rolled up to the desk, opened the bill drawer, grabbed the checkbook and calculator, and prepared to get down to business. However, the vision of her parents kissing kept distracting her from bills on the desk. A small smile tickled the edges of her lips with the hope that things might get back to normal, that her parents would once again love each other, that her father would heal enough to take over the farm. The glimmer of hope died.

Unless a miracle happened, he would never be able to run the farm. It was up to her to keep it alive and prosperous. And she would. At the beginning, after her father's accident, a thought had manifested itself. She had wanted to sell the place, split the money with her family, and return to Sioux Falls and try to get her old job back. She had even dreamed of moving out of South Dakota entirely and getting a job with a big news corporation and traveling the country and world. The past few months had taught her many things. The most important: she belonged here. She unchained those creeping thoughts from the basement of despair and breathed freely, knowing they would never claw at her mind again.

She reached for the checkbook, switched on her laptop, and brought up the bank account. After fifteen minutes of computing, writing, and talking to herself under her breath, she leaned back in the chair and studied the ceiling. She closed her eyes and rubbed her temples. The wheat harvest had been a success, but she needed the soybean harvest to turn a profit. She needed every acre to yield its maximum potential.

Her eyelids popped open at a familiar scent tickling her nose. She opened the top desk drawer and touched Baxter's handkerchief lying there, drenched in Old Spice. Smiling sadly, she picked it up and brought it to her nose. How she could ever bring herself to go to the elevator, she would never know. Her eyes burned with unshed tears as she tucked the treasure back in the desk drawer.

Her cell chirped. She glanced at the lit-up display screen and smiled.

Hey, babe! Remember if you're angry, I know a great guy who can take care of that for you.

She bit her bottom lip. With deft fingers, she typed, *Who? Luke?*

Five seconds later, her screen lit up again. *TOO SOON!*

She rolled her eyes. *You're right. Sorry. I wouldn't want to take my frustrations or anger out on anybody but you.*

Now we're talking. I'll talk to you later, babe. I've got to do some harvesting for my dad before I'll be over. Maybe a couple of hours.

Corrie texted her goodbye and put her phone down then stared at it before closing her laptop. She had work to do, and sitting around mooning over a man wasn't about to get it done. She ran her tongue over her lips. Although it sure was fun thinking about that man and the way he kissed. Maybe, just maybe, he would kiss her again in the middle of the soybean field in a couple of hours. A loud bang crashed above her head, and Corrie's skittering heart jumped out of her chest. *Violet.*

Corrie hopped out of her chair, ran down the hallway, and bumped into her parents at the bottom of the staircase. The look of worry on their faces surely mirrored hers.

"I'll go." She laid a comforting hand on each of their shoulders. "I'll call if I need any help."

Not waiting for a reply, she bolted up the steps, taking two at a time. She ran down the hallway and pushed Violet's door open. Violet sat on the floor next to a dresser drawer, surrounded by stray underwear and bras—castoffs from Nikki and new ones Corrie had bought her after Violet's arrival.

"Are you okay?" Corrie dropped next to Violet and took the weeping woman into her arms. "What's wrong? Are you hurt?"

Violet shook her head, her wild black tresses tickling Corrie's face. "I don't know." She turned to Corrie, her panicky eyes rolling in her head. "I need to leave."

"What?" She scrambled for Violet's hand. "Why? What happened?"

Violet jerked from Corrie's grasp and struggled to get to her feet. She latched onto an ugly green suitcase, which sat on the floor amid the lingerie, then tossed it on the bed and began reaching down and grabbing handfuls of intimate apparel and shoving them into the suitcase.

"Please, tell me what's going on." Corrie jumped to her feet and restrained Violet's hand as it went in for another load. "You look as if you've seen a ghost."

Violet quit fighting and sank to the mattress that seemed to swallow her small frame. "Please don't ask questions," she whispered. "I just need to leave. Being here any longer only puts you in danger."

Corrie struggled to grasp what Violet meant. "What do you mean? You're safe here. You can't leave."

Violet's gray eyes pierced Corrie's soul. "You're not safe with me here. I can't let anything happen to you. You guys are the only real family I've ever had. I have to go." In a rare show of affection, Violet leaned over and kissed Corrie's forehead. "I wish you were my real sister."

Corrie sputtered, trying to find words that made sense. But nothing came. She stood in silence as Violet replaced the top dresser drawer that had fallen then continued to collect the clothes donated to her or bought since her arrival and put them into the old suitcase.

Violet looked at it sheepishly. "I hope you don't mind me borrowing it. I found it in the attic."

"I wish you'd tell me what's going on. Is it George? Did he do something to you?"

Violet's eyes shimmered with tears. "No," she whispered, her voice rasping in her throat. "Please don't ask any more questions. Just know that the longer I stay here, the more you and your family are in danger."

"But, Violet, you are family."

Violet's hand trembled as it grasped Corrie's. "That's why I have to go."

Corrie sank to the bed, stupefied, as Violet finished packing and lugged the suitcase off the bed. Violet bent over in agony, groaning.

"Violet!" Corrie lunged for her and eased her onto the bed. Violet curled up in a fetal position and whimpered. Corrie tucked a blanket around Violet's shivering form. "I don't care what you say, you are not leaving this house. You and your baby are too precious to us. I will deal with whatever comes my way. Do you understand?"

Beads of sweat glimmered on Violet's pasty skin. "I can't stay."

"I don't think you have a choice right now." Corrie brushed at Violet's bangs that had plastered themselves to her forehead. "You rest. I'll be back later to check on you." She planted a kiss on Violet's head and slipped from the room. She crossed the hallway into her room and sank onto her bed. Letting a sigh escape, she lay across her comforter and studied the texture markings on the ceiling. If she looked close enough, she would find the old sticky goo from her glow-in-the-dark stars. They had long been taken down or fallen down, leaving only glue to collect microscopic dust motes.

Corrie's mind just couldn't compute Violet's strange behavior and willingness to put her life and the life of her unborn baby at risk. Corrie shifted her attention out her window. The wooden skeleton of a new machine shed met her eye. She loved the fact that another building was being born. Its gleaming silver tin would soon greet her, and she couldn't wait to park the equipment in its new home. Ever since the fire... She bolted upright in bed, her eyes glued to the cement floor peeking out through the six-by-six wood beams. The gray surface was pristine, as if smoke and fire hadn't tainted it.

The conversation she'd had with Violet the day after the fire seemed like an eternity ago, but every word and facial expression came screaming back. Her fear and panic and her words, *It's my fault,* echoed through Corrie's mind. Corrie launched herself off her bed and tiptoed to Violet's room. The young woman lay sleeping, her breathing heavy and even.

"What do you know that you're not telling?" Corrie whispered to the sleeping form, unable to keep the dread she'd experienced right after the fire from snaking up her spine again. Leaving Violet to sleep, Corrie made her way downstairs and into the kitchen, where she found her mom, a blush shining on her mother's cheeks and the slightest of smiles spread across her face.

"Mom, Violet's having some pain again. I tucked her in and told her to rest. Could you look in on her later?" She squeezed her mother's shoulders when the smile slipped into a worried frown. "Oh yeah, she's also acting pretty weird. Just don't let her leave."

"Weird?"

"Yeah, she's claiming that we're all in danger because of her. She actually stole your ugly suitcase and was packing."

Cynthia cocked her head. "That is weird. I'll keep an eye on her."

"Keep two eyes on her. I've got to go." Corrie started to walk out of the kitchen. She halted just inside the door. "Do me a favor, okay? Could you lock the doors after I leave?"

Confusion clouded her mom's face.

"I think someone's out to hurt Violet. We need to keep her safe. Just be careful, and as soon as Nikki and Nathan get home from school, send them to the field. I'll need them today."

"Don't you worry, hon." Cynthia pulled her into a hug. "Your father and I will take good care of her." Her mother squeezed hard before letting go. "Be safe. Say hi to Aaron for me."

Corrie's face warmed at her mother's wink. "Yeah, sure." She grabbed her thermos and a lunch cooler filled with ham and scalloped potatoes then bolted into the yard. She had work to do, and she wasn't about to let some specter of Violet's imagination get in the way. As she made her way to her pickup, she hoped the ghost haunting Violet didn't reveal itself in all its glory. She didn't do well with ghosts, especially ghosts that might be very real.

Chapter Thirteen

Corrie peered through the dust, concentrating on the header and the dried-up soybean stalks getting sliced and then the little round yellow beans being led to their demise by air tubes blowing them farther into the header's grasp. Squinting against the fading sunlight streaming through the dusty chaff, she adjusted the header when a rock—which had rejected its pummeling into the earth by the bean roller in the spring after planting—jutted up in all its glory. She cursed the rock and the low visibility.

After avoiding the rock, she tried to piece together the mystery of the machine-shed fire and Violet's odd behavior. Someone had set fire to the machine shed. She chewed on her bottom lip and reached for her water jug off the floor. Taking a sip of ice-cold water, she understood one thing. Violet knew who it was. *Could it be George? Or someone from Violet's past?* Corrie placed the jug back and wiped away water that had dribbled down her chin. *But why would someone from Violet's past want to destroy my machine shed?* Either way, the heebie-jeebies that had started plaguing her right after the fire were firing on all cylinders.

Shifting in the combine seat as she came to the end of the field, she lifted the header, turned the machine around, lowered the header, and continued harvesting. Going this way was worse. She couldn't see past the header.

"How can you see anything?" Aaron's voice over the radio sent a hot flash sizzling through her body.

"I can't. I'm thinking of calling it quits pretty soon if the wind doesn't die down. If the combine were to create a spark, we'd have some issues."

"Sounds good. Do you need to dump yet?"

She glanced over her shoulder at the little window into the hopper. Tiny soybeans were just starting to cover the entire window. "Yeah. That would work. After you get back, then we'll fill the truck and then fill the grain cart as well. Where are you?"

"Right here, babe."

Corrie peered out the glass combine door and squinted through the haze. She could barely make out Aaron in the tractor.

"If you couldn't see it, I just blew a kiss at you," he teased over the radio.

She chuckled. With her right hand, she flipped the switch to extend the auger and then another switch to start it, then she emptied the hopper load into the waiting grain cart. She usually didn't have difficulty driving alongside the tractor during these transfers, but with the conditions, she was terrified she would run into the tractor's wheels. She let out a pent-up sigh after the hopper fully emptied.

"We're done," she called over the radio.

"Why? What did I do now?" He laughed.

"Hardy har-har!" Corrie giggled. "Sadly for you, I don't plan on ever being done with you."

"How will I ever bear the hardship?"

"Some of us were born to be grenade jumpers. Sucks to be you, doesn't it?"

His chuckle melted her insides to jelly. "Some might actually say you're the grenade jumper in the relationship. Why, just the other day, Luke called me grandpa."

"Lucky for you, I love older men. Now, shoo. Oh, and I'd like a Snickers bar, please."

"That'll cost you, you know."

She licked her lips. "You'll receive adequate payment upon receipt of product."

"I love it when you talk all businessy to me. Don't stop."

"I give bonuses depending on the promptness of delivery."

"Consider it done, Boss Lady. I'll be back before you can miss me."

Sighing, she placed the radio receiver down. "Too late," she whispered as she readjusted the header and prepared for another turn. She missed him every second she wasn't physically with him. If she couldn't feel his hand in hers or his lips on hers or see his eyes peering into her soul, she felt unsettled. As if something was missing. This only made the moments when they were together so much sweeter.

She lost track of time. Dried-up soybean leaves flew through the air, scuttling against the windshield like a thousand beetle feet scurrying across the ground. Watching the header's monotonous motion put her in a brief trance. Blinking against the hypnotic effect, she peered through the haze, struggling to see much of anythi—flames! Flames, orange and red, devoured the bean field, one acre at a time.

Corrie screamed and brought the combine to a rocking halt. She jumped the cab, climbed to the top of it, and gaped at the fire inching through her unfinished field. Toward her. The wind, which had persisted all day, fanned the fire, giving it the oxygen it needed and the speed it desired. Shielding herself from the invading smoke, she raised her T-shirt collar over her mouth and squinted. She had to act fast. But before she could formulate a game plan, a dark figure moved against the flames then fell. A human form. She gasped and, for a split second, panicked. Fear, akin to the feeling when she found out about her dad's car accident, gripped her insides and squeezed.

Fighting to breathe against the emotion and smoke, she forced herself to think logically. Before climbing down, she whipped out her cell from her jeans pocket and checked for service. She had enough to call 911. Knowing the volunteer fire department would take a little while to arrive, she fought the urge to flee and drove the combine toward the fire and the human figure she'd seen fall. She kept the combine running and descended the ladder as fast as she could. Second-guessing herself the entire way, she sprinted toward the inferno and the figure. Heat surged around her—an intense heat that tightened her skin in fear. Smoke invaded her lungs, and she coughed and gagged on noxious air. She skidded to a halt next to the figure and screamed.

"George?" She fell to her knees beside him and jostled him. His eyes blinked open and stared at her.

"Corrie," he croaked. His tongue darted out and licked his chapped lips. His face, streaked with smoke and dirt, looked pasty under the filth. His mouth opened and shut several times before he was able to make another sound. "I'm sorry."

She looked at him, at the approaching fire, at the combine. She shushed him when he started to talk again. "Listen to me. I am going to need you to get up. Can you do that?"

George shook his head and moaned.

She turned his head toward the flames. "That is your fate if you are unable to get up and walk. I can't carry you."

"Leave me."

"No. I'll help you, but we've got to go. Now!" Yanking on his arms, she begged him to get up.

Lodging his palms into the dirt and soybean chaff, George hoisted himself into a sitting position.

She squatted next to him. "I don't care if you have to crawl. We're doing this. Together. Now move."

He began to crawl. Slowly at first, but the heat of the approaching fire's breath had them both panting in desperation, her tugging at his shirt wet with sweat and darkened by soot and smoke, and him whimpering as the ground and dry plants sliced at his palms.

"We're almost there. Come on. You can make it." She gave one last heave, and after what seemed like an eternity, they reached the combine ladder. "Climb, George."

He sprawled on the ground under the ladder. "I can't. Just leave me. I don't deserve to live, anyway."

"Nonsense." She studied the ladder. She sure couldn't carry him up it, so maybe he could just hold on to it. "Okay, here's the plan. You are going to step up on the first step and wrap your arms around the ladder. You must not let go. I'll go slow, but we need to get out of here."

He nodded weakly and got to his hands and knees. She placed his hands on the lower ladder rung and assisted him as he hauled himself up. With seemingly every ounce of his energy, he pulled his body up the ladder and gave a massive grunt as he brought his feet up to the bottom rung.

"Good. Now hang on for dear life, because if you let go, you're a dead man."

The look in his eyes told her he knew the enormity of their situation. She maneuvered around his frame and scampered up the ladder and into the combine cab. With a shaking right hand, she pushed the joystick forward, slowly so as not to jerk him off the ladder. The combine's engine revved and whirred to meet the speed she demanded. She was never so thankful for the smooth bean field. She pushed the joystick all the way to the little rabbit insignia and prayed George could maintain his hold on the ladder. Through the side mirrors, she watched the flames continue their destructive path, following her. Looking out the windshield, she knew that if the fire department was unable to stop the fire, it would eat up the next field and the field after that. It would dine on a veritable smorgasbord of ready-to-harvest soybeans, corn, and sunflowers.

After coming to the end of the field, she brought the combine to a gentle stop and clambered out of the cab. "George?" She peeked down the ladder. His bloodshot eyes seemed to glow out of the blackness smudging his face. "You okay?"

He shook his head. His hands slipped from the ladder, and his body crumpled to the ground.

Gasping, she slid down the ladder and dropped to his side. She placed her pointer and middle finger to his neck and felt his pulse, weak and unsteady, thrum up against her fingers. Glancing at her surroundings, she noticed Aaron's pickup nearby. Measuring the distance in her head, she couldn't imagine it was much more than twenty feet. She stood and, placing herself by George's head, slipped her arms under his armpits and pulled.

"Crap!" Corrie exclaimed as her body came to a jolting stop due to George's heavy frame. She dropped his arms and wiped at the sweat beading on her forehead. "Okay. You can do this, Corrie Lancaster. You work out. You lift weights. There's a fire, woman!" She stretched her neck to the left and right, cracked her knuckles, and squatted next to his head again. Feeling her thighs tighten, she wrapped her arms around his armpits again and yanked. This time, he moved. Slowly, she slid him across the harvested bean field toward Aaron's pickup. Groans, grunts, and swear words exploded out of her as she yanked and tugged. George, unresponsive, didn't make a sound while his body jerked across the dirt and soybean chaff.

Finally, sirens wailed in the distance. Relief flooded through her, but she kept moving, dragging him to her final destination. She glanced at the combine and choked down panic. The flames she'd driven from were closing in on her new machine. No way on God's green earth was she going to lose another combine to fire. With a final push, she reached the temporary safety of the pickup just as the firefighters arrived in the field.

"Corrie!"

Corrie turned to the voice hailing her. "Derek." She hardly recognized her mechanic friend in his bunker gear. She'd forgotten he had joined the volunteer fire department. She had teased him about leaving the auto mechanic shop and abandoning his precious Smarties to vandalizing children. "I've got to get the combine."

His wrestling build seemed to expand in front of her, as if to block her view of the machine. "No. You're not. The fire is too dangerous now."

She could never outmatch him, but she could outrun him. "Yeah. You're right." As soon as he relaxed a little, she made a run for it, bolting out of his reach and sprinting toward the combine and the fiery inferno creeping up on it. Behind her, Derek yelled at her to stop. Beside her, the brush trucks dashed toward the flames so firefighters could begin battle. The roar of the fire rumbled as it ate up her crop. The heat crackled from its voracious flames.

She kept her eyes on the combine and soon mounted the ladder, whipped open the door, and fell into the seat. Glancing out the windshield, she screamed as flames began to lick the header, tasting it before swallowing it whole. Panic surged through her veins, and she pushed the joystick to the rabbit with such force the combine seemed to jump. Leaving the flames behind, she maneuvered the combine to the approach, crossed the gravel road, and drove it into her neighbor's unharvested cornfield. She winced driving over the corn, but given the circumstances, she didn't have much choice. The fire wouldn't jump the road. Hopefully.

She dashed out of the cab and ran back across the road, only to be brought to a sudden halt by strong arms grabbing her waist. She whirled around and threw herself against Aaron. Allowing the tears to come, she lost herself in his chest and didn't come out until several minutes passed. The smell of his cologne refreshed her sense of smell, burned and bruised by the acrid smoke. Her eyes burned as tears poured out and soaked his T-shirt.

His hands caressed her hair and back. Every touch seemed to leach out the toxic stress building up inside her.

"We need to go, babe." His voice purred in her ear.

Not wanting to let go, she pushed herself farther into his chest.

"Corrie, someday I'd like to die with you. But I'd rather it be in our bed at the age of a hundred and one and not burned to crispy bacon before I'm able to truly make you mine."

She released her death grip on him and allowed him to lead her to his pickup.

Luke's pickup skidded to a halt on the gravel road. He and Gerome jumped out and jogged over to where Corrie and Aaron stood. "What can we do?" they asked in unison, their eyes never leaving the growing fire.

She rubbed her temples, trying to make her brain make sense. Brush trucks and firefighters waged war on the flames hissing with anger when water touched their fiery tentacles. Paramedics loaded George into an awaiting ambulance. She would need to get all the equipment to safety.

She spun back to the three men. "Gerome, could you please take the grain cart across the road? I don't think Leonard will mind. Luke, could you take Aaron's pickup over there, and Aaron, could you move the semi from the road and into Leonard's field? I'll bring your truck, Luke, and we'll figure out what to do from there."

Before getting into Luke's truck, she dashed over to the paramedics as they shut the back door. The same ones who had loaded Baxter's body weeks ago turned to her as she hailed them.

"Wait, please." She puffed as she skidded to a halt. "How's he doing? I don't know how much smoke he inhaled before I pulled him out."

"We're not sure yet." One of them smiled kindly, her eyes crinkly at the corners. "You'll have to contact his family later to find out."

"But George doesn't have any family nearby."

"Are you a close friend?"

Corrie paused and swallowed hard. "He used to be my hired man."

The paramedic touched her arm. "You'll just have to contact the hospital in Sweetwater later, then. Maybe they'll be able to tell you something." The female paramedic hopped in the driver's side and drove the ambulance out of the field and down the gravel road.

Coughing on the smoke, Corrie ran to Luke's pickup and drove it out of the field and across the road before parking. She hopped out and ran to Aaron then nestled in his awaiting arms. She felt secure as he rested his strong, chiseled, smooth chin on her hair.

"You, my dear, smell." He sputtered against the stench of smoke emanating from her hair and clothes.

"That's romance, old man?" Luke teased as he joined them.

"Age is relative, Luke." Gerome came to Aaron's other side and touched Corrie's shoulder. "Are you okay?"

Corrie studied Gerome's kindly face. A much older version of Aaron met her gaze. The same dimpled chin, the same blue-green eyes, just slightly weathered by life, peered into hers. She nodded, afraid speaking would open the floodgates to the torrid emotions inside her.

"What was George doing in the field with you?" Gerome wondered aloud.

She shrugged, asking herself that question as well for the first time. Aaron's arms tightened around her, and the nagging suspicion she'd had since the machine-shed fire came to light. George. George was the arsonist.

She jerked her head up and stared into Aaron's eyes, trying to decipher what he knew or suspected. Swallowing against the tears, she croaked, "You know, don't you?"

He cupped her face with his large, calloused hands. "I don't know anything definite. That's why I never voiced my fears. George has seemed to have it out for you from the beginning." He shifted to the fire hissing and spitting in defeat. "There's only one reason George would be in the field with you."

Amid the ringing in her ears, she heard Gerome spit out a rare curse word. She concentrated on Aaron's eyes to keep from passing out.

"Corrie? Stay with me," he ordered. "Now is not the time to faint. You can faint later. We've got to get you home."

She didn't move, couldn't move. Her legs would not obey.

Aaron, seeming to sense her paralysis, lifted her in his arms and carried her to his truck. "Don't worry about a thing. From the size of the growing crowd, we'll get people to help move the equipment to the farmyard."

She didn't even look at the people gathered on the gravel road, watching flames devour her bean field. She refused to see the pity in their eyes over the poor little farm girl who gave it her best but, in the end, had failed.

AT THE SOUND OF FOOTSTEPS and heavy breathing, Aaron stepped out from the Lancaster kitchen, holding a cup of hot coffee. "Where are you going?"

He couldn't help but wince at Violet's tearstained face and bloodshot eyes. An ancient green suitcase sat at her feet, its worn handle clutched securely by a shaking hand. He blew into his coffee and studied the young woman before him. She seemed ready to bolt at the slightest sound. Her eyes looked at everything but him.

"Where you off to?"

"I have to go," she whispered hoarsely. She met his eyes, terror emanating from their depths. "Corrie should have let me go earlier."

He approached her and laid a hand on her shoulder. "What kind of trouble are you in, Violet? Let me help. Let us help. You can't go." He glanced at her growing baby bump. "You have to think of your baby."

She ripped herself from his gentle grasp. "You don't understand. I have no choice. Corrie could have died today. All because of me."

"What *are* you talking about? George is at the hospital right now under armed guard. He was out there. He's the one who set the fire."

"George might be a male chauvinist pig, but he's no killer." She pinned him with a stare. "But I know who is."

Aaron's stomach clenched, and he swallowed the rising bile in his throat. His heart thudded, and he zeroed in on Violet. Piercing her with his gaze, he spoke slowly and softly. "Violet, you need to have a seat in the living room. I'm going to call the sheriff, check on Corrie, and then we are going to get to the bottom of this." When she hesitated, he squeezed her shoulders. "Go."

She waddled into the living room and perched precariously on the edge of the couch, her feet tapping, her hands wringing.

Before heading upstairs, he made a call to the sheriff and then double-checked to ensure the doors were all locked. Nathan and Nikki would be home soon, and they would need to be filled in. He bounded up the stairs two at a time and rapped on Corrie's bedroom door. A soft voice welcomed him, and he tiptoed into the semi-darkened room to find Cynthia and Jake huddled around Corrie's bed, each holding one of Corrie's hands.

Aaron shivered at the look of fear in Jake's eyes as the older gentleman turned from his daughter's bedside.

"George did this?" Jake whispered, as if afraid to wake his sleeping child.

"We're not sure yet, Mr. Lancaster. Too many questions right now." Aaron stepped next to Corrie's bed and gazed at her torrid face finally showing tranquility. He jumped at the soft hand on his shoulder.

"Sorry. I didn't mean to startle you, but Jake and I will leave you alone for a bit. Nathan and Nikki should be here any minute now." Tears clung to Cynthia's eyelashes.

"Violet is threatening to leave. She says she knows who did it."

"What?" Cynthia gasped then slapped a hand to her mouth. Peeking at Corrie's still form, she asked again, more quietly, "Did she say who it is?"

"She won't tell me, but she's terrified of someone, that's for sure."

Cynthia nodded. "I'll have Jake sit with her."

The two began walking out of Corrie's bedroom, hand in hand. He almost smiled then frowned. "Oh, and the sheriff is coming from the hospital too."

"Thanks, Aaron, for everything." Cynthia smiled and shut the door.

Aaron fell to his knees at Corrie's bedside. He clutched her hand and cradled it between his. He studied her pert little nose, the freckles adorning her high cheekbones, and her full lips relaxed in sleep. He had kissed those lips many times, and every time, the wonderment they gave him still took him by surprise. He rose and laid a light kiss on her lips. They stirred underneath his, and he glanced up to find her chocolate-brown eyes gazing at him.

"Hey," he whispered, afraid to break the spell.

"Straw." A smile tickled the side of her mouth.

He brushed her bangs off her forehead. "How are you feeling?"

"Better." She frowned. "I feel like such a fool. I had no business fainting and being all damsel-in-distress. I don't like those women."

He kissed her nose. "Does that make me your knight in shining armor?"

"Who wants a knight in shining armor?" She wrinkled her nose. "I want my knight dirty and smelly and banged up, proving he's actually done a thing or two."

"So I qualify for the position?"

She laughed and pushed him away, swinging her legs over the bed and sitting on the edge of the mattress. "Sir Aaron, I would like my flip-flops, please."

He bowed low to the ground and grabbed the pink shoes from the floor. Slipping them on her feet, he smiled up at her. "Anything for you, m'lady Corrie."

When she playfully shoved him and stood up, stretching to her full length, he averted his eyes from the lithe, slender body arching catlike before him. He certainly didn't miss the gaze she gave him as she sauntered to her window and opened the shade.

"What is the sheriff doing here? I thought he was supposed to be guarding George." She pressed her face to the window.

Aaron moved in front of her and hugged her to him. He tucked her head under his chin and rocked back and forth, hoping the soothing would assuage the trembling woman in his arms.

Before too long, she pushed him away and glared up at him. "I told you I don't want to be a damsel in distress. I can handle this. Tell me what's going on."

He followed the side of her face with his index finger. "Violet knows who did it. The fire today and the machine-shed fire."

In an instant, Corrie dragged him from the room, down the hall and steps, and into the living room. There, the sheriff, Jake and Cynthia, Violet, Nathan, and Nikki, with the addition of Xavier, were talking in hushed tones. Their conversation halted as soon as Aaron and Corrie sat on the loveseat facing the already-occupied brown leather couch and two recliners.

Nikki released her hold on Xavier's hand and flung herself into Corrie's arms. Aaron kept his arm around Corrie, afraid to lose contact with her. He heard the words of encouragement she whispered to Nikki as the girl clung to Corrie's neck. After several minutes, Nikki sat at Corrie's feet, Xavier by Nikki's side, her hand in his. Nathan remained unmoving from behind Corrie, much like a sentry guarding a treasure.

Corrie glanced at Xavier. "You should probably go home."

Xavier's Adam's apple jumped. "Can I stay?" At Corrie's raised eyebrow, he stammered, "I-I came to help Nikki on a project for history, but I guess that's not going to work right now." He glanced around the room. "I, uh, I'd like to stay. Please. For Nikki." His face broke into a smile at Corrie's nod.

When a knock sounded at the front door, they all jumped. For several heartbeats, no one moved. Sheriff Steve bounced to his feet. "Stay."

No one needed to be told twice, and they collectively held their breaths until a familiar voice greeted Steve—Luke. After a few moments, he stepped into the room, his face a mask of pastoral calm. Aaron was not fooled. His brother's clenched fists and whitened knuckles betrayed the rage simmering under Luke's skin.

"Steve just filled me in. Tell me how I can help." Luke's eyes sought Violet's, paused there, then scanned the room.

"Pray." Cynthia clasped her hands together.

"Done." Luke set himself up on the edge of the family circle, an angel of protection against the unseen demon.

Sheriff Steve cleared his throat. "Corrie, I'm glad you are safe and secure." His two-tone eyes studied her, and a flash of regret or guilt emanated from them. "I feel like I'm to blame for all this. I should have done a better job protecting you and your property."

"No!" Violet blurted, causing everyone to jump. "It's my fault and my fault alone. If I hadn't been so ashamed and so distant, this would never have happened. So now it's my job to fix it." She paused for breath, and the vein in her neck pulsed beneath her white skin. "Several years ago, I met a man. A man who I thought loved me for me, you know?" Her breathing hitched. "I've been a foster kid all my life. In and out of homes, kicked out of some. I wasn't your model child by any means. I spent my teenage years finding love in all the wrong places. Until Frank, or so I thought.

"The beatings didn't start until I was pregnant with our first child. He beat me until I lost it." This time her voice broke, and quiet sobs racked her body. The only person to move was Corrie, who brought Violet into her arms. After taking several deep breaths, Violet continued, "He apologized, of course, told me how sorry he was, but I couldn't go making him angry and not expect him to correct me. In my naïveté and stupidity, I believed him. I got pregnant a second time, and this time, I landed in the hospital. Same old song and dance."

Violet rubbed her belly. "This little guy or girl is number three and my salvation. I didn't even tell Frank. I just ran. Stole his car, his cash, drugged his whiskey, and took off." Her voice died to a strained whisper. She looked at each of them. "I'm so sorry." She turned in to Corrie's shoulder and wept.

Luke moved to Violet's side, his hand resting on the crown of her head.

"So that's how you came to us?" Nathan whispered from behind Corrie.

Violet nodded. "The day I arrived at this farm was the day I ran away from hell. I had one chance to escape, and I took it. He was becoming suspicious when I started to show. Asked what I was eating, tracked my food intake. I made a run for it. After I had drugged him and stolen the cash, I headed out with nothing much more than the clothes on my back. As soon as I hit the border of Montana and South Dakota, I got off the interstate and took back roads." Violet's speech diminished into a whisper. "I never thought he'd find me. Not here." Her voice hitched. "I wanted all of them. All my precious babies."

"How do you know it's him? Why would he set fire to property that doesn't belong to you?" Aaron asked.

Violet's face whitened until Aaron feared she would faint. "Because I'm his property, and he needs to correct my misbehavior. He's punishing me by hurting you." She choked, gazing at the Lancasters, her eyes locking with Luke's. "That's why I need to leave."

"And go where?" Cynthia furrowed her brows. "If what you say is true, he will find you, and—"

"Kill me," Violet whispered.

"Let us help you," Luke interjected, his hand slipping from her hair to the nape of her neck. "He won't get to you. Or us."

She grew quiet, her toes drawing circles in the carpet. "How will I ever repay you?"

"You don't have to repay us. This is just what families do for each other," Corrie said.

"Um, if we're all family, we're going to need a bigger living room," Nathan chirped from behind the loveseat.

Corrie's gaze circled the room. "You know what? You're right. Put all your learning in shop to use and build an addition." Her glance lingered on Luke's hand resting protectively on Violet.

"All we're building is stupid snowmen. Why does everybody have to skip Thanksgiving and jump right to Christmas?"

Aaron chuckled at the boy's exasperated sigh and asked, "So, what now?"

Sheriff Steve pinched the bridge of his nose. "We wait."

Chapter Fourteen

Corrie chafed at the confinement. She hated waiting. Always had. Biting her lip, she eased her bedroom door open, aware of the creaky hinges. If she didn't get out of the house in the next several seconds, she'd be bat-crap crazy. She tiptoed down the hall and steps, cognizant of the fifth and seventh steps from the top. The little tattle-tales.

She rounded the corner and headed down the hall toward the front door only to spy a deputy sitting on a chair inside the living room. She swore under her breath, retraced her steps, and entered the kitchen but stopped at the silhouette of another deputy sitting outside the double patio doors to the garden. With a hiss of frustration, she spun around and crept toward the office. The dark room was empty and the ground outside the window unoccupied by law enforcement.

Double-checking for her cell phone in the back pocket of her jeans, she opened the window and crawled out. She was grateful for the sweatshirt she'd grabbed as the cool fall evening enveloped her body. She breathed in the scents of dead leaves and wood-burning furnaces churning out smoke from nearby farmhouses, relishing it. All of it. The colors, the scents, the rest fall gave the land. She would love it more if there weren't some deranged lunatic stalking her.

She twisted sharply, her heart stuttering. Placing her hand on her chest, she talked herself down from her fright and leaned against the house. Clouds played hide-and-seek with the yellowish moon, casting strange shadows on a place she knew every square inch of. This farmyard was her childhood friend but had become a hiding place for an enemy she didn't know. Feeling like a mouse stalked by one of the farm cats, she took one last breath of fresh air and shimmied back into the window.

"Caught you!"

"Goodness sakes!" she squeaked, losing her balance on the windowsill and toppling onto the office floor. Her sister's giggles and her brother's chuckles met her ears. Seething, she stood to her full height, hoping to intimidate her younger siblings.

"You scared me near to death, you two little funguses!" She scowled.

"Serves you right for sneaking out, anyway." Nikki violently chewed on a piece of gum. At Corrie's stare, she sighed. "If I don't chew something, my nerves will cause me to crumble to little bits. It's this or my lip. Do you want me to have a bloody lip by the time this is all over?"

"At least chew with your mouth closed. You sound like an old cow chewing her cud."

"Hey! That's not very nice!" Nikki pouted.

"And it wasn't very nice to scare me, now was it?" Corrie softened her tone and winked at her sister. She pinned Nathan with a glare. "Was this your idea?"

He shuffled his feet. The big grin on his face gave him away.

She walked up to him and placed her cold hand on his warm, slightly fuzzy cheek. "Remember, my dear, dear brother. Revenge is best served cold." She walked out of the office, her siblings in tow.

Nikki grabbed her elbow and whispered, "What were you doing outside, anyway? Mom gave us strict instructions to not leave the house after dark."

"I couldn't sleep, and I just needed to get out. But trust me, it's not so inviting outside."

"Afraid of the boogeyman?" Nathan teased as they crept up the stairs.

"Yup, and crazy lunatics by the name of Frank." Corrie bid them good night and entered her room then shut the door behind her. She took off her sweatshirt and jeans and crawled into her bed under the warm comforter and willed herself to sleep.

CORRIE woke up to cries reverberating through the house. She bolted upright and squinted at the clock. Eight. Another cry ripped through the house. She tugged on the pair of jeans still lying on the floor, ran down the hall, and took the steps two at a time, holding onto the banister. She rounded the corner and skidded to a stop at the sight of Violet bent over, hugging her bulging belly. Corrie's parents stood nearby, slipping into light jackets and shoes.

Corrie sprinted over to Violet and laid a gentle hand on the young woman's midnight-black hair. Sweat beaded on Violet's forehead, so Corrie ran to the kitchen and wet a dishcloth with cool water. She placed it against Violet's forehead and hugged Violet, taking the pregnant woman's weight into hers.

"It's okay, Violet. Everything's going to be okay," Corrie murmured into her ear.

"I'm scared," Violet squeaked as another contraction racked her tiny body.

Corrie supported her as she crumpled into Corrie's side. "It's okay to be scared, but you are the bravest woman I know." She lifted Violet's chin after the contraction subsided. "You can do this."

Violet bit her lip and nodded weakly, leaning again into Corrie. Corrie caught her mother's eyes, and the concern they both had for mother and baby passed between them. Corrie kissed Violet's temple and led her to one of the living room recliners. The late-morning sun glared into the room, casting rainbows through the crystal prism hanging from the curtain rod. Corrie eased Violet into the chair and walked back to where her parents spoke quietly.

"The baby is early." Concern etched in the furrowed lines on Jake's forehead.

Cynthia looped her purse over her shoulder. "Corrie, we'll take Violet into Sweetwater. I'll keep you updated as soon as I know what's going on." Her mother's hand shook as it caressed Corrie's cheek. "Hold down the fort, my dear. You do remember the combination to the gun safe, right?"

"I don't think I'll need it with all the deputies posted around here."

"Do you remember it?" Her urgency made Corrie's skin crawl.

"Yes, Mom, I remember it."

Her mother and father kissed her cheek then gathered up Violet and an overnight bag.

Corrie rushed to Violet's side and hugged her. "I'll be praying for you and your baby. I'll see you soon, okay?"

Violet hugged her back with such intensity, Corrie felt as if her ribs might crack. Without a word, Violet waddled out the door, Cynthia supporting her. Jake, bringing up the rear, closed it behind them. Corrie clicked the dead bolt into place and stood in the empty hallway.

Loneliness crept into her. Corrie tried laughing the feeling away, but she proceeded to tiptoe into the kitchen, afraid of making too much noise. With her mom and dad with Violet, and Nathan and Nikki at school, it was her and only her in the house. Normally it wouldn't have bothered her, but today was different. Today was still haunted by the unseen presence of evil, probably lurking until the right moment to attack her precious farm or her even more precious family.

She yanked open the fridge door, retrieved a can of Pepsi, cracked it open, and took huge gulps. "Breakfast of champions," she mumbled. After taking the milk out, she snatched the Honey Nut Cheerios off the counter, poured the cereal into a bowl, added the milk, and walked to the table with it and her Pepsi. She sat with her back to the wall and her eyes set firmly on the patio door. One of the deputies remained posted just outside, sitting in a lawn chair, his head turning once in a while like an owl's.

When her cell phone vibrated in her back pocket, Corrie jumped. She yanked it out and read her new text message.

Hey, babe, how are you doing this morning?

She smiled at the cute emoji he'd added. Her thumbs flew across the screen as she replied that she was fine.

You're not very good at lying.

She scowled at the text sprawled across the screen and rolled her eyes.

You just rolled your eyes, didn't you? came his next text. *You want me to come over?*

Her fingers automatically started texting the word yes, but she stopped herself. *No. I'm okay, and I know you have stuff to do.*

She sat and waited for his reply, but none came. Shaking off the hurt feelings, she ate her cereal, now drowned and soggy from swimming in a pool of milk. She polished off her Pepsi, put her dishes in the dishwasher, and ran upstairs to get ready for the day. She was mid-tooth-brush when the doorbell rang. Her heart stammered, and without removing her toothbrush from her mouth, she ran to the office, opened the gun safe, and grabbed her father's Smith & Wesson revolver.

The doorbell rang again, setting her nerves on edge. She peeped through the curtains covering the window flanking the front door. There, Aaron stood, hands in his back pockets, rocking back and forth on his sneakered feet. The sheriff stood next to him.

She shivered at the weight of the loaded gun in her hand. Before opening the door, she stashed the gun in the entryway table. Butterflies erupted in her stomach at Aaron's smile.

"Hi," he said as she stepped aside so he could enter. "You coming in, Steve?"

"No." The sheriff glanced at her. "How are you doing, Corrie?"

She forced a smile and spoke around the toothbrush in her mouth. "Good. Do you want something to drink? Do any of the deputies?"

"We're good. Please let me know if you need anything, okay?" He drummed his fingers on his firearm and walked down the porch steps.

She shut and locked the door and immediately found herself drawn into Aaron's arms. Not wanting to stab him in the neck with her toothbrush, she plucked it out of her mouth, swallowed the toothpaste coating her mouth, and used the back of her hand to erase any residual paste on her lips. She melted into his embrace and reveled in the strength of his chest and arms. He tucked her head securely under his chin, and she vowed not to leave this spot for at least another five minutes.

His husky voice vibrated her ear when he spoke. "Corrie, please don't ever lie to me again."

She broke her vow and lifted her head. Cocking it to one side, she frowned at him. "I didn't."

"You're not fine. You don't have to pretend with me. You know that, right? Please don't feel there is anything more important to me than you." He caressed her hair then ran his fingers down her cheek.

Her entire body responded to his touch. A disturbing thought, which had been nagging her since Violet's revelation, came to light once more. As stupid as it seemed, he was the one person she could rely on to not laugh at her.

As if ripping off a Band-Aid, Corrie spoke quickly. "I want to go see George."

Aaron's eyebrows shot up almost to his hair. Her heart faltered and sputtered along for five beats—not that she was counting—before his eyebrows settled into their normal place. He grabbed her hand and gave it a gentle squeeze.

"When do you want to go?" His thumb caressed the back of her hand.

"Right now, if you don't mind. Besides, we can check on Violet as well."

"Violet? Is she all right?"

"I suppose you can consider having a baby an all-right thing." Corrie giggled when Aaron's mouth fell open, and he sat on the wooden bench next the entryway table. The gun lurked in its drawer, but she didn't dare draw it out before Aaron to put it away. He would think her a harebrained, skittish woman. Slipping on her shoes, she placed her toothbrush on the table and brought him up to speed on the morning's events.

"You've had a busy day so far." He put his hand to the small of her back and guided her out the door.

She made sure the door was locked then walked hand in hand toward Aaron's truck. "Yeah. I'm really ready for this whole thing to be done. As soon as I return, I've got to start combining too." She sighed and rested her head on his shoulder as he drove down the long driveway.

"Let me, Corrie," he pleaded, turning slightly to kiss her forehead. "Please, let me. I can make do till Nathan and Nikki get home. You need rest."

She wanted to say no, to refuse his offer, but she also knew that being a stubborn old cow wasn't going to get her anywhere. "Okay."

Corrie laughed at Aaron's surprise and concerned look. He felt her forehead. "Are you feeling okay?"

She laughed again and brushed away his hand then sighed deeply. If felt so good to laugh. "Remember when you told me I had to let others help? Well, I'm finally taking your advice. I'm learning to let go." A frown creased her forehead. "I'm afraid if I don't, I'll be crushed under the weight of this farm and all its responsibilities." She relaxed when he placed a hand on her thigh. "I suppose I'm scared of failure. I'd hate to see this farm destroyed, especially because of me." The high-pitched squeakiness in her voice sent her cringing. She gave him a wobbly smile. "Thanks. For everything."

He took his eyes off the road and beamed her a smile. How she loved the way his eyes crinkled at the corners when he did that. "You don't give yourself enough credit. I have a suspicion that, once you've set your mind to something, nothing gets in your way."

She lay back on the headrest as the prairie's fall landscape flew by her window. Pastures, once alive with green verdure, lay brown and brittle, simply waiting for a blanket of snow to protect them from the temperatures forecast in the breeze whistling through the dead grasses. Trees were already shedding their vibrant foliage, and leaves of orange, yellow, and red trickled off the branches, floating to the ground, where they were left to rustle in the chilly autumn winds. She groped for Aaron's hand, and once her fingers intertwined with his, she closed her eyes, refusing to think of the lurking danger and her impending visit with the man she detested.

CORRIE'S first order of business was to check on Violet. She met her parents just outside one of the hospital rooms. Aaron held her hand, squeezing it occasionally.

"How is she?" she asked, breathless with anticipation.

"We're not sure. The doctor is examining her now."

Cynthia rubbed her hands together and leaned into Jake's side. He stumbled slightly but righted himself, propped his hip against the beige wall, and put his arm around his wife.

"What are you two doing here, though? I was going to call you soon."

Corrie gaped and then stuttered, "I, uh, I..."

Aaron, seemingly taking advice from Jake, wrapped his arm around Corrie and hugged her into his side.

"I'm going to see George."

Cynthia's mouth fell open, and her eyes grew to twice their original size. "You are really going to visit that odious man?"

Jake patted his wife's upper arm. "It's okay."

"No, Jake, it's not okay. That man betrayed us all, and even if he didn't start the fires, he deserves no such attention from any of us, especially Corrie."

Cynthia sniffed and tried to wrench herself from his side. Jake, however, did not relinquish his hold, and for the first time since his accident, strength seemed to creep back into his bones. She eventually gave up and wilted into her husband. Fat tears slid down her face.

Corrie's heart weighed heavy. She hated bringing her mother pain, but she knew the right thing to do. She had to get answers, and she had to get them from the source.

She hugged her mom. "I'll come back as soon as I'm done and check in on Violet, okay?"

When Cynthia nodded but said nothing, Corrie latched onto Aaron's proffered hand, and they walked down the quiet hospital halls. Smells of antiseptic and cafeteria food mingled in the air. Trying not to inhale too deeply, she continued until she reached George's room. The wooden door was shut, but the nurse had informed her she could go in.

For several seconds, Corrie stood, still and unmoving. She heard nothing but her own heartbeat swooshing in her ears. Her mind flashed to the field fire. Her skin tingled at the heat trying to sear her. She again saw the flames licking the header, tasting the green metal before taking the first big bite. Her nose wrinkled against the smell of smoke and burning soybeans.

"Corrie?" Concern vibrated in Aaron's voice, and his hand caressed her back.

She shook herself like Bacon did after getting wet. Reaching out, she knocked and then turned the doorknob.

George, in all his corpulence, sat up in his bed, his eyes homing in on her. Some soap opera blared from the television hooked to the wall. Apparently, Hot Actor X was having an argument with Hot Actress Y. George grabbed the remote and muted the noise, canceling out the overacted words and emotions.

With a little nudge from Aaron, Corrie moved toward the bed, stopping feet from it. All her anger for the man in the bed bubbled to the surface. His grossness, his sexist words and actions, his betrayal of her family, her suspicions of him all torpedoed her senses.

Instead of yelling as she so badly wanted to, she tamed her tongue and in a steady voice asked, "How are you doing?"

George blinked as if still trying to figure out why she of all people was standing in his room. "I'm doing fine."

"Good. Good." She fiddled with the string on her SDSU hoodie. "I, um, came to see how you are."

"So you said." He studied her. She fidgeted under his eyes but didn't see leering licentiousness glowing from them, as was the norm.

"Yeah." Corrie sighed. "Look, George, I came to apologize." The words burned as they exited her windpipe, made their way through her vocal cords, and slid over her tongue.

"Apologize?" He sat up a little more and winced. "What could you possibly have to apologize to me for?"

Aaron rested his hand at the small of her back. His strength reinforced her own, and she took the plunge. "Because I hated you."

George's face grew purple. His bulging eyes bugged out even farther. Then he settled back in his bed and smoothed the bedsheets covering his ample stomach.

She waited for the swear words, waited for the insults, waited for the demands for her to leave his room. But they didn't come. Instead, a remorseful look crossed his bulgy face, making all the creases and wrinkles even deeper than usual.

"You have every right to," he said, a slight vibration in his voice. "Thank you, by the way, for saving my life. You risked your own life to save me."

She swallowed. "Why were you in the field?"

George dropped his gaze and for several seconds remained motionless. He cracked his knuckles. "I came to talk to you again about selling the farm."

"Then why were you in the middle of the field, surrounded by flames, almost dead from smoke inhalation?"

His face lost all color. "I saw him, Corrie. I saw the guy who set the fire. I thought I could stop him, stop the flames, but by the time I got there, he had disappeared, and the fire was spreading faster than I anticipated." He turned his eyes upon her, sheer terror coming from them. "I didn't set the fire. You have to believe me. I might be a terrible person—and I sure haven't treated you right—but I'd never do something like that."

She remained quiet. Her hatred for him had been so palpable, so tasty, really. She'd almost relished it. It had fed her, motivated her. But as she stood looking at him, all pitiful in his hospital bed, the hatred began trickling out from her heart. She couldn't truly hate a man as lonely and lost as George. She put herself in his beat-up work boots and realized what a miserable creature he was. Jealousy and envy had been his only friends.

He began fidgeting beneath her prolonged silence. His mouth opened and shut as if wanting to say something more. Finally, he spoke again. "Everybody thinks I set your machine shed on fire, too, don't they?" At her nod, he beat his fist against his mattress. "I didn't do it! I swear to God, I didn't set any fires. Why would I? I wanted your farm. Why would I purposely damage it?"

"Why do you want my farm so badly?"

His throat worked for several beats. "Because I didn't think you could handle it. Because after everything I did for your father and family, I thought I deserved a piece of the pie, and I didn't want the farm after you ran it into the ground." He looked away from her.

She squelched the black words on her tongue. At least George had used the past tense. She calmed herself down. "George, let's get one thing straight. I am never selling the farm. Ever. Not to you, not to anyone. Understand?"

A rare smile cracked George's lips. "You truly are your father's daughter, aren't you?"

Shoulders drooping, body tired and weak, she grabbed a chair and waited until Aaron pulled one up beside her before sitting down. "Yes, I am. Stubbornness is in the Lancaster genes." She rested her elbows on her knees and brought steepled fingers to her chin. "What did the man look like, the one who started the fire?"

George screwed his face up, his forehead fissuring into large crevices. "He was rather short, I thought. Stocky build, not fat, but you wouldn't want to meet him in a dark alley. I couldn't see his face real well because he was wearing a hat. I've already told the sheriff all this."

"I know. Thanks for repeating it." She stood. "I, uh, hope you recover soon."

He held his arm out, offering her his hand. "Corrie, thank you. And whenever they let me out of this darn place, I... I could help you out if needed."

She hesitantly shook his hand, remembering that one of the last times she'd touched him, it had been her fist to his nose. His hand felt clammy, and she released her hold as soon as was polite. "Just concentrate on getting better" was all she could bring herself to say.

Aaron guided her out of the room, his large hand on the small of her back again. Once they reached the hallway and shut the door behind them, she propped herself against the wall and rested her head on it.

"I don't know what to think," she said.

Aaron rubbed his thumb across her cheek. "If I didn't know any better, I'd say George has had a change of heart."

"Not lasting, I suppose." She chewed on her bottom lip.

"I'm not a betting man, babe, but if I were, I'd say the George we saw today might be the new one. Who knows, though." He shrugged. "Once back in his own habitat, he may revert to his mean, old, nasty ways."

She sagged into Aaron and breathed in his scent. "Let's go check in on Violet." She rubbed her temples then stopped. "Oh, have you called Luke about her?"

"No, why?" Aaron peered at her. "Should I?"

She patted his cheek. "Yes, you should, because I have a strange feeling that your brother is very interested in the well-being of our little friend."

His eyes twinkled. "Good. That means my competition is completely out of the game."

Corrie winked. "But that doesn't mean you've won." She turned on her heels, flicked her hair over her shoulder, and marched down the hallway, smiling to herself, delighted with the butterflies waltzing through her tummy.

Chapter Fifteen

Corrie nodded to the deputy sitting on her front porch next to a pot of dying pansies. She made a mental note to dump them and all the other potted flowers in the compost pile. Cool fall weather and chilly nights had done their work.

After entering the front door, she locked it, clutched the handgun still in the small table and the toothbrush lying on top, shoved both in the waistband of her pants, and moseyed into the kitchen, where Nathan and Nikki were eating cookies.

"Hey, you two. How was school?" Corrie nabbed a cookie from the nearly empty container, hoping her T-shirt kept the bulge of the revolver a secret.

Nathan rolled his eyes. "Same old, same old."

"You're just upset because you got sent to the principal's office today." Nikki shoved the rest of her cookie in her mouth and chewed triumphantly.

"What?" Corrie glared at him. "What did you do?"

"Why do you assume I did anything?"

"Spill it," she commanded, her hand at her waist. She sent a death glare to Nikki, who had begun opening her mouth. "And you zip it."

Nathan stared at his hands before looking up at her. "Some guy was pestering my girl. He wouldn't leave her alone and kept messing with her hair during band today. I told him to knock it off, but he called me a name and continued to bother her. That's when I grabbed his arm." Nathan rubbed his cheek. "He swung at me. Hit me hard. So, I swung back." A smile slithered across her brother's face. "I hit harder. Bloody nose, actually."

"Nathan!" she exclaimed.

"Well, he deserved it! He is such a jerk all the time and to everybody." He turned his face away.

The beginnings of a bruise blotched the assaulted cheek. Corrie wanted to be angry, knew she should be angry, but she understood all too well that a person's limits could only be pushed so far before they snapped. Pulling up a chair beside him, she looked at Nikki and signaled for her sister to leave. After pilfering two more cookies, Nikki left with a huff and a swing of her long blond hair.

Corrie placed her left hand on Nathan's arm. He flinched.

"Nathan." She hoped her calm voice would coax him out of his shell. "I totally understand why you punched that boy today."

"You do?" He stared at her. "You're not angry?"

She smiled and moved her hand from his arm to his cheek. The peach fuzz that met her hand caused a twinge of sadness to reverberate through her heart. "No, I'm not. Disappointed, yes." Seeing his face fall again, she gave his cheek a small pat. "Don't get all pouty on me again. You know the rules about physical violence."

"But you punched George."

She swallowed hard. "I did. And it wasn't right for me either. However, listen closely, okay? If you are sure someone is in danger or you feel truly threatened by someone, please feel free to use physical violence. I just don't think the band room was the time or place. Was it?"

"No," he grumbled, moving his head away from her touch. "It's just Casey is a complete idiot, and I thought he was hitting on my girl."

"Must be mating season," Corrie said under her breath. At Nathan's confused look, she shook her head. "Nothing. Just promise you won't punch somebody again unless your life or the life of someone is in danger."

"Okay." At her raised eyebrow, he mumbled, "I promise."

"Good. Now you can pack a lunch for Mom and Dad. They're at the hospital with Violet."

"Is something wrong?" His eyes darted to the seated deputy still posted in front of the patio door.

"Nope. She's going to have a baby."

The color dripped from his face. "Why don't you take the lunch to them?"

"Because I have a load of beans to take to the elevator, and you can't drive the truck. Besides, Aaron's combining, and Nikki can run the grain cart."

"Why can't Nikki take Mom and Dad their stuff?" Nathan heaved his arms across his chest.

"I thought you liked to drive?" She put the cookies back in the cupboard and poured herself a glass of milk.

At first, she couldn't hear him with his voice dropped so low. Finally, after asking him several times to repeat himself, he yelled, his voice squeaking, "What if she has the baby while I'm there?"

She couldn't laugh at her brother's blotchy face. She set her glass down and walked over to him and ruffled his hair. "She's not going to have it anytime soon. It will be a while. No baby is going to come out of her and run around the room chasing after you." Corrie couldn't help adding the last part. "Now, do as I asked." She gave one final pat to Nathan's head, went to the bottom of the steps and called for Nikki, then walked out of the house, handgun securely tucked into her jeans waistband.

CORRIE held her breath as she turned in to the elevator. Part of her expected Baxter's wrinkled face to pop up in her window and greet her with his smile. But she knew better. Baxter would never greet her again, would never ride on the truck's running board, chatting her ear off. Fighting the tears, she drove onto the scale, waited for the green light, then pulled off in the direction of the bin. After dumping, she drove back on the scale and waited for her ticket from the weigh house. A young man she didn't recognize bounded down the steps and hopped up on her running board. She wanted to scold him, tell him that wasn't his place, but she bit her tongue.

"Here you go, miss."

"Thanks," she mumbled as he hopped down and ran inside. She didn't even glance at the ticket before pushing the parking brake and shifting the semi into gear. Corrie nearly reached the end of the elevator driveway before the same young man ran her down, waving his arms.

He jumped back up on the running board and handed her a smudged and dirty envelope. He panted. "This is for you. Sorry. Some guy dropped it off this morning."

She took it and studied it. "Do you know who the man was?"

"No. But I'm new here myself."

"Thanks, uh...?"

"Brad. Brad Cunningham."

"Thanks, Brad. And welcome to Sandy."

He smiled again and hopped down. Checking to make sure no other trucks were behind her and waiting to pull onto the highway, she ripped open the envelope and plucked out a note scrawled in black ink. Her blood froze as she read the message: *Third time's the charm.*

She flipped the paper over, but empty whiteness met her eyes. She shook the envelope, but nothing came out. When she flipped the paper over again, those four words stared at her with their angry little letters.

Blood boiling and nerves firing at machine-gun pace, she drove to the field. The brown prairie zipped by her window.

What's next? He'd already destroyed one building, a combine, and a tractor, and burned a field of precious soybeans. He had probably watched the entire thing.

Corrie's skin tingled. He had. She just knew it. A pyromaniac loved any kind of flame, even one he didn't start himself. That was the turn-on, the arousal of it all. Set something on fire and watch it burn. *What if I start the next fire?* She thought of ways to bring a fox out of his den. This was, after all, her farm. She knew every nook and cranny, and she was determined to use every weapon in her arsenal to eradicate the fox stalking her family.

AARON TOOK HIS EYES off the bean header long enough to catch Corrie, sitting in the buddy seat next to him, playing with the chipped pink nail polish on her thumb. The color reminded him of her pink dress and matching heels that brought to mind an icy glass of lemonade. Soon, he would take her on a real date so she could wear that dress again, and he'd watch her brown hair fall in waves over her bare shoulders across from him at a candlelit table. He swallowed against the thirst burning his throat. This wasn't a thirst for lemonade.

"... set fire to the tree belt."

"You want to *what*?" Aaron heard his voice crack. He brought the combine to a stop and grasped her hands. The calluses on her palms scratched against his skin. "Are you crazy?"

"Excuse me?" Her head reared back.

He brought her hands up to his lips and kissed them. "Please don't take this the wrong way, but this idea of yours is, well, let's just say it isn't very good."

She yanked her hands free and crossed her arms over her chest. "What do you mean? We have to smoke him out. I'm tired of waiting. I'm tired of being on the defensive." She sighed. "You know very well from the note that he plans on attacking again."

He eyed the detested note, neatly folded on her lap. Bringing his hand up, he brushed aside an escaped strand of hair and planted a kiss on her forehead. He undid her ponytail, freeing her hair from its prison, then threaded his fingers through it and brought her lips to his. All the fear, all the anger came out in this kiss. He heard her sharp intake of breath then felt her reciprocate the passion and emotion. Aaron lost track of time. He didn't care, though. Hours in this woman's arms felt like only minutes. Soon his frustration and anger had fully vented itself, and he ended with a slight nibble on her bottom lip.

"Sorry," he murmured against her lips.

He felt her smile. "You should kiss me like that more often."

Aaron kissed her gently on the nose and released his hold on her. "You should talk to the sheriff about your idea." He engaged the machine, and the combine shuddered underneath him. As he flipped the switch to start the header, she gathered her hair back into its ponytail.

"My kiss convinced you?" she teased, her smile tantalizing.

"I'm sure you could persuade me to do anything with your set of skills." He loved the blush working its way up Corrie's face. "Seriously, you should talk to Steve about this." When she leaned against him, his heart dipped down to shake hands with his stomach. "At the end of the field here, I'll drop you off, okay? Text me, though, right away about what he says."

"Trying to get rid of me so soon?" She batted her eyelashes.

"Yup. You're nothing but a distraction. I bet I missed about an acre of beans back there."

She swatted his arm then curved her body against his again. The end of the field grew closer and closer. If it were up to him, he would never let her go.

CORRIE squirmed under Sheriff Steve's gaze, feeling like a naughty kindergartner caught snatching an extra cookie at snack time rather than an adult with a brilliant idea. The nagging suspicion that her idea was the opposite of brilliant crawled into her mind.

"Corrie, we've searched every inch of this farmyard. Nothing." Steve exhaled and blinked his different-colored eyes. "I'm not saying he's not out there, but I don't see how your idea will work. What do you have around here to start on fire?"

"The tree line." She pointed behind him toward the rows of trees.

"You can't be serious!"

"Very, Steve. Listen, please. I'm tired of being the mouse in this dangerous game. We don't know when or where he'll strike, so I say we choose. I'm assuming he's a moth that can't resist a good flame."

"But your tree line. Are you willing to destroy it? What happens if we can't stop it and it destroys all your equipment with it? We can't remove it because it would be a major red flag to this guy. He'd know something's up."

She leaned on one of the porch railings and studied the tree line in question. Cottonwood, elm, and maple trees, dotted by the occasional scrubby-looking chokecherry tree almost bare of leaves, stood stark and naked before the setting sun. Rays of gold and red stretched throughout the expanse as if setting the trees alight with flame. Shivering with the idea of actually setting her beloved trees on fire, she imagined the hands of her great-great-grandparents planting every infant tree. In one fell swoop, she would destroy them.

Shaking her head, she turned to Steve. "You're right. I can't. We'll just have to keep watch." She rested her head against a porch railing. "I'm just tired. I'm tired of watching over my shoulder. I'm tired of worrying about my family."

"We'll do everything in our power to make sure we catch this guy. Do you have any idea where he could be besides this farm?"

"I haven't the faintest idea. I'll keep thinking, though." She pushed away from the railing. "I've got to get back to the field. My parents and Nathan are still with Violet at the hospital, and Nikki will be out in the field with me."

"Stay safe and don't do anything stupid."

"Who, me?" She infused an innocent squeak to her voice.

The sheriff cocked an eyebrow at her and sauntered off the porch toward a deputy posted around the corner. She walked to her pickup and couldn't help peering in the back seat before hopping in. Sighing, she drove off, carefully inspecting the tree line for signs of a hidden adversary the entire length of the driveway.

BLANK, SHARKLIKE EYES glowed at Corrie from the shadows of a metal skeleton. Hidden within the iron innards, the eyes stared, unblinking, until the orbs glowed red and orange with tongues of fire. She opened her mouth to scream, but the sound never came. It curled within her mouth like vapor and filled her with a horrible sound only she could hear. The eyes glowed hotter, hotter, until Corrie's skin began to soften and slip. Then they spoke her name. "Corrie."

She plugged her ears to her name, to her scream.

"Corrie."

She sat upright in the semi seat, her neck stiff and sore from an impromptu nap, her chest heaving.

"Corrie!" Aaron's voice crackled over the radio.

She shook the echoing scream from her head and grabbed the receiver. "Yes?"

"Are you okay?"

"Yeah. Just peachy." Corrie released the button and ran the receiver across her forehead, trying to make sense of her dream. The iron skeleton must have been the windmill. She'd only had pleasant, albeit forbidden, dreams of her favorite childhood haunt. She shivered. Those empty eyes were the eyes of a killer. A chill swept through her, and she gasped. *The windmill.*

"It's the windmill," she croaked into the radio.

"What?" Aaron replied. "What's wrong with the windmill?"

"Nothing's wrong with it. That's where he's been hiding." She whipped out the cell phone from the pocket of her hoodie and dialed the sheriff. Drumming her fingers on the steering wheel, she waited for him to pick up. On the fourth ring, he did.

"Steve." She panted into the phone, breathless over her epiphany. "It's the windmill."

"What is?"

Corrie rolled her eyes. "He's at the windmill. Where else could he be so well hidden yet know everything that's going on? That windmill is about thirty feet high. He could see the whole farm from its vantage point."

A slight pause ensued as the sheriff seemed to register the information. "We'll look. Is there a place at the base, though, where he'd be hiding?"

"The base is so overgrown with weeds, it's essentially its own thicket. But there is a watering trough where the water used to be pumped into, and not too far from the windmill is an old dugout." She chewed her bottom lip. "It has to be all fallen in, though. I never went in it as a kid. Too scared of it collapsing on me."

"Thanks for the info. I'll keep you posted."

She hung up and dialed her parents, updating them. In return, her mother brought her up to speed on Violet's progression.

A baby in a few hours. Corrie placed her phone in her hoodie pouch. A seed of panic sprouted inside her and sent tendrils throughout her body. It was all too much to bear. *How much more can I handle before breaking in half?* She could feel herself bending more and more each day. She knew the balance in the farm account. The farm loan had to be paid off very soon. The consequences of defaulting on the loan—unthinkable.

But it wasn't her. She hadn't failed. She had an enemy. An enemy who wanted to destroy her. The cold bite of steel in her waistband reminded her of the handgun she carried. A doubt surfaced. *Would I—no, could I—look someone in the eyes and pull the trigger?* Closing her eyes, she brought back the dead, vacant eyes from her dream. In the middle of them, two fires raged, each destroying an integral part of her farm.

Chapter Sixteen

Corrie fell into her bed, a moan escaping her lips. She grasped her phone, several text messages lighting up the screen.

From Mom: *It's a girl! Violet and baby are doing great. Will keep you posted. Nathan will drive back with Dad. Love you.*

From Aaron: *Hey, babe. Thinking about you. Sleep tight. See you in the morning.*

From Steve: *Corrie, we found supplies and food at the windmill. No sign of him, though. There's an emergency in Sweetwater. I have to call back a few of my deputies from your farm. Will leave two.*

Corrie closed her eyes. Knowing her father, sister, and brother were home safe and tucked in their beds filled her with little comfort. Leaving only two deputies at the farm gave her enemy the chance he needed. Whatever was going to happen would happen tonight. In spite of the exhaustion gnawing at her bones, she stumbled out of bed and slipped on a clean pair of jeans and a T-shirt. She pulled her sweatshirt over her head, grabbed the gun off her nightstand, and made her way downstairs, suddenly afraid of the house she'd grown up in. The familiar shadows and creaks were no longer old friends—they were strangers, drifting in and out of her piqued senses.

She paused at the kitchen doorway. The entire room looked eerie, as if a horror-movie production crew had set up the lighting. A reddish haze permeated the space, and seconds passed as she computed the new environment.

Fire. But it wasn't in the house.

She stepped into the kitchen and to the glass patio doors facing the garden, the willow tree with the tire swing, and the tree line bordering the farmyard on the west side.

"Dear God," she whispered. "Please don't let this be happening. Please," she begged in prayer, but nothing changed. Flames reached into the sky, bursting and exploding as the hungry fire gulped down tree after tree. Without thinking, she yanked open the porch door and tripped over the body of a deputy. Swallowing a scream, she dropped next to the man and felt for a pulse. A weak one drummed against her fingers. She gagged against the smell coming off the man's uniform. She'd smelled that scent so often, but panic blinded her to everything but fight or flight. No sight of the other deputy. Her throat closed. *Now is not the time to be allergic to fear.* Dialing 911, she reached for the handgun in the waistband of her jeans and wrapped her palm around it, her index finger placed on the trigger guard.

"911, what's your emergency?"

"This is Corrie Lancaster, and there's a fire on my farm. Again." She swallowed against the smoke in the air, nearly gagging on it. "Come quickly, please."

After giving the address, she hung up her phone and tucked it in the back pocket of her jeans. Holding the gun with both hands, she surveyed the area, inching closer to the fire roaring in its desire to consume everything in its path.

"Not today," she growled. Her beloved willow stood there, its dried tentacles burning in the night as if a million red fireflies had landed upon its droopy branches, fluttering and flapping their tiny, angry wings. She couldn't save the fire-eaten tree line, but she could save her beloved tree. Racing back a few paces to the edge of the garden, she scoured the ground for the garden hose, yanked at it with one hand, and ran to her tree.

"Crap!" she yelled as the water hose stayed limp in her hands. Stashing the gun in the waistband of her jeans, she sprinted in the dark, made her way to the house, turned on the faucet, and raced back to the hose end. Water sprayed from the nozzle and hissed as it hit the tiny flames encircling each willow branch. Smoke belched forth from the tree as water engulfed and suffocated the tiny flames.

She clenched her teeth and kept spraying the tree, wishing she could use the garden hose to put out the fire raging beyond her reach.

"You like my work, don't you?"

She whirled around and faced her enemy—Frank. His teeth flashed in a sudden grin. She grappled for the gun stuck in her pants. It wasn't there. *No, God, no. Stupid, stupid!*

"Not really." How calm she sounded. "I prefer my fires chained to a firepit." She needed to find the gun. She moved a step closer and prayed he wouldn't see her foot sweep out to feel for her weapon.

"That's too bad." He pulled out a box of matches. "Because I have a special show for you." He was startlingly handsome. Corrie could see how a woman could fall for that face. The face of an angel before he plummeted from the heights of heaven to the depths of hell.

She sniffed.

"I wondered when you'd smell it," he purred. Then he struck a match and let it burn down to his fingertips, where it sputtered and died against his skin. "Gasoline."

Corrie swallowed at the rising bile. She took another step and swept out her foot. Nothing.

"Want to get a good seat, I see? Well, my shows are on fire." He laughed. "Tough crowd. Critics of my work are usually haters. I've grown a thick skin." As if to prove his point, he lit another match and let it burn. "Can you guess where the gasoline will lead my fire?"

She couldn't speak, but her eyes betrayed her answer.

"Your precious home. And family, too, of course. All tucked in safe and sound. Am I right?"

The gun. She had to find it. Had to stop him from destroying the essence of her existence.

He lit a match. "Ready?"

Knowing he had no intention of letting it burn out in his hand again, she wailed a warrior's cry and pile-drove her body into his. Her forehead smashed into his nose, and her breath whooshed out of her as she landed on him. Stunned by the force, she was helpless when he brought his legs up and kicked her in the stomach, launching her backward to crunch on the ground. And on something metallic.

He swiped at the blood flowing from his nose. "You stupid little bit—"

Panting, she whipped the gun from the ground and aimed the barrel directly at his chest. All the peripheral commotion dimmed. Only the man in front of her mattered. His black eyes blinked in surprise but for only a second before they taunted her, dared her to pull the trigger. Her finger begged her to comply.

He never broke eye contact and jiggled the box of matches he still clutched. "See, that's what people don't understand about fire. Fire doesn't like to be tied up. It likes to be free."

"Well, aren't you a kind and considerate person." Her fingers twisted tighter on the gun. "Why don't you go give it a big hug and kiss right now, then? I'm sure it would love to show you its appreciation."

His laugh ripped through Corrie. He pulled another match from the box. "All in good time. But first, you have something of mine, and I'd like it back."

Corrie's heart fell. He didn't seem to even notice the gun pointing directly at his chest. He was freaking crazy. "If you're talking about Violet, she left."

"You're not a very good liar, are you? Don't worry. When she gets back from the hospital with our useless baby, I'm sure you'll hand her over."

"Shut up!" Corrie hissed and pointed the gun at his head.

He stroked the match like a lover. "You see, you have a choice. Your family or Violet? There is so much gasoline on your house, there will be no chance to save your dad and siblings. And that poor deputy?" He jerked his head at the still-prone officer. "He's practically doused in it. You want him to die too?"

Corrie had never wished someone to hell before until now. She steadied her gun, her finger itching to pet the trigger. "You cannot have Violet."

He struck another match. "You have no idea the kind of woman you've been letting hole up in your house. She's nothing but a—"

She aimed the gun slightly to the left of Frank's head and pulled the trigger. The gun jumped in her hand, and the bullet whizzed past his ear. He cursed and fell on his stomach, the match winking out before hitting the tributary of gasoline leading to the house. A string of insults and four-letter words spewed from his mouth. After months of experience with George, she didn't bat an eyelash. Earlier, she had questioned whether she could look a man in the face and bring his life to an end. She had her answer now. Hell yes. A sense of calm eased her tremors, her breathing slowed, her eyesight sharpened, and her tongue honed with razor-like efficiency.

"Now, Frank, I'll be honest with you," she crooned as he struggled to his feet. "When I was just twelve years old, I won a target-shooting contest. And not to freak you out or anything, but I only got better with time. So, here's the deal. If you run, I can and will shoot you, hitting you with dead accuracy."

He scoffed, "You couldn't shoot me."

"What is it with the male chauvinist pigs in my life?" She tsked. "First George, now you. Trust me when I say this, Frank. I'm not the type of female you seem to think all women are. Besides"—a movement stalked behind him—"I'm not sure I'll have to shoot you."

He opened his mouth, and it stayed that way as a hoe handle came crashing down on his skull.

"Dad!" Corrie pocketed her gun and ran to her father, who had stumbled and gone down next to Frank. "Dad? Are you okay?" She reached her father and helped him up, his feet struggling to find steady ground.

Fire engines blared their way down the highway parallel to the farm. In a minute or two, they would be there, battling the flames still gorging on the feast of trees.

"I'm okay," Jake mumbled, leaning heavily upon her. "You okay?"

She glanced at Frank, lying prone on the ground. "Yeah. I'm okay." She let out a shaky laugh. "You did well, Dad."

He nodded. "My farm too."

Fire trucks and two ambulances, along with the sheriff's car, halted in front of the fire. The firemen bolted into action.

"Steve," Corrie hollered and pointed at the house. She sprinted over to the deputy, just now coming to.

Steve knelt beside the man and rested his hand on the officer's badge for a second. "Stay still, Jackson. Wait for the paramedics."

The deputy groaned and succumbed to unconsciousness again.

The same female paramedic from before ran over, two other EMTs bringing up the rear with a gurney and medical bags. "Fancy meeting you here."

Corrie couldn't help grinning. "Do I get a prize or something?"

"Paramedic humor. I like it." She began assessing the deputy. "Name's Christy. Figured you could just ask for me by name next time."

Christy barked orders to her colleagues and within minutes had the unconscious officer on a gurney and loaded into the ambulance. The other deputy, apparently knocked out on the front porch, had weathered the attack better and limped into the back of the ambulance before it sped out of the yard.

Standing tall, Corrie took in the organized chaos, wishing for Aaron's comforting and strong presence. Many times, she whipped out her phone to text him only to put it back again. *You promised.* Her conscience was right. For once. She whipped off a quick text, prayed it woke him up, and trudged back to the lifeless body of Frank. Her father, still brandishing the hoe, stood guard.

"I'm so sorry, Corrie." Steve massaged his neck. "I never figured he'd take out both my deputies." He toed Frank's body. The man moaned. "He's not dead?"

Corrie snickered at the disappointment edging the sheriff's voice. "No, but he'll have one whopper of a headache when he wakes up." She winked at her dad.

Steve rolled Frank over, brought Frank's arms behind his back, and handcuffed him. Straightening up, Steve nodded toward the fire hissing and spitting against the water. "They'll have it out soon. It shouldn't get to your equipment."

Her siblings ran out of the house and toward her, cutting off her reply. She hugged them to her and reassured them everything would be okay. Nathan and Nikki jumped from Frank's unconscious form.

"Don't worry about him. Dad knocked him out cold."

"Really?" Nathan's face lit, and he turned his gaze toward his father. "That's totally cool!"

Corrie rolled her eyes and tousled Nathan's bedhead hair. "Please take Nikki and Dad inside."

Nathan grasped his father's arm while Nikki took Jake's other side. Jake supported himself against his son, and all three trudged to the patio door. At a signal from Steve, the second ambulance pulled up. Corrie moved aside while medics approached Frank. Steve uncuffed him, and the medics rolled him over, placed him on the gurney, and wheeled him to the awaiting ambulance after Steve recuffed their patient to the gurney.

"You going to be okay?" Steve placed a hand on her forearm.

Corrie forced a smile. Her stomach hurt from being horse-kicked by a crazy wackadoo, and her head felt numb. "Yeah. I'll be okay."

"You and your dad did most of the heavy lifting. I'll be by to-morrow to get a statement from both of you. You get some rest." He sauntered off, stopping periodically to shake hands with someone or slap someone else's shoulder on his way to his car. In a few minutes, both the ambulance carrying Frank and the sheriff's car were noth-ing but fading taillights.

Suddenly weary, she sank to the ground, hugged her knees to her chest, and observed the last of the fire dancing and writhing. Once it was out, smoke billowed in plumes into the night sky, obliterating the stars and snuffing out the moonlight. The wind, in her favor the entire evening, carried most of the smoke away from the farm, over the highway, letting it dissipate over dried soybean, corn, and sun-flower fields.

A hand caressed her shoulder, and she jumped, letting out a screech.

"It's just me," Aaron crooned in her ear as he sat next to her. "Are you okay?"

Melting into a puddle of tears, she curved into him and wept. She didn't know what exactly he whispered and murmured in her ear, but it didn't matter. All that mattered was that he was there.

"I'm sorry I wasn't here. I didn't know anything about it until my dad woke me up and I saw your text." Aaron wiped away the tears streaking down her cheeks. "I should have been here, protecting you."

Smiling through the tears, she whispered, "Maybe you can make that your full-time job." She curled into him. "Might be the toughest job you've ever had."

"I like a challenge," he whispered back, bringing his lips to her forehead. "You must be exhausted. Let me help you in the house."

She accepted his offered hand and held it all the way to the house, where the kitchen light burned brightly. The room was empty, though, and she sank into one of the kitchen chairs. He poured her a glass of water and sat next to her, encouraging her to drink it. She reached into her waistband, pulled out the handgun, and plopped it on the table.

"Whoa! I like a girl who packs some heat."

She blushed at his wink and ducked her head. "I would have shot him, I think." She licked her dry lips. "I was so calm and so steady." She lifted her right hand, shaking and trembling. "Now look at me. I can hardly hold a glass of water without spilling some on myself."

"Yeah, you're probably right, but I also know you would have only done so if you felt you had no other option. You did the right thing." He grasped her shaking hands and rubbed his thumb along the backs of them. "I'm very proud of you. You are the strongest person I know. Don't you ever doubt it."

She put her head on his shoulder and soaked in his strength. She certainly didn't feel very strong. She felt like a spaghetti noodle boiled a bit too long. "My willow tree is gone." She held her breath against a fresh onslaught of tears.

Aaron didn't say a thing. He grabbed her, lifted her up, and sat her on his lap. Cradling her, he rested his face in her hair and sat like that for what seemed like hours. Glorious hours.

She allowed the tears to come. Allowed them to cleanse away the debris left in Frank's wake. Before she wanted to, Aaron stood up, placing her on her feet. Without a word, he guided her up to her room.

"Good night," he whispered, giving her a gentle kiss on her lips. "I'll see you in the morning. Don't worry about combining. I'll take care of it."

She waited to shut her door until the front door clicked closed. Without a single thought, she undressed, slipped on her pajamas, and fell into bed.

TWO days after the fire, Corrie finally had the guts to inspect the damage. A quarter of the tree line, black and crispy, braced against the chilly autumn wind whistling through the gaps and holes. The skeletal remains of tree bodies stood as a silent reminder of the havoc revenge could wreak upon its victims. She hugged her arms tighter around her stomach and ambled closer. Her work boots crunched over burned debris. The acrid smell of scorched wood stung her nose, and she sneezed.

She hadn't been brave enough to face her willow tree and tire swing. Rather, she'd hidden her face from it as she approached the tree line. The time had come, though, and she steeled herself for the shock of seeing her childhood sanctuary destroyed.

Taking a deep breath, she turned then almost fainted. She blinked, rubbed her eyes, and stared at the empty spot where a tree used to be. A giant stump jutted out from the ground, the only reminder that a tree once stood there. Blackened grass circled the stump, and she shivered.

Her footsteps heavy, she strode into the circle, the fire's hardened black ghosts exploding under her feet. When she reached the stump, she sat upon it and remained motionless, staring into the distance across the pastureland behind the house. The windmill peeked over the tree belt behind the property.

Bowing her head, she prayed. It had been a while since she had, and it felt good to talk to her Lord again. Even though she'd had much taken from her, she still had much, including her family. She brought her fears for the future before the throne of God. A peace washed over her. She opened her eyes and surveyed her farm. God never promised her a perfect future, but he did promise he would be there when times got tough. With a renewed soul, she left the fragment of her childhood behind. She didn't need it anymore. A secret smile skipped across her lips. Her next safe haven just happened to drive onto her farm.

AARON'S heart clenched as Corrie walked away from the stump of her tree. Had he done the right thing? Although too late to question his actions, he prayed she would forgive him when she understood. Putting that to the back of his mind, he hopped out of his truck and made his way to where she waited with a huge smile.

"Hey." She grabbed his hand.

"Straw." He enveloped her in a hug. He released her and studied her face. "You look absolutely beautiful this morning."

She beamed at him, her eyes shining. Their brown depths, once murky with all that life had thrown at her, sparkled and shimmered in the morning sunshine. The freckles under her eyes seemed to dance as she smiled.

"Thank you. You're not looking too bad yourself this fine morning." She pulled him inside the house. "I've got a surprise for you. But you must be very quiet."

He already knew—courtesy of his brother, who'd called him—but he played along and followed her, enjoying the way she walked, tall and proud, afraid of nothing. He wanted to kiss her lips when she held a finger up to them as they entered. Instead, he made the gesture back, reassuring her of his compliance with stealth and catlike motions. She gestured into the living room, and he peeked around the corner.

Violet sat in the rocking chair, cuddling a bundle of pink. He could barely make out the fluffy little head poking through the blanket. Not wanting to disturb the new mother, he attempted to un-peek around the corner. But Violet's head popped up, and she grinned when her eyes met his.

"Aaron," Violet whispered, "how good to see you." She jerked her head to the loveseat next to the rocking chair. "Please, come in."

He slipped off his shoes and walked in, followed by Corrie still clutching his hand. "Hey, Violet." He perched on the edge of the small couch. "Congratulations."

Her lips twitched up, and she'd never looked so beautiful. Her cheeks took on a rosy glow, and despite her obvious exhaustion, her eyes twinkled with a delight he hadn't seen before. "Do you want to hold her?"

He hesitated, unsure he wouldn't smoosh the poor thing to pieces in his giant hands. At Corrie's nudge, he nodded and reached for the baby, who gave a tiny squeak as Violet tucked the swaddled bundle in his awaiting hands. He brought the baby to his chest, looked down at the pink face, scrunched in sleep, and felt a tug on his heart. When he brought his lips to the top of her head, the fluffy hair tickled his lips.

"What's her name?" he whispered.

"Iris." Violet's smile widened. "It means 'rainbow.' Kind of like the rainbow after the world got a fresh start." She gazed at her daughter, nestled against his chest. "She's mine."

"That is a beautiful name." He turned to Corrie. "You want to hold her?"

She chuckled. "I've been holding her since five this morning. This little girl doesn't know what sleeping in means. You can keep spoiling her. I'll go help Mom with lunch." She patted his knee, bent over and gave Iris a kiss on her head, and walked out, leaving him alone with Violet.

"So." He cleared his throat. "Has Luke stopped by yet?" From the color exploding on her cheeks, he'd asked the wrong question. "I, uh, well, he said he was going to, so I, uh, just wanted to know..." His voice petered out.

She fiddled with the hospital bracelet still circling her wrist. "No, he hasn't. I was hoping he'd stop by, but I understand he's a busy man."

He's an idiot. "I'm sure he'll stop by. Don't worry." Aaron focused on the baby sleeping on his chest. "Why don't you go get some rest? I can hold her for a while."

Violet smiled her thanks and gave her daughter a peck on the tip of her petite nose before walking out.

He touched her clenched hand with his finger and jumped a little when the tiny fingers grasped his. "You've got quite a grip, don't you, little one?"

Iris hiccupped in her sleep, and for a few seconds, her eyes opened, revealing dark-blue eyes.

"Well." He patted her and whispered, "What do I do with you now?"

Her lips pursed, and a tiny sigh escaped them. Thankful it wasn't a cry, he double-checked to ensure he was entirely alone and started singing "Twinkle, Twinkle Little Star" to his little audience. He watched, fascinated, as Iris's eyes drooped shut again, her mouth still working and pursing in her sleep.

"I didn't know you had such a good voice," Corrie murmured from the doorway.

A blush tingled its way up his face. "I was just singing her to sleep. That's all."

"I think it was precious." Corrie sauntered across the living room and kissed his lips. "I think you'll make a great father someday."

"Probably adequate at best," he teased, trying to ease the sudden tightness in his chest. He studied Corrie as she stood in front of him. Her eyes watched him, as if she were trying to figure out his thoughts. He knew exactly what he was thinking and precisely what he wanted. "I should go and start combining. I think we're almost done."

"That's great. I'll be out in about an hour to run the truck in."

"Actually, you don't need to. I've had people knocking down my door to help with your remaining fields." He chuckled at the confusion mottling her face. "By tomorrow, all your beans will be in."

"That's not possible. I have, like, five hundred acres left."

"You hired Superman, remember? Besides, no one would take no for an answer, so you have nothing to worry about."

"B-but... I..." She stopped, her mouth opening and closing. "I can't pay them."

"They don't want payment. They are neighbors who want to help, no strings attached."

Her forehead began to furrow.

"And no, they don't think you can't handle it just because you're a girl." He ignored the glare sent in his direction and kissed her still-furrowed brow. "Relax. Take care of your friend. I'll make sure everything's taken care of." Aaron handed her the baby, trailed an index finger down Corrie's cheek, and ended its journey with a little tap to her chin. "Let me take you out. Away from it all. Well, as far as Mabel's, anyway."

"But the combining?"

"I told you, I have men talking care of that. It's time someone took care of you." He dropped his lips to where they were only a breath away from hers. "I'll be by at six." He kissed her bottom lip.

High on kisses, he dang near skipped from the house to his pickup. He looked in the back at the remains of Corrie's willow. It was time to create a new beginning for her tree. But first, a date.

Chapter Seventeen

Corrie smacked her lips and wiped a smudge of maroon lipstick from the indent in her top lip. Applying a touch more blush to her cheeks, she studied herself in the mirror. It was as good as it was going to get. Not normally a jealous person, she wished she had her sister's perfect complexion. She dotted concealer over a pimple that had sprouted the night before, hoping Aaron wouldn't notice it.

A knock on her door interrupted her beauty regimen. Violet peeked around the door. "Can I come in?"

"As long as you give me your honest opinion." Corrie stood and smoothed out the dress she'd chosen for the evening, disregarding the twenty other dresses strewn about her room, outcasts of her closet.

"Oh my." Violet sucked in a breath. "Teal is your color."

"You think so? I can always change."

"Don't you dare. Aaron will melt when he sees you." Violet touched the dress's lace sleeves. "It's so delicate and fine." Longing lit in her eyes.

"I know I'm ten times your size—"

"Are not!" Violet scolded, smacking Corrie's arm lightly.

"Um, yeah. Me size ten, you size zero."

"Two, to be exact."

Corrie rolled her eyes. "Anyway, as I was going to say, Mary is an excellent seamstress. Did you want to take some of my dresses and see if she can alter them to fit you?"

Violet's eyes shimmered. "Oh, I couldn't ask that of you."

"You didn't. I'm giving them to you." Corrie swept her arm toward the dresses lying dejected on every available surface. "See all these? I never wear them. Pick any you want, and we'll see if we can have Mary work her magic."

"I don't know how to thank you."

Corrie shrugged. "That's just what sisters do." She gasped when Violet's arms encircled her in a bear hug.

After Violet released her, Corrie swiped a finger under her eyes. "I'll have to redo my mascara now."

Violet picked up a cream-colored wrap dress. Swirls of pink and purple embroidered the skirt in loops and spirals. She held it to her face. The sound of Iris crying and the doorbell ringing had them staring at each other before they took action.

Violet snatched the dress and left the room, leaving Corrie standing stock-still in the middle of her bedroom. Butterflies—no, they were more the size of sparrows—darted and swirled in her stomach. Aaron's voice sailed up the steps. She smoothed her hands down the dress, loving the way the soft material moved and hugged her body. After slipping on a pair of silver heels, she marched out of her room and down the steps.

Goodness gracious! Aaron looked yummy in his gray pinstripe suit. The mint-green shirt brought out the color of his eyes, and she couldn't imagine staring at anything else all evening. She placed a hand over her stomach to shush the butterflies and sparrows and whatever else was making her insides squishy. His gaze raked her and left her mouth dry and her knees weak.

"Hi." She should say something else, but her tongue had stopped working, and her synapses refused to fire correctly.

Aaron approached and enfolded her hands in his. "You look absolutely stunning." Laying a kiss on her lips, he played with a curl she'd so painstakingly created. When his finger brushed her collarbone, she sucked in a sharp breath.

She playfully pushed him away. "You don't look so bad yourself, mister."

"Yeah, I've been told I clean up pretty good."

She fingered his crew cut. "I like the new style."

"You don't miss the shaggy-dog look?"

She would miss playing with the curls at the back of his neck. She chewed on her lip then stopped herself before she gnawed off her lipstick. "I think you look sophisticated and—"

"Not so old," Nathan piped up from the kitchen doorway. A cookie dangled from one hand, and a glass of milk tipped in the other.

Aaron narrowed his eyes. "Don't you have somewhere to be? Like getting your butt whooped by your sister in Monopoly?"

"Preach it!" Nikki yelled from the kitchen. "Come on, sissy pants. I need to bankrupt you so I can call Xavier."

"Stupid name, anyhow," Nathan mumbled as he saluted them with his half-eaten cookie and trudged into the kitchen.

Corrie crinkled her nose. "Sorry. I don't normally claim them. My parents found them on the side of the road."

"Understandable. I don't claim Luke either." He slipped her black peacoat on her, his fingers caressing the lace covering her arms.

Goosebumps exploded on her skin as she waltzed out into the evening. Crisp air met her lungs. "I really think October is the best month ever."

He kissed her lips. "Because you were born in it."

"That was *the* worst pickup line I've heard in a long time."

"Really?" He cocked his head to the side. "That bad, huh?"

She patted his cheek and held his hand as they headed to his truck. "That's okay. Lucky for you, I'm a sucker for cheesy lines."

"In that case, do you like water?" He shut her door, walked around the front, and hopped in.

"Um, yeah."

"Then you already like seventy-five percent of me."

She snorted. "What about the other twenty-five percent of you? How do I feel about that?"

"Probably tolerate at best." He reached over and tucked another curl behind her ears.

She slapped his hand away. "Pay attention to the road. I can't enjoy cheese buttons if I'm dead."

"Or my stunning personality either."

"True." She linked fingers with him as they drove through the night toward the twinkling town lights.

AARON'S SKIN TINGLED as Corrie slid her hand into his. Fear warred with anticipation and excitement as Sandy came into view. "I never appreciated this place till I moved away."

"Me either. It's so good to be back."

"You know that we'll be the talk of the town tomorrow."

Corrie winked at him. "So let's give them something to talk about."

Nothing clever came to him. His flirt machine experienced a breakdown, and he knew he would be a bumbling fool most of the night. After parallel parking his truck in front of Mabel's, he made up for the deficit by pulling her to him for a kiss.

She reached up and swiped her thumb over his lips. "You got a little lipstick on you," she whispered, her minty breath and perfume intoxicating him. "Looks good on you."

Heat exploded in his core. "Any interest in skipping dinner?"

She bit her lip. "Tempting. But my stomach would never forgive me. Besides, I can smell the fried chicken from here."

Helping her out of the truck, he looped his arm around her. Jingle bells announced their arrival when he opened the glass door. The restaurant, big enough to comfortably sit forty people, grew silent. Every occupant swiveled and stared, eyeing them with curiosity. Placing a hand on the small of her back, he led her through the maze of tables and chairs to the far corner, where a white linen–draped table sat unoccupied, a crystal vase exploding with roses and delicate white baby's breath.

She fingered the crimson rose petals. "They're beautiful, Aaron. Thank you."

"So are you," he murmured in her ear as he pulled her chair out for her.

"Well, you two lovebirds sure make a sight for sore eyes."

Aaron's shoulder blades touched at Mabel's resounding greeting. He plastered on a smile as the dumpling-shaped woman waddled to their table. With her tagged along the scents of dough, yeast, butter, and fried goodness.

"Good evening, Mabel. The table looks great."

Mabel nudged Corrie's arm. "This man wouldn't quit pestering me about tonight. Actually wanted me to shut down the place so you two could have it all to yourselves. Imagine that!"

He prayed. Prayed a hole the size of one of Mabel's cheese buttons would swallow him alive into the mysterious underbelly of the ancient building. Feeling the curious bystanders boring holes into his body, he shifted his chair slightly and concentrated on Corrie's face. Her brown eyes sparkled in the candlelight he'd paid Mabel an extra five dollars to provide. But it was the best five dollars he'd ever spent. His fingers begged to wrap her curled tendrils around them. Her laugh made his heart jump. His rapt audience disappeared. The curious eyes didn't matter. All that mattered was Corrie.

Mabel bopped him on the head with a pen. He blinked and stared at the offender.

"Now, Mabel, was that really necessary?"

"It is when I've asked you six times what you'd like to drink."

"Lemonade." He licked his lips and glanced at Corrie. "Yeah, I've been wanting that for a long time now."

Mabel cocked her head to the side and studied him for a beat. "Sure. So, one lemonade and one Pepsi for the lovers."

"Does she have to be so loud?" muttered Corrie as Mabel stalked away, taking with her their dignity and privacy.

"I'm thinking her volume button is stuck on maximum."

"Yeah, just like this place is stuck in the seventies. It's a hopeless cause." She tapped her fork on the edge of the table. "Actually, I'm thinking this place is a time capsule for every decade from the twenties. Who has black Formica tabletops, confetti-colored floor tiles, and barstools the color of a rotten orange?"

"Mabel's."

"It's the perfect ambiance, really, for a first date." Her lips twitched.

"Company's pretty good, though, I hear."

She shrugged, and one side of her mouth dipped. "So, that's the word on the street? Not what I heard."

He leaned forward, plucked a rose, and played the velvety petals down her cheek. "What'd you hear?"

"That it's the best in the state. I look forward to a five-star experience."

"It's pretty epic. Kind of like my hired-man proficiency. Top-notch."

She reached across the table and intertwined her fingers through his. "Speaking of which, you never cashed the check I gave you, did you?"

"Nope."

"You should."

"You're right. But I'm not going to."

Pink colored her cheekbones. "You're stubborn."

"Pot calling the kettle black?" His heart tripped over itself at her giggle. He squeezed her hand. "I'm not interested in your money, Corrie. I'm only interested in your heart."

"Now, that's a pickup line." Her eyes twinkled at him. "I believe payment has been delivered, then." She took a sip from her water glass. "I can't believe you even put up with me after my breakdown after Baxter died. Thank you. Thank you for not giving up on me and giving me a second chance."

"You left me with no choice. I was putty in your hands the moment I saw you swinging on your tire swing." He paused as Mabel set their drinks and side salads in front of them. "Thanks." He brought the lemonade to his lips. The sweetness coated his tongue and trickled down his throat. It was worth the wait. Just like the beautiful woman across from him. "Have you been to Baxter's grave yet?"

Her face whitened. "I'm scared."

"I can go with you, if you want." He traced the veins on the back of her hand. "You don't have to do everything on your own."

"I know." She ducked her head and studied the blue cloth napkin scrunched in her hand. "I think this is something I need to do alone, though."

"Just let me know if you need me, okay? I will always be here for you." And after gazing into her eyes and seeing into her soul, he promised himself that he would never leave her side.

SHERBET-COLORED WASHBOARD clouds blanketed the morning sky as Corrie parked her truck in front of the cemetery. Moving through the gate, she stepped gingerly over dew-covered grass. Baxter's grave scarred the earth. No grass covered his final resting place, and no pretty suncatcher dangled from a shepherd's staff like that of his neighbor Gladys Bowman's.

Ignoring the wet grass, Corrie sat cross-legged next to the mound of dirt and plucked a weed that had dared to grow. She'd picked a few wild sunflowers from the ditch that very morning, and she placed them on the tombstone he shared with his beloved wife. *Terrance Baxter: husband, father, grandfather* shared the same space as *Annie Marie Baxter: wife, mother, grandmother*. A John Deere combine and a stalk of wheat for each of his children were engraved in the smooth gray marble on his side of the stone.

"Hey, Baxter." She traced the wheat stalks. "I, ah, had a date last night. I know you always rooted for Luke, but Aaron kind of stole my heart."

An inquisitive prairie dog stuck its head out of a hole and chattered at her from a distance. Knowing Baxter used to shoot the things, she smiled at the memory of him telling how, as a boy, they would collect the tails and keep them in a tin can to turn in to the Game, Fish, and Parks department for money.

"I miss you, you know. There's a new kid at the elevator. He seems to think he can hop up on my truck any old time he wants. I'm tempted to shove him off one of these days." She gathered her knees to her chest and rested her head on them. "I hope you don't mind, but I have one of your handkerchiefs." Her breathing hitched. "I'm sorry I couldn't save you." Violent sobs broke from her body, bending her in half. Somewhere in the midst of the torrent, peace washed over her. She felt lighter and found it easier to breathe. She whispered a prayer of thanks, basking in the peace at Baxter's grave.

A meaty hand landed on her shoulder. Corrie screamed and pivoted. She thumped her hand over her heart. "George!"

George's face turned purple. "Simmer down, woman. You purt-near gave me a heart attack."

"Me? Give you a heart attack? I'm not the one sneaking around on people in cemeteries." She swiped at her face and glared at him.

He had the decency to look chagrined. "Sorry. I just heard you crying over here and thought I'd come check on you. That's all."

She pushed to her feet, refusing his belated hand of assistance, and brushed her pants off. "What are you doing here, anyway? Shouldn't you be in the hospital?"

"I'm right as rain. The doctor kicked me out. Said I was eating all the food and they couldn't afford to keep me." George spat on the ground. "Don't know why people make a fuss over doctors."

She cringed. His manners sure hadn't been fixed during his stint in the hospital, but something was different in his face. Kinder, it had lost much of its defiant anger. Still, she debated on the wisdom of being alone with him. Some wounds went too deep. She turned her body and faced the ornate metal cemetery gate. "So, you come to the cemetery to celebrate not being here permanently?" Even as the acrid words passed her tongue, she wanted to take them back.

His face softened, and for the first time, George looked peaceful. All the wrinkles and crags in his face seemed to roll out and away. "It's my daughter's birthday today." His voice shook. "She would've been twenty-five."

"I'm sorry, George." Corrie extended a hand and lowered it when he shied away. "I didn't know."

He jerked a shoulder.

"Can I... may I... visit her?" She picked at the dirt clinging to her palms.

George began walking away, and since he hadn't shot her down, she followed him to the far eastern side of the cemetery reserved for the congregation's smallest members. She sidestepped a stone lamb with a blue ribbon about its neck. Jeffrey Mullins never saw the age of three. Not paying attention, she bumped into George's wide back. He grunted but said nothing, and she came to his side and looked down.

Her breath clogged her throat. She'd seen this gravestone before, even commented on its beauty, but now, standing next to the father who'd ordered it made for his little girl, she felt like weeping. Pink quartz glinted in the emerging sunlight. Elegant cursive stretched across it and bore the name Ella May. The short timeline of little Ella's life was engraved in the space below: April 10, 1990–September 24, 1993. An angel carved from the same pink stone held a small child to her bosom, her wings covering and protecting the girl.

"I know her dash is small and short," George whispered. "But she filled my life with such joy."

"What happened?"

He shuddered. "I didn't see her. I swear to God, I never knew she was there."

Corrie's heart dipped, and she reached for George's hand and squeezed it. "George, I'm so sorry."

"Some around town say I killed my wife." He didn't pull his hand away. "They're right. She never could cope with Ella's death and hated me till the day she died. A month later, by her own hand."

"You don't have to carry this burden. God—"

He yanked his hand away. "Don't talk to me about God." He blew out a breath and stared at his daughter's headstone. "I don't want to know a God that lets this happen." He walked off, stomping through the cemetery and out the gate.

Corrie touched the angel's wingtip. "Ella, say hi to Baxter for me. He's probably the guy handing out suckers." With a final glance in the direction of her old friend's grave, she left the cemetery, closing the gate and leaving her guilt behind.

AARON FLICKED HIS TONGUE out and ran it across his lips as he carved a curlicue into the freshly sanded wood. It was coming together. His stomach clenched at the idea of Corrie using it, running her hands along the carvings, her fingers tracing markings he'd made. His ears pricked at crunching gravel outside the shop. He pulled a tarp over the wood and ambled outside.

"Hey, babe." He hugged Corrie to his body and inhaled her scent. She'd changed it. His mouth watered at the scent of caramel-covered apples.

"I visited Baxter's grave this morning," she murmured against his chest. "You were right. I needed to see it. Talk to him one more time." She toyed with a button on his overalls. "George was there."

He tensed. "Who won?"

She scowled. "We are civil to each other. Now." Her face softened. "Did you know he had a daughter? She'd be my age if she had lived."

He smoothed her hair and grasped her hands. "I think maybe I did know. I remember my parents discussing it after it happened."

"No wonder he's such a crotchety old fart." She clasped a hand over her mouth. "That wasn't very nice to say, was it?" She buried her face in his chest, and her warm breath puffed through his sweatshirt. "I can't imagine losing a child and being the one responsible for her death."

"He could have chosen to not become a jerk, though," he grumbled as he glared over Corrie's head at Kentucky. He waved his arm at the bird, hoping it would get the hint to hightail it.

"He's so lost and lonely." Shaking her head, she brushed wood shavings off his sweatshirt. "I got to go. Iris has an appointment later, and Violet wants me to come along." She brushed a kiss over his lips. "Oh, and I'm tired of Violet moping around the house like a lovesick puppy. Your only job is to get that stubborn brother of yours to realize his love and affection for her."

He tapped her nose. "Do I have permission to use physical force?"

She rolled her eyes and sashayed to her truck. "Desperate times call for desperate measures."

"It's so hot when you use clichés," he yelled over her truck's diesel growl.

"They're better than your pickup lines." She waved out the window and barreled down the driveway.

He shoved his hands in his pockets and began whistling. His entire body tingled with anticipation for the day when she'd become his in every way. First, she had to say yes. Not allowing doubt to run rampant through his head, he sauntered into the shop, swooped off the tarp, and began carving Corrie's past into what would hopefully become the future for both of them.

Chapter Eighteen

Corrie hefted the large machine shed doors closed and tucked her combine away for the winter. She wanted to skip, to dance, to do a somersault. After checking for an audience, she did all three and landed squarely on her bum on the third.

"Not as spry as I used to be," she muttered as she limped to the house and back to her office.

"Dad?"

Jake sat tall in his office chair, his eyes glued to the computer screen.

"You okay?" She walked over and stood next to him. The bank account balance gleamed back at them, and she bent to see his reaction. She'd been up most of the night before, doing bookwork, and finally finished in time to get a tiny bundle of tears and drool shoved in her arms. She rubbed her eyes, promising them the precious sleep they so desired.

He clasped her hand in his and beamed up at her until she ducked her head. "So proud."

Her heart grew too large for her chest. She took a deep breath. "It's in my veins, isn't it?" She took to her knees beside his chair. "Do I make a good farmer? Did I do a good job?"

He cocked his head to one side and studied her. She felt like a little girl again when her father's hand descended on her hair. "Better than me."

"No." She snorted. "But I did learn from the best." She raised herself up and kissed his bristled cheek. "Keep in mind, we had several setbacks, but the crops did amazing this year. We should have a nice balance after the loan is paid off."

"Aaron?"

"I've already factored in his pay. The stubborn man won't cash the check, though."

Jake's face screwed up in frustration. "Aaron?" This time he pointed his finger at the upper left part of her chest.

She blushed and gazed out the window behind the desk, where massive evergreen tree branches used to scratch the pane, seeming to beg entry into the house. In its stead now was a baby-blue spruce, its tiny needles soaking up all the rays the fall sun could offer.

She turned back to her father's expectant face and nodded. "I think so."

"Aaron is good man."

"Yes." She got to her feet. "Yes, he is." The homey smell of tomato soup and cheese sandwiches wafted down the hallway. "I think lunch is done. I'm starving."

Jake pushed shakily to his feet, and she positioned herself on his side to help him regain his balance. She looked back at the computer and smiled. She had done it. But she hadn't done it alone. Walking her dad down the hallway, she realized she'd had it all wrong from the beginning. People hadn't been waiting to see her fail. They'd simply been waiting for permission to help. *A life lesson learned a smidgen too late.*

Iris's cry brought Corrie to a halt.

"I think Violet's still in the shower." She patted her father's hand. "Go on without me. Tell Mom I'll eat later."

To the tune of her stomach growling, she padded into the living room and lifted Iris from her bassinet. Corrie's heart melted, and her insides jumped. Iris had found her hand and was sucking vigorously on her fist, squeaks and chirps coming from her tiny mouth. Unsummoned memories assailed Corrie as she held her. Her baby would have been eight this year. *I wonder what it would have felt like to hold my baby, feel its tiny heartbeat flutter like hummingbird wings?*

She closed her eyes and breathed in Iris's scent. Her baby would have smelled like this—warm, milky, and new. *Would Luke have married me?* If so, Aaron wouldn't be in any equation. Her heart lurched.

Frustrated and confused with memory lane, she closed off the past and began pacing the living room, humming random tunes into Iris's ear. Instead of going back to sleep, though, Iris opened her tiny mouth, and a fearsome cry tore from her throat. She suckled on her tightly clenched fist and cried again.

"I know, little one. Your mommy is coming. Just hang on for a few minutes." When Iris continued to wail, Corrie dipped and danced, trying to quiet the fussing infant. "I'm hungry, too, you know, but you don't see me fussing, do you?" She placed her lips on Iris's fuzzy head and continued to dance around the room, trying to soothe the baby.

"Thank you," Violet cried as she entered the living room, her hair still dripping from her shower.

"No problem, but you do have one very hungry baby girl on your hands." Corrie handed Iris over, made sure mother and baby were situated comfortably, and dashed into the kitchen before her stomach forced her to bellow in wails loud enough to outdo Iris.

CORRIE pulled the chain saw cord, and the machine gurgled and buzzed to life. The vibration traveling up her arm invigorated her, and with a newfound sense of energy from her recent nap, she approached the nearest charred tree. The chain saw's blade took the first bite, slicing into the blackened skin and sinking its teeth into the meaty center. Her body became one with the chain saw, and she maneuvered her arms wherever she felt the blade wanted to go. Anticipating the final cut, she made the last incision, and the tree succumbed to gravity and toppled to the ground.

"One down, one hundred to go," she sighed as she moved to the next tree.

"You need help?"

She whirled around, wielding the chain saw like a sword. "George." Upon seeing her visitor, she hesitated but then turned off the chain saw and set it on the ground.

"I came out to see if you needed any help."

Behind her, rows and rows of trees needed to be cut down. She eyed George. Even though she'd forgiven him and understood where his bitterness stemmed from, she still pictured every horrible moment in his presence. She ground her teeth. "Are you sure you're well enough for hard labor?"

"Corrie." His ruddy face grew even redder. "I know I don't deserve a second chance, and to be honest with you, it wasn't easy for me coming here. But after the cemetery, seeing Ella's grave... I, ah, I owe you quite a bit." He scratched his belly. "If you could just let me try to make things up, for being such a... a..." He faltered, seeming to have trouble finding a nonoffensive swear word.

"Jerk," she offered, her right eyebrow cocked.

"Yeah." He took a huge breath. "That." He peered at her, and she squirmed under his gaze. "You have stronger words for me, don't you?"

She blushed. "Maybe."

"Good. I couldn't respect you if you didn't think the worst of me."

Corrie raised both eyebrows this time. "In that case, George, you must have the utmost respect for me, then."

A smile creased his face in all the wrong spots, like a shar-pei with its entire face scrunched and smooshed with wrinkles and fur. The uncanny resemblance made her giggle. Clearing her throat, she shrugged. "There's an extra chain saw in the barn. Just promise you won't keel over again. I don't feel like dragging your sorry hind end anywhere."

He mock saluted her and waddled off to the barn.

Yup. She turned back to the tree line. *Very much like that shar-pei. I think his name was George too.* Snickering, she started the chain saw again and began working on what used to be her favorite pine tree.

Before too long, George strutted up a little farther down the line and began to slice into a crispy elm.

Corrie shook her head. God really did have a funny way of providing help. With a prayer of thanksgiving, she made the last cut, sending a needleless evergreen slamming to the ground, its charred outer bark exploding in every direction.

LATER THAT AFTERNOON, Corrie sat across from Steve at the kitchen table and stared into the sheriff's bicolored eyes. "Violet's sleeping. I'd hate to wake her."

Steve spread his hands across the table. "Sorry, Corrie, but I've got to ask her some questions."

"It's okay," Violet said from the kitchen doorway. "I'm up, anyway." She yawned and sank into the chair next to Corrie. "What can I do for you, Sheriff?"

"First of all, congratulations on your baby." He pulled out a small spiral notebook from the pocket of his uniform. Clicking his pen open, he studied Violet. "How did you know Frank again?"

Corrie felt Violet tense. Even the poor woman's arm hair stood at attention. "I, um, he was..."

"Steve, she already told you about her past and her relationship with Frank."

"Don't make me kick you out of this room, Corrie." His gaze swept back to Violet. "Please tell me again."

"He was my fiancé," she spat out. She cracked her knuckles and began chewing on her thumbnail.

"Where did you get the car to escape?"

Her face blanched. "I stole it from him." Her voice, barely audible, cracked.

"He claims he never even had a car."

Corrie folded her hands and stuck them between her thighs. It would do Violet no good for Corrie to slap the sheriff silly.

Color rushed back into Violet's face, replacing the bleached whiteness to maroon. "Do you really believe him over me?" she gritted out between her teeth.

Steve sat, tapping his pen on the table. "No."

"I did what I had to do to escape the hell I suffered. Arrest me if you want, but I swear I would do it all again to get away."

Steve's face, which had long since turned the color of oatmeal, twitched. He folded his lips together and seemed fascinated by a certain word on his notepad. Scratching his neck, he blew out a breath. "I'm sorry, Violet, but I have to ask, did you call anyone when you got here? A friend?"

"I didn't want to." Her eyes searched Corrie's. "Really, I didn't, but after my phone was charged, I just had to text my friend. She was the only one who mattered to me anymore, and I wanted to let her know I was safe."

"Did you tell her where you were?" Steve steepled his fingers and rested his chin on them.

Violet removed her hand from Corrie's grasp. "Not at first, but then I did." Her forehead furrowed. "I just felt so safe here after a while. I never thought he'd come all this way. I just never thought." Her voice faded into a whisper, and she closed her eyes. They snapped open. "Oh dear! My friend! He must have gotten to her. She was the only one I ever told. I swear."

"What's your friend's name?"

"Rebekkah Joleaf." She clutched at Corrie's hands. "I haven't heard from her. Something's wrong, I just know it."

Steve snapped his notepad shut. "Thank you, Violet, for answering my questions. I'll try to find out about your friend. Frank hasn't been very talkative, but I'm much more stubborn than he is." He got to his feet. "And Corrie, I appreciate your self-control and not punching me in the face."

"I don't look good in orange or stripes, so basically fashion made me keep my hands to myself."

Steve's lips quirked to the side. "Does Aaron know what he's getting himself into?"

"I sure hope not."

He chuckled and left the kitchen, the door clicking shut as he exited the house. Silence coated the kitchen.

"I'm sorry," Violet breathed. "For the darkness I brought with me."

Corrie wrapped her arm around Violet's shoulders. "No, you didn't. It found you, through no fault of yours. You were being a good friend. Frank is the one to blame, not you. And even if you had a thousand fiancés wanting revenge, I'd get Dad to whack them over the head with a hoe."

Violet gaped at her. "I've never met anyone like you before."

"That's probably a good thing. Too much of this crazy could cause the world to end." She stood up and placed her palm against Violet's cheek. "In all seriousness, though, I'm sorry you suffered like you did. I don't know what else to say. Sorry seems so stupid and lame."

Violet drew her into a hug. "Do you think there's ice cream?"

It was weird not feeling the baby bump anymore, and Corrie was glad she didn't have to worry about a tiny foot kicking her in the gut. "If not, I know of a really hot neighbor who might have some."

CORRIE'S heart melted into her chest. There she was on a lazy Sunday afternoon, lying on the crispy grass next to the garden with her head in Aaron's lap. His fingers played with her hair, sending her blood roaring through her body. She took in his strong features, sharpened by the clean-shaven look he'd recently adopted. Reaching up, she ran her fingers across his smooth cheeks, missing the slight stubble that usually met her fingertips. She trailed her index finger along his cheek, across his chin, and nestled her finger in the dimple centered there.

Aware of his eyes watching her face, she smiled as she brushed her finger down his neck, her heart skipping a beat when his Adam's apple bobbed violently beneath her touch. She rested her fingers over his pulse point. Her heart paced to match the staccato of his.

He captured her hand and brought her fingertips to his mouth and kissed each one.

"Two can play this game, Corrie." Passion darkened his green eyes.

She giggled and yanked her hand away to play with a stray curl that flopped onto his forehead. "And what game might that be?"

"You shall be my undoing." He groaned and shifted his body.

She raised her head slightly then put it back down, resting her neck on his muscled thigh. She sighed as he began caressing her hair again. Closing her eyes, she savored the floating-midair feeling. Wishing she could lie in his lap forever, she breathed in deeply. The smells of wood fires from neighboring chimneys and drying vegetation soothed her, but the smell she loved the most was the slight cologne scent coming from her man. Her man. She bit her lip. To think that Aaron Tuttle was all hers.

A sudden memory torpedoed her happiness. Her stomach churned. *Does he know that I once carried his brother's child inside me?*

Guilt and fear wiggled into her conscience. She had to tell him. *He'll reject you. No one needs to know.* She chewed on her lip some more as the good angel on her right and the devil on her left argued. The angel won. She would have to tell him and pray he would forgive her, because now that he was hers, she wasn't sure she could let go.

"You really shouldn't do that." He broke into her ruminations.

"Do what?" She peeked one eye open and peered owlishly at him.

"That lip-biting thing you do."

"And why is that?" She gazed up at him with both eyes.

"It makes me want to kiss you."

She smiled and very slowly bit her lip again. He growled, dipped his head down, and kissed her until she thought their lips had permanently melded with passion. Her conscience reared its ugly head.

She detached herself from him, putting her fingers on his lips. "Aaron?"

Confusion clouded his eyes. She sat up and faced him, her hands resting on his thighs. Playing her fingers over the jeans material, she toyed with a loose fiber surrounding a rip in the denim. As if it held the answer to all life's questions, she stared at it. Looking up would only mean meeting his eyes, and she wasn't quite sure she could.

His finger pressed under her chin and elevated her head. His trusting gaze pierced her.

Not so long ago, she had put pain in those very eyes. She wasn't looking forward to doing it again.

"What's wrong?" Aaron's finger traced her chin.

"I have to tell you something, and I'm not sure how." Corrie's heart vibrated, and sweat beaded down her back.

His white teeth flashed against his tanned skin. "You're not breaking up with me, are you?"

"Never. But after what I tell you, you might be the one breaking up with me." She shifted, refusing to look him in the eyes, and his finger halted on its journey back and forth across her chin.

"Corrie," he murmured, "look at me, please." He lifted her chin again, cocked his head to the side, and seemed to peer into her soul. "I don't think anything you can say would ever make me walk away from you. In fact, I'm pretty sure I'm in—"

"Don't. Don't say it." Panic snaked up her spine. If he said those words to her then walked away, she could never bear it. Best if she never heard them from him if she were only to lose him.

"What's wrong?" Worry etched across his face. "Please tell me."

She wanted nothing more than to wipe the worry away and allow him to say the words she wanted so badly to hear. Swallowing the fear coating her tongue, she blurted, "Do you know the whole story of Luke and me?"

"I suppose so. You guys ended on a sour note. I guess I never really knew why."

She quit playing with the jeans fiber and folded her hands, willing them to stop shaking. "Luke got me pregnant."

Aaron's body jerked, and his breath fanned her face as he exhaled slowly. After the initial impact, the earth seemed to quit spinning. Even the air seemed to still, filling her ears with silence. Terrible, quiet silence. She sat there in front of Aaron, not touching anything but the grass under her and not hearing anything but the roar in her ears. Too afraid to look at him, she concentrated on the blades of grass beginning to show their descent into death as autumn took its hold.

Finally, Aaron's voice, gruff and hoarse, pierced the quiet. "He didn't take advantage of you, did he?"

She snapped her head up and looked into Aaron's face. His eyes—a mixture of anger, jealousy, and confusion—peered into hers. "Oh, heavens, no! We are both to blame. We were young and dumb and succumbed to misplaced passion. Please don't be angry at Luke. If you need to be upset at someone, it should be me."

The anger died in Aaron's eyes. Confusion and jealousy warred in the green depths. "I could never be upset with you. Especially about something that happened so long ago. We've all done things we regret." He reached for her and drew her into his arms and tucked her head under his chin. "What happened to the baby?"

The tears came then. She didn't bother stopping them. They trickled down her face and plopped onto his shirt. "I lost it."

His arms tightened around her, and she relished their strength holding her, securing her against her painful memories. "Oh, baby, I'm so sorry. That must have been terrifying."

"That's not the worst part. Part of me wanted the baby, but I can't lie, part of me was happy and relieved when I miscarried. Can you image being happy over the death of a baby?" She shook her head violently, sniffling. "I was a horrible person."

"No. Never think that. You were a terrified teenage girl whose stupid, immature boyfriend had seduced her." Aaron kissed her hair. "You were brave to have wanted the baby. That's the memory you have to hold on to. You would have cared for that little person with your whole being."

She wriggled from his arms and looked at him, wiping the tears from her face. "So, you're not angry with me? I was so afraid you'd hate me after you found out. Afraid you wouldn't want me after you knew I... well, you know... carried Luke's child."

He caressed her face.

She bit down a purr growing at the back of her throat.

"Nothing could stop me from wanting you." He pursed his lips and scowled. "But I can't promise I won't punch Luke in the face when I see him next. What an idiot!"

She hiccupped. "Remember, it takes two to tango, so technically, I'm an idiot too."

"True, but here's the thing." He cupped his hand around the back of her head, bringing her closer to him. "I'm very much in love with you, Corrie Lancaster."

The words washed over her. She felt weightless yet unable to move at the same time. Wanting to speak but finding her tongue paralyzed, she laid her hand behind Aaron's neck and drew him in for a kiss.

"Is this an I-just-want-to-be-friends kiss?" he teased as he ended the kiss.

Finally finding her tongue working again, she smiled. "Not a chance. It's more a what-took-you-so-long kiss."

"At the beginning, I never thought you'd actually want me, much less love me. I guess I was afraid of taking the first step."

She caressed his face. "Let me put your fears to rest. Not only do I want you, Aaron Tuttle, I love you with all my heart. In fact, I'm pretty sure I've been in love with you for quite some time. I guess I was afraid you wouldn't want me either."

His smile almost broke its confines. His eyes darkened, and she imagined herself swimming in the tropical waters, gently tugged at by a kind riptide summoning her to its mysterious journey.

"There's nothing about you I don't want," he huskily whispered as he hauled her into his lap and kissed her until she knew nothing but the taste and texture of his lips.

LATE THE NEXT MORNING, Aaron glared at Luke's truck as it roared up their parents' driveway. Aaron set down his glass of chocolate milk and stomped across the farmyard and into the barn. He wouldn't be able to share airspace with his little brother for quite some time. *Years, probably.* With eyes narrowed, he glared as Luke ambled from his truck to the house. Kentucky clucked at Aaron's feet. Ignoring his pet, Aaron raked a hand across his head. After Corrie had revealed the truth about her and Luke, he'd hidden his rage well, but he seethed within. Clenching his jaw, he continued working on his present for Corrie. He brushed his hands over the wood, grabbed fine sandpaper, and rubbed with the grain until the loose and jagged fibers wore completely smooth.

His mind churned with nauseating images. His heart broke for the woman he loved. Corrie should never have had to deal with the guilt and shame caused by his—

"Hey, Aaron, what are you working on?"

Aaron spun around and pounced. Grabbing Luke by his shirt collar, Aaron pounded his brother into the shop wall. The bang echoed through the building. "You good-for-nothing scumbag!"

"What the—" Luke squirmed against the hold, his hands pressing back Aaron's shoulders. When Aaron didn't budge, Luke narrowed his eyes. "Let go."

"Nope." Aaron tightened his hold on his brother's shirt. His fist pushed against Luke's windpipe. "I forgave you for kissing my girl. But I'm not sure I can forgive you for taking advantage of her and piling a load of junk at her feet she'll have to deal with her whole life."

"Let go of me, Aaron," Luke croaked past the obstructing fist.

"Why should I?"

"Because we both know I can take you down, *old man*."

Aaron released him. "Prove it." He crouched, his fists up, body balancing from leg to leg. Dodging a flying fist, Aaron spun and punched up, connecting with Luke's stomach. "How. Dare. You." He puffed, evading a fist to the face. "How dare you hurt Corrie like that."

Luke lunged, but Aaron swept his legs out from under him, bringing his brother crashing to the floor. Aaron swiped at his sweaty brow and backed away. "Stay down if you know what's good for you."

With a growl, Luke jumped and tackled Aaron, pinning his back to the floor. "Knock it off. What do you want me to say that I haven't already said? What do you want me to feel that I haven't already felt?" Luke's spittle sprayed Aaron's face. "It killed me to walk away from her, you know that? My insides shriveled up until I was face-down in a bottle." Luke shoved him again. "What I did to Corrie will always haunt me. I'll never meet the baby—*my* baby—that I made with her. There is nothing you can say to me, brother, that will make me feel any more convicted than I already do."

Aaron shoved Luke away, swiping his hand under his nose. The rage that had billowed into an inferno cooled. "Why didn't you tell me?"

Luke snorted a laugh. "You were off in your own world, doing your own thing. Caleb didn't need the pressure of a loser for a brother on top of fighting in Afghanistan." He shrugged, lowering himself to the floor next to Aaron. "I took my guilt out on alcohol and girls."

"Who dragged you out?"

"Dad."

"Does he know?"

"No." Luke heaved to his feet and reached for Aaron's hand. "There's only two—three—people I need forgiveness from, and I've got the first two covered."

Aaron stared at his hand and wanted to swat it away. Taking it, he jumped to his feet. "Who's the third person?"

"You."

Aaron ground his teeth. Feeling the will of God descend upon him, he bowed his head. *Lord, you certainly don't make it easy on a fellow, do you?* He flexed his right hand, releasing the tension, and instead of fisting it, he laid it open and reached for his brother's. "I'll forgive you only if you forgive me and my attempts to kill you just now."

Luke's face broke into a toothy grin. "Deal." He pulled Aaron into a hug, slapped his back three times, and released him, putting manly distance between them. "Besides." Luke smirked. "We both know you'd never succeed. Old-timer."

The dinner bell clanging through the farmyard stopped Aaron's retort. Deciding to keep his mouth shut, he strolled out of the shop, brother in tow. Kentucky came running up to him, squawking her greetings.

"Does Corrie know you have a pet chicken?" Luke eyed the fowl keeping step with Aaron.

"Nope."

"You going to tell her?"

"Nope."

"Good idea. She might think you're ready for a room at the nursing home."

Aaron slapped the back of his brother's head. "One more old man joke, and I'll find very creative ways of making your life a living—"

"Aaron!" Corrie hailed him from his parents' front porch. He took in her skinny jeans, calf-high brown boots, and oversized sweater. Her hair, free of its normal confines, blew in the breeze, sending small tendrils sailing across her rosy cheeks.

He raced up the steps, drew her to him, and tucked her hair behind her ears. "To what do I owe this pleasure?"

"Just wanted to see your face."

He peered into her eyes and saw a flicker of doubt. Time to stomp it out. "Go out with me again. Tomorrow night. We'll go to Mabel's Café. She's got her chicken-and-strudels special."

Kentucky clucked low in her throat. Aaron expelled a breath. *Really?*

Luke slapped his back on his way into the house. "I bet they serve great food at the local home," he murmured before escaping through the door.

Aaron glowered at the door then down at his chicken.

"Who's this?" Corrie asked, her lips twitching.

Rolling his eyes, he gestured to Kentucky. "Corrie, this is Kentucky. Kentucky, this is Corrie."

Corrie squatted down. "Kentucky, it's nice to meet you." She giggled when the chicken ruffled her feathers and stalked off. She straightened up and wrapped her arms around his neck. "I think she's jealous."

"What can I say? I give all the girls I meet what they need."

"What does Kentucky need?" Corrie played with his hair.

"Corn nuts. Any kind will do, but she really loves ranch." His tongue felt thick, and his mind struggled with formulating any cohesive thought.

"What do I need?" Her minty breath washed over him.

He surrounded her face with his hands and kissed her. By the time he was done, she would only remember the feel of his lips on hers, and no one else's.

Chapter Nineteen

"**H**ey, watch where you're going!"

Corrie reached out with gloved fingers, attempting to pat at Nikki's face, but couldn't see past the itchy wool covering her eyes. "Sorry."

"That's my eye." Nikki swatted at Corrie's hand. "What are you two doing, anyway?"

Corrie shook her head. "Honestly, I have no idea. Ask the man who is abducting me. But more importantly"—she turned her face to where she assumed Xavier stood—"what are you and Mr. Palinski doing out here?"

Aaron, the man stealing her from the Christmas festivities, chuckled behind her. "I believe they were using their imaginations and conjuring mistletoe where there isn't any."

Corrie didn't need to see the boy to know he was blushing. That was all he did around Nikki. It was kind of cute. "Just make sure that's all you're conjuring. Understood?"

Nikki's snort of derision contrasted with Xavier's politely frightened "Yes, ma'am."

Stepping off the porch steps with Aaron's helpful hand for guidance, she scrunched her nose against the itchy wool. "Where are you taking me?"

"Keep your eyes closed," Aaron commanded as he guided her out the front door and into the chilly winter evening.

"You have me blindfolded, remember?" she retorted, cuddling in her downy jacket. "I can't see anything with this ridiculous hat over my eyes."

"I have to use my mother's gift somehow. This just seemed like the perfect opportunity." He walked next to her, their snow boots crunching in the snow.

She wished she could see the million tiny snowflakes twirling and spiraling from the sky and landing on the white ground. Straining her ears, she heard nothing except their footfalls. The cold air refreshed her, and she took a deep breath, inhaling it, relishing it.

"Here we are." He led her into the machine shed. The smell of machines, oil, and dirt replaced that of the pure snow, leaving her unsure which scent she preferred. "Don't take off the blindfold just yet."

He stomped away, and she could hear him fumble for the lights. Fluorescent light seeped through the wool over her eyes, yet she saw only shadows. Aaron stepped to her side.

"Are you ready?" he breathed.

"As ready as I'll ever be," she quipped, her body tingling with excitement.

"Ta-da!" He whipped the hat off her head.

She clasped her hands over her mouth. "It's beautiful." Corrie approached the rocking chair wrapped in a big red bow. She removed her gloves, ran her hand over smooth pale wood, and traced delicate carvings in the armrests with her index finger. "Did you make this?" She turned to gaze at Aaron, his face beaming.

"Yeah." He walked to her side. "Do you like it?"

"Like it? I love it, Aaron. It's amazing. Thank you so much." She kissed his cheek, allowing her lips to linger a little.

"I, uh, used the wood from your weeping willow. I hope you don't mind."

Her heart dipped to her toes, and her skin tingled as she brushed her fingertips over her old tree friend. The same tree that had rocked away all her worries for countless years and would for countless years to come. She wanted to laugh but needed to cry. Throwing herself in Aaron's arms, she did both. She clung to him, knowing no matter how hard she tried, she could never hold him tight enough. "Thank you." She released him only enough to allow her to squish his face between her hands. "Thank you." She brought his forehead to hers and stood there breathing in his scent.

"Merry Christmas," he whispered and captured her lips with his.

"I feel bad now for giving you a pair of socks," she grumbled, pulling slightly away. "I'll have to knit you a very ugly sweater to make up for this present exchange."

"Actually, could you do me a favor and try out the rocking chair?"

She eyed Aaron, whose voice squeaked on his last word. "Quality control didn't test for comfort? Well, it's the least I can do." She began untying the ribbon so she could sit. Something on the ribbon sparkled. There, with the red ribbon through it, suspended a diamond ring, twinkling in the machine-shed light.

She whirled around, her heart pounding. He smiled and got down on one knee, his clean jeans landing in a big oil spot. Feeling as if the world would never stop spinning, she centered herself by gazing into his face, taking in every feature, every small scar, every gray beard hair poking from his shaved skin. The possibility that all this would be hers fascinated her, and before he even spoke, she placed her hand on his cheek, enjoying the texture of his cold skin against her warm palm.

"Corrie." He swallowed. His Adam's apple bounced up and down. "Will you marry me?"

Surely her face would shatter from her smile. "Yes!"

He whipped her into a hug and twirled her in circles. She giggled into his neck, storing every moment in her memories. Aaron released her, removed the ring from the ribbon, and shimmied it on her ring finger.

"It fits perfectly." The large diamond, surrounded by tiny ones, glittering and winking, mesmerized her.

He ducked his head. "I have a confession to make. I had your mom steal one of your rings for me."

"Sneaky."

"I didn't want to go sneaking into your room." He dug in his pocket and handed her the pilfered item.

"You didn't?" She ran her finger along the collar of his Carhartt coat, her fingertips brushing his skin. "That's too bad."

He growled low in his throat, sending an electric current to her very center.

"If I get a pretty little bauble like this, you can sneak into my room anytime."

His gaze burned into hers. "I don't think your parents would approve. I might not be able to resist the prettiest thing in there."

She blushed, and her insides went all watery. "My old Barbies would certainly find you irresistible." Squealing with delight, she ran from Aaron and his face that promised a good, old-fashioned kissing. "We're missing my mother's pumpkin pie, you know."

"Well, I wouldn't want you to miss your favorite part of Christmas, now would I?"

"Correction"—she held up her left hand— "second favorite part of Christmas. Something has surpassed even my mother's pie."

After they put their gloves on, Aaron pulled his ugly wool hat over her head. He reached for her hand, and she clung to his, afraid this moment would end all too soon. They exited the machine shed and trekked to the house, where Xavier and Nikki apparently shared their last kiss before the boy skipped down the steps and into his car. He waved at them as he drove off to his own family's Christmas meal.

"Stop," she whispered, afraid to break the spell. Hardly breathing, she took in the night she had been blinded to before. Candles shone through the windows, beckoning all guests, promising a cheery welcome. White icicle lights twinkled from the gutters, and every porch railing sparkled with hundreds of colorful twinkle lights dancing in the cold night. And the star of the show, the Christmas tree, stood just beyond the picture-window pane, its lights abstract and blurry through the sheer glass shut to the dark, snowy night.

She curved into him as he encircled her side with his arm.

He rested his head on top of hers and whispered, "Merry Christmas, my love."

"Merry Christmas," she murmured, enjoying the soft snowflakes kissing her exposed face. She turned to face Aaron, encircled her arms about his waist, and stretched a little farther to make up for the extra padding provided by their bulky winter jackets. "I'm thinking this is certainly a contender for the best Christmas ever."

"I wonder why?" A sly smile touched his lips. "I know I'm super pumped about my new socks."

"You're never going to let me live that down, are you?"

"Nope." He tapped the tip of her numbed nose with his gloved finger. "I believe you'll be able to compete against Rudolph if I don't get you inside soon."

She nestled against Aaron's coat. "One more minute like this."

He held her, and even though she couldn't feel her face or the tips of her fingers, her entire body felt warm and steamy. In a dreamy state of mind and through slitted eyes, she watched thousands of snowflakes twirl and whirl in their descent.

Her minute up, she grabbed Aaron's hand and held it as they ascended the porch steps and entered the house. Smells of Christmas turkey and all the trimmings still hung in the air. The scent of pumpkin pie taunted her. After taking off her winter gear, she leaned against the door to the living room. The Christmas tree glowed in magnificence, an angel with golden hair and translucent wings perched atop it. Ornaments hung and dangled off green boughs, reflecting and refracting the lights behind them.

Nathan and Nikki lay under the tree, gently shaking and rattling the presents, trying to guess what was in each. Cynthia sat next to

Jake on the loveseat, their hands intertwined. Little Iris, all decked out in Christmas finery, lay on a white blanket near the tree. Her dark eyes never strayed from the lights and ornaments.

Corrie smiled wistfully. Next year, Iris wouldn't just be gazing at the tree; she'd be attempting to climb it. Moving her gaze around the room, Corrie didn't see Violet. Or Luke, whom Aaron had invited to join them for Christmas supper.

Turning to Aaron, she laid her left hand on his chest, admiring how nice her ring finger looked. "Go on in. I'll look for Violet and Luke."

Aaron kissed her cheek and sauntered into the living room with a loud "Ho Ho Ho!"

Corrie bit her lip and shook her head, love for him pouring through her entire body. Peeking into the kitchen, she saw no one but was tempted to snatch a piece of pie cooling on the counter. Knowing her mother's wrath when it came to her pies, Corrie refrained and walked up the stairs. Violet's room was empty.

Grunting, Corrie clambered down the steps and along the hallway toward the office. Nothing. Stomping down the hallway this time, she checked her steps at the entrance to the kitchen and, turning spy-like, snuck through it toward the patio door. Plastering her face to the cold glass, she glimpsed two figures embracing next to her mother's snow-covered lilac bushes bordering the garden.

Her breath caught, and for a second, the white fog from her breath, which had obscured her vision, disappeared. Beyond the glass, Luke's head descended, and his lips touched Violet's. Feeling like a sister watching her big brother kiss a girl, Corrie backed away, blissful that the big lout had actually taken the plunge.

Playing with the diamond ring on her finger, she returned to the living room and lay down next to her siblings. Snatching a box, she gave it a good shake.

"I believe Luke and Violet will be in shortly." She casually reached for a box with her left hand in front of Nikki's nose. Nothing. Corrie huffed then yawned, stretching, making sure her diamond ring whizzed right past Nikki's face.

"Oh. My. Gosh!" Nikki squealed, grabbing Corrie's hand and yanking her out from under the tree. Nikki paraded her around, shoving the ring under everyone's noses, even little Iris's. Iris simply drooled and sucked on her fist.

Cynthia stood and embraced Corrie, giving her a hard hug. "I'm so happy for you, my dear," Cynthia whispered into Corrie's ear. "You couldn't have found a better man."

Tears pricked the back of Corrie's eyes as her father took her in his arms. Some of his strength had returned, and nearly a year after his accident, she felt that the man she used to know was slowly emerging from the depths. "My baby" was all he said.

Nathan merely punched her in the shoulder, studying his socked feet. "Good luck."

She rolled her eyes and reciprocated the shoulder punch, surprised by how much muscle her fist met. "You'll be needing the luck. It'll just be you and Nikki in the house in a few months."

"Where are you going?" Nathan's head jerked up. Dismay and panic contorted his face.

"Um, after the wedding, I'll be living with Aaron," she said dryly.

"That's stupid." He jerked his head toward Nikki, who was dragging Aaron around the room, making sure he got the proper congratulations from everyone, including Iris. "What am I supposed to do with just her? She's weird."

"Then you two will be perfect together." Corrie ruffled her brother's hair. "Besides, I won't be far. I'm still going to farm this land. Maybe we can build a house right next door."

"Then can I live with you?"

"Do you really want to live with Aaron and me? I plan to kiss him. A lot."

Nathan's face turned as red as the poinsettias scattered about the living room. "Yuck. I think I'll live with Nikki."

Corrie crossed her arms over her chest and gave a mock frown. "You mean to tell me you haven't kissed a girl yet?"

"It's different. You're old."

She made a move for him and laughed when he shrieked and ran from her, bolting out of the living room and into the kitchen.

"Nathan Jacob Lancaster, if you touch the pie, I'll... I'll... just don't touch the pie," Cynthia weakly ended, giving Corrie a wink. "I never could really punish that boy, could I?"

"Nope, I do believe he's your—"

A yell of frustration cut off Corrie's statement. "Does everybody plan to kiss tonight? Gross! Luke and Violet are outside swapping spit." Nathan's voice echoed through the house.

Feeling an evil grin, Corrie quickly whispered her plan to everyone in the room, and as Nathan reentered the living room, he found his parents in a fond embrace on the loveseat and Aaron and Corrie locking lips under the mistletoe.

"Feeling left out, little brother?" Nikki asked innocently before attacking him and laying a slobbery kiss on his cheek.

"Ewwww!" He pushed her away. "When everyone's done trading germs, I'll be in my room. Come get me for pie and presents."

Corrie broke away from Aaron and grabbed her brother's arm before he could leave the room. She gave him a resounding kiss on the other cheek. "We're just kidding you, you big baby," she teased, pulling him toward the tree. "We still haven't figured out what the big present is. The one from Santa to Mom."

"It better not be another kiss," he mumbled, glaring about the room.

Corrie tilted her head and smiled at her parents, whose shoulders were shaking with silent laughter. Violet and Luke stepped into the living room. Their noses and cheeks were rosy, their clothes and hair were dusted with snow, and their eyes had trouble looking at anything except each other.

"We, ah, were enjoying the night air," Luke stammered, his cheeks growing redder.

When Nathan began to scoff, Corrie kicked at him. Searing him with a glare, she nodded, accepting the lie.

"Yeah, it was quite refreshing." Violet blushed as she placed Iris in her arms and began swaying back and forth. Violet looked angelic with her black hair curled and sweeping around her shoulders. A pink shrug complemented the cream-colored dress she'd picked out from Corrie's closet.

"I'm sure it was." Corrie pinched her lips together. "How did you two manage to stay warm, though? You didn't take your coats."

Nathan grumbled, "Body heat."

Luke and Violet exchanged nervous glances. Feeling sorry for them, Corrie jumped up from where she was sitting on the floor and showed them her ring. Another round of congratulations began, and when Luke hugged her, she whispered, "It's okay, you know, loving Violet."

He hugged her tighter. Corrie waited for the old memories and old feelings, but they didn't come. "Thank you. I do love her." He released her. "Iris is pretty special, too, isn't she?"

Corrie placed her hand on his cold cheek. "You have two very special ladies in your care. Don't screw it up." She patted his cheek.

Tears shimmered in Violet's eyes. Corrie whispered, "What's wrong?" After fetching Iris from Violet's arms and handing the baby to Cynthia, Corrie dragged Violet into the hallway and wiped the tears away. "Why the tears?"

Violet's lips trembled. "They're happy tears." She looked down at her feet. "You saw us kissing, didn't you?"

"Yup, and it's about time too. I was ready to lock you two in a room and not let you out until you had."

Giggling, Violet placed her hands over her mouth. "I can't believe this is happening." Sobering up, she clung to Corrie's hands. "I don't deserve this. Not after everything I've put you through, not after everything I've done."

"We've talked about this before. You didn't bring Frank here. His revenge brought him here. You should never regret coming here. Do you hear me? Ever. Besides, you are a part of this family. And if that doesn't make you feel all warm and fuzzy on the inside, just remember that Frank is in prison right now, lying on a hard cot with not a present to be seen. And as for deserving Luke, he's a stubborn, bull-headed man who will make you want to pull out your hair. But he's kindhearted and sweet, and you most certainly deserve a man who will love you all the days of your life and treat you right."

"But, my past—"

"If Luke doesn't care, why should anyone else? And from the way he's been looking at you lately, I don't think he cares two figs about your past. Now, you go back in there. We have presents to open."

Violet wiped the remaining tears off her face, entered the living room, and latched on to Luke's hand. Luke gazed down at Violet and brought her hand up, kissing the back of it with tenderness.

From the entryway, Corrie caught Aaron's gaze. He flashed a grin at her, and her heart performed several flips before settling in her chest. What that man could do with just a smile... Her body tingled at the idea of him using all his powers on her. Anticipation shivered through her. Taking a deep breath to cool her boiling imagination, she stepped into the living room, a room full of laughter, teasing, and baby cooing. Somewhere in the background, Bing Crosby sang

Christmas tunes, serenading them with tradition and hope. Hope for a better tomorrow.

Gazing at the people before her, she knew, given the choice, she would choose the hard road again just to have them in her life. She waltzed up to Aaron, intertwined her fingers with his, and laid a large smooch on his lips to the tune of Bing Crosby... and her brother's groaning.

Acknowledgments

To my siblings: I stole your personalities for my characters, whether you like it or not. Thank you for being your quirky selves and fodder for my book.

To my mom: Not many women can shepherd two churches, grow eighty-five tomato plants, operate a combine, and drive a truck (in heels). Thank you for being so awesome.

To my dad: I get to write this story because of you. Thank you for raising a farm girl.

To my husband: You're the love interest in the story of my life. Thank you for... well, everything.

To my four minions: You are the cutest distractions an author could ever ask for. Thank you for putting up with crabby Mommy.

To my publisher: you took a chance on me when so many wouldn't. Thank you!

To my editors, Jessica A. and Angela M.: You made my writing sing. My eternal gratitude is yours.

About the Author

Jessica Berg, a child of the Dakotas and the prairie, grew up amongst hard-working men and women and learned at an early age to "put some effort into it." Following that wise adage, she has put effort into teaching high school English for over a decade, being a mother to four children (she finds herself surprised at this number, too), basking in the love of her husband of more than fifteen years and losing herself in the imaginary worlds she creates.

Read more at https://www.jessicabergbooks.com.

About the Publisher

Dear Reader,

We hope you enjoyed this book. Please consider leaving a review on your favorite book site.

Visit https://RedAdeptPublishing.com to see our entire catalogue.

Don't forget to subscribe to our monthly newsletter to be notified of future releases and special sales.